West to Moora Moora

Mark Morgan

Published in Melbourne, Australia by Bible Tales Online.
www.BibleTales.online

Series: Beyond the Western Margin
1. **Beyond the Western Margin**
2. **West to Moora Moora**

This book: West to Moora Moora
ISBN (Paperback): 978-1-925587-44-9
ISBN (eBook): 978-1-925587-45-6

Last modified: 8 January 2026.

Shelving categories:
English literature
Religion / Christianity
Religious /Christian fiction
Religious / Christian / Young Adult Adventure

Typesetting information:
Title: Merienda Bold, 30pt.
Part headings: Roboto Regular, 18pt.
Chapter titles: Merienda Bold, 20pt.
Body text: EB Garamond Regular, 10.5pt.
Headers: EB Garamond Italic, 10pt.
Footnotes: EB Garamond, 8.5pt.
Footers: EB Garamond Regular, 10pt.

Cover:
Photo of Moora Moora Reservoir by Mark Morgan (2024).

To my ever-patient wife, Ruth.

Contents

Foreword

This story is entirely fictional, although it is set in many real locations in the state of Victoria in south-eastern Australia. While the plot was prompted by the COVID-19 pandemic and my experience of closed borders, lockdowns, masks and social-distancing, the situation presented in the story is just one of an infinite number of possible futures. I hope that everyone can simply enjoy the story without either believing that it is a prophecy of an inevitable future or accusing me of criticising governments for mishandling the pandemic! That is not my intention.

All of the characters are fictional and any similarity with any existing people or names is purely coincidental. The existence of groups of terrorists trying to cause havoc in the Grampians National Park and elsewhere is simply part of the story and not intended to reflect on any individuals.

Particular thanks go to Ruth, my wife, who helps me find time to write, patiently reads what I write, and humours me when I spend inordinate amounts of time on research into minute details.

No manuscript is ever without errors, but early readers have helped eliminate many typos, bad grammar and uncomfortable usage. Cathy, my oldest daughter, has tirelessly undertaken the thankless task of proof reading the entire manuscript more than once. Thanks, Cathy.

I have a request to make of you, dear reader: if you find any errors; typos, spelling errors, poor grammar, or any other fault, please let me know.

Mark Morgan
January 2026

Online information

Extra information about the book, including maps and photos, are available on the Bible Tales website as listed below. Use the links on the left or the QR codes on the right.

"West to Moora Moora" page
https://www.bibletales.online/west-to-moora-moora/

Map of the World and Australia
https://www.bibletales.online/west-to-moora-moora/#MapOfAustralia

Map of Victoria
https://www.bibletales.online/west-to-moora-moora/#MapOfVictoria

Map of the Northern Grampians
https://www.bibletales.online/west-to-moora-moora/#MapOfNorthernGrampians

Map of Moora Moora
https://www.bibletales.online/west-to-moora-moora/#MapOfMooraMoora

Map of Australia

Dan and his family live in Australia in the southern hemisphere, where summer fills December, January and February and winter lasts from June to August.

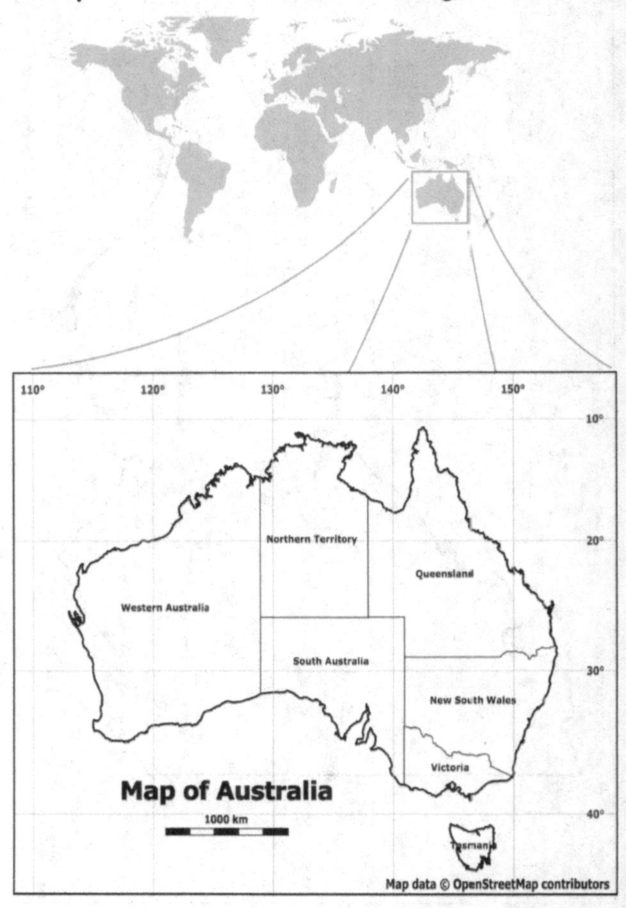

Map of Victoria

In the southeast corner of Australia lies the state of Victoria, the smallest of the mainland states.

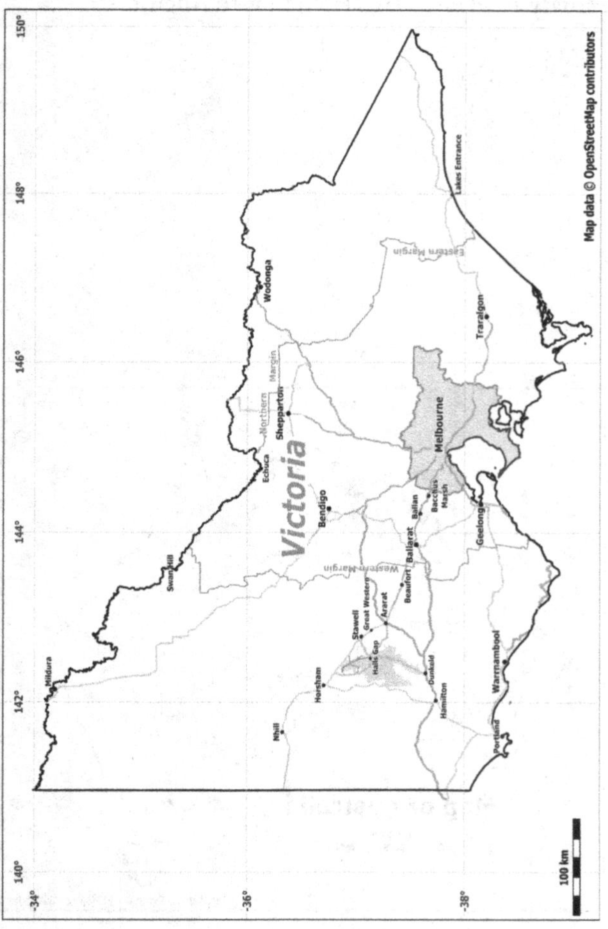

Map of the Northern Grampians

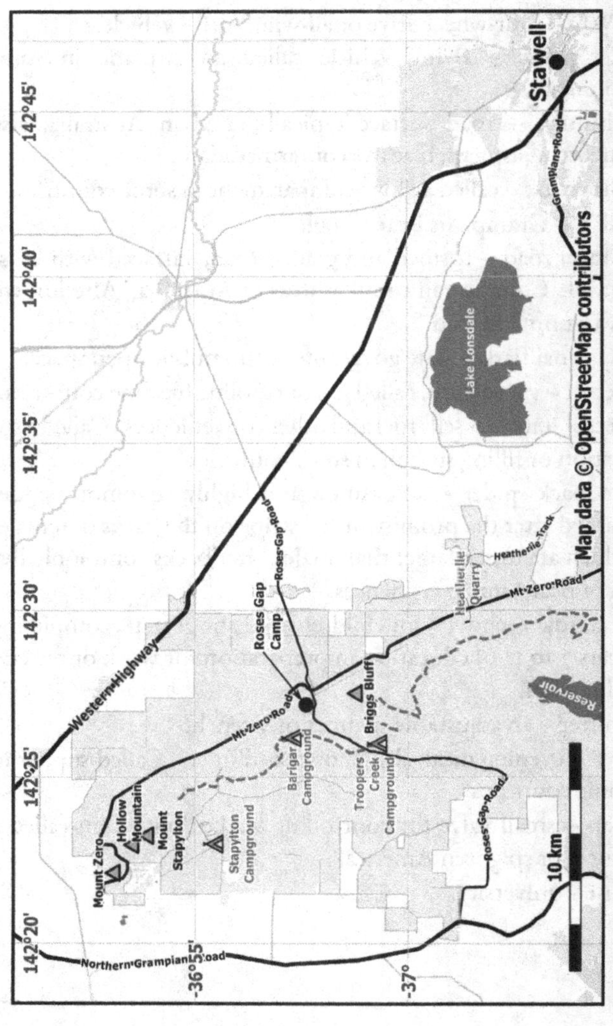

Glossary

4WD – four-wheel drive or all-wheel drive vehicle.

Aeroplane – flying vehicle called an airplane in some countries.

Bitumen – road surface typically used in Australia, also known as asphalt, blacktop or tarmacadam.

Glovebox – called a glove compartment in some countries.

GPT – Grampians Peaks Trail.

Gravel road – formed and graded road, surfaced with loose gravel. Common in country areas of Australia. Also known as an unmade road.

National Park – state government-run public open space.

Petrol – petroleum, called gas or gasoline in some countries.

Petrol station – sells fuel and other conveniences. Called a gas station or filling station in some countries.

Redback spider – a common and highly venomous spider named after the prominent red stripe on the backs of females which are much larger than males. Redbacks commonly live in or near human residences.

Secondary school – for children aged about 12-18, completing years 7 to 12 of education in preparation for work or tertiary education.

Shifter – an adjustable spanner or wrench.

Tea – evening meal, also known as dinner. Called supper in some countries.

Tap – small valve for controlling water flow, often called a faucet or spigot in America.

Uni – university.

Chapter 1

Another Camp Ends

Dan and Dave were examining sports equipment at the Roses Gap Camp before putting it away into storage. It was a wet day in the middle of March and they were huddled in the equipment shed out of the rain.

The Turner family had managed six camps at the campsite since arriving in November. This was the final day of what was to be their last camp for some time.

"That's the last helmet," said Dan. "Now we've only got to check the harnesses and do a visual inspection of the ropes."

"I've had a great time learning how to look after this equipment – and use it too!" said Dave. "Much better than being stuck at uni in Adelaide."

"Or locked down in Melbourne," agreed Dan.

The cousins had spent the last three months together working with Alex and the rest of the family to keep the Roses Gap Camp open when the owners, Steve and Sylvia, had been forced to go to Melbourne for Sylvia's cancer treatment. It had been expensive and they had feared that the campsite would have to close, but the Turners and Alex had shared their reward for the recovery of NK2's stolen gold and this had covered the cost. Now, instead of shutting down the camp, they were planning upgrades using the funds gained from six successful camps and the knowledge that the Turners and Alex were available to continue helping run the campsite.

As a result, everyone had agreed that there would be no camps until the start of May.

Steve and Sylvia would stay at the campsite while the Turners finally took the camping holiday they'd planned when they left Melbourne. Much to Dan's satisfaction, Dave would come with them.

"I'm looking forward to camping," said Dave, picking up one of the harnesses they were inspecting.

"Yes, we've spent enough time here in Roses Gap," said Dan. "Time to head for the hills."

At that moment, Alex hurried into the shed, eager to escape the rain. "How's the inspection going?" he asked.

"Everything looks pretty good so far," said Dan. "One carabiner was badly cross-threaded and the spring on the gate of another was broken, so we'll need to replace them, but that was all. Oh, and one of the campers said that a rope was looking a little frayed. I'm just about to start inspecting the ropes so I expect that we'll find it soon."

"Have you written it all in the log book?"

"All except for the rope."

"Well, make sure you put that down too. It's not a formal report, but if a camper mentions something, we always need to check it."

"I'll do it now." Dan made a note in the log book while Dave began to inspect the strong but soft and flexible climbing ropes. Soon, Dan joined him. He loved the smooth bulk of the ropes that gave such a feeling of solid reliability. He knew by now that climbing with ropes demanded caution, but felt a deep-seated confidence in their reliability when used properly. He had never done any rock climbing before coming to Roses Gap and had thoroughly enjoyed learning from Alex, who had taught him many of the technical requirements for climbing and for supervising climbing and other sports activities. Visually inspecting the ropes and running them through his hands to make sure there was no internal damage was something he enjoyed. He had found that his fingers were very good at identifying any unevenness or fraying in ropes, and it wasn't long before he found the rope the camper had mentioned. Alex inspected it as well and decided that the rope should be taken out of service – there was enough fraying that it might get caught in carabiners or other devices.

Inspections complete, the three made sure that the equipment was neatly stowed and ready for the next camp. Alex locked up the shed and they hurried back to the living quarters, getting out of the rain as soon as they could.

The car park was still full of vehicles, but within minutes, the campers would begin departing and another successful camp would be over.

The campers were students from a secondary school in Horsham, and they were hurrying backwards and forwards between the cabins and the several buses that would take them home. Laughter and happy shouts showed that they had enjoyed the camp, despite the unseasonably heavy rain that had dampened their spirits over the last two days.

"Is there anything else for us to do?" asked Dan as he led the way into the office where his mother Tanya and his sister Belinda were finalising the paperwork for the camp organisers.

"We're just making sure the final invoice is correct," said Tanya. "Belinda is going through it one last time to make sure nothing has been left out."

Belinda had enjoyed the varied work they had all done at the campsite, but she had been surprised at just how much she had enjoyed the administrative work and accounting chores – particularly when it was rainy or extremely hot!

"Nice to work inside where it's dry, hey sis?" teased Dan.

"Well, someone has to do the work indoors instead of playing around outside."

"Would you like to swap places then?"

"No thanks, Danny-boy," said Belinda, smiling sweetly. "This job needs someone who can add up numbers properly."

"Ah, so that's why Mum's with you?"

"Children, children," said Tanya, exasperated. "We've only got a few minutes to finish this. If you want to be helpful, Dan, go and find your father and help him. I think he's in the kitchen with Steve. Something to do with pumps and the dishwasher."

As Dan, Dave and Alex headed out into the rain, Alex stopped and said, "I'll go and clean the solar panels. Your dad said they need cleaning and the rain will make that easier."

He went back inside to get his rain jacket while Dan and Dave made their way to the kitchen. There they found Dan's dad, Nathan, and Steve, the owner of the campsite, easing the large commercial dishwasher away from the wall. A steady stream of water was running out from underneath and pouring into the drain in the middle of the floor.

"Can we help?" asked Dan.

"We've got to find out where this leak is coming from, and that means moving the dishwasher," said Nathan. "We've undone the hold-down bolts and moved it away from the wall a bit, but now we need to disconnect the pipes so that we can move it away further and see what's going on. Dan and Dave, can you disconnect the pipes while we go and turn off the power for this room? I also need to show Steve a few things that have changed since we came."

"Sure," answered Dan and Dave together.

Nathan and Steve left the kitchen and Dan went to look behind the dishwasher. There wasn't much room behind it, or much light, either.

"Lots of spiders' webs," commented Dan, peering behind the machine. "They might be redbacks. I'll get a broom."

He fetched one from the cleaning cupboard and began to clear away the dust and cobwebs, keeping an eye out for spiders – he hated spiders and had no wish to get bitten.

Dave, meanwhile, had knelt down on the other side of the dishwasher and was looking under it, using his phone torch.

"There's a pipe underneath that leads towards the wall. It must be the drain."

"Is the water coming from there?"

"Doesn't look like it – in fact, it looks like it's running down the wall. You might be able to see it better from your side."

Once Dan finished clearing away the cobwebs, he looked down at the water supply pipes – just as the lights went out.

"Hey! How come... oh, I suppose Dad just turned off the power." He took out his own phone and the extra light made it clear that Dave was right. "Yeah, the water's coming out of one of the supply pipes and running down the wall." Seeing the blue fittings at each end of the pipe, he added, "It's the cold water pipe."

By that time, Dave was shining his phone torch from the other side of the machine and a sudden reflection from something on the floor caught Dan's attention.

"Hey, Dave, can you hold your phone still for a moment? I think there's something under the dishwasher – jewellery maybe."

Dave held his phone still for a moment while Dan looked, then moved it around a little to get a better look himself.

"You're right, Dan. I think it's a necklace or a bracelet. Some bits are metal: gold, probably."

Dan knelt down on the floor and reached in to where he had seen the flash of light. Before he'd reached very far he felt something hard and metallic lying on the floor. It didn't feel like jewellery! Pulling it out, he found that it was a large serrated knife.

"That's weird," he said. "Look at this, Dave."

"A knife! Someone must've dropped it when they were putting it in the dishwasher."

"Mmm. Probably."

Dan handed the knife to Dave then looked carefully as he reached under again. He had to stretch as far as he could before his fingers closed on a small cold, metallic object attached to a band. Taking it out carefully, he found that it was a bracelet, mostly made of braided leather, but with gold-coloured attachments for fastening and a single star in the middle.

"I wonder who lost this?" he asked.

"And how long has it been there?" queried Dave.

"It can't have been there long," said Dan. "The leather is in good condition and there are no cobwebs or dust on it. It looks almost brand new."

"Perhaps one of the school kids dropped it this week."

"I guess so, but how could it get so far under the dishwasher?"

"Maybe it just rolled under, and perhaps whoever lost it was trying to use the knife to pull it out. With the dishwasher back against the wall, they wouldn't have been able to reach right under like you did."

"Good thinking, Dave. We'd better go and give the bracelet to the coordinator before they all leave."

"I think we need to check this water leak first," said Dave. "There's a lot of water just running to waste at the moment."

"True." Dan put the bracelet in his pocket and looked behind the dishwasher again. His torch showed that water was pouring out of the pipe close to where it was screwed onto a tap on the wall.

"Could you unscrew the pipe from the tap?" said Dave.

"Possibly, but I'll try turning the tap off first," said Dan, reaching behind the dishwasher and finding the tap with his fingers. It wasn't easy to start, but he finally managed to turn it clockwise until it was turned off. The water flowing from the hose slowed and stopped.

"That did it!" exulted Dan.

"But why was the hose leaking?" asked Dave.

"Dunno," said Dan. "I'll see if I can undo the hose and have a look at it."

Once more he reached in behind the dishwasher and tried to turn the plastic wingnut attaching the hose to the tap. He was still trying unsuccessfully when Nathan and Steve returned.

"We stopped the leak," said Dan, "but you won't be able to use the dishwasher until the cold water hose is fixed."

"What's wrong with the hose?" asked Steve.

"We can't see properly, but it's leaking near the tap end," said Dave.

"And I can't get the nut undone," said Dan.

At that moment, the door banged open and a student rushed in. "Ben just slipped over near the buses and hurt his elbow badly. Is there a nurse anywhere?"

"My wife is a nurse," answered Nathan, hurrying to the door. "Follow me and we'll find her."

The student ran after him, while Steve made his way directly to the carpark, Dan and Dave close on his heels.

It was still raining gently, but three teachers and several students were clustered around a student who stood on one leg, holding his elbow. Clearly the elbow wasn't all he'd hurt.

One of the teachers was carefully rolling up the boy's sleeve despite his objections, "I'm alright. Don't worry about me. Everything's fine."

The blood seeping through his sleeve told a different story, however, and Dan also noticed a matching patch of colour on his trouser leg.

Tanya came out of the office and hurried towards the crowd.

"Are you a nurse?" asked a teacher, and Tanya nodded.

"Then I'll defer to you," he said.

Tanya turned to the boy. "Your name's Ben, isn't it?" The boy nodded and Tanya continued, "Tell me what's wrong, Ben."

"It's not important," he answered, shaking his head.

"So you normally walk around with blood on your shirt and trousers? Is that it?"

"No, but they'll be alright. I'll clean them up when I get home."

"I think they'll recover quicker if we clean them up now and check if you need an ambulance."

"How could you call an ambulance nowadays, anyway?" protested the boy weakly. He was sounding less definite.

"You're right, Ben," said Tanya, "but if we need to, we can get you to a doctor in Stawell quicker than you'll get home, or find a doctor in Horsham. Now, let's have a look."

She pushed back the sleeve and looked at the injury. "How did you do this?" she asked.

"I was running around the back of the bus and I... I fell over."

Dan, watching the boy as he spoke, felt that something didn't seem quite right. The boy had glanced at the crowd around him as he spoke, briefly locking eyes with another boy. But Tanya was busy examining the injury and didn't notice his hesitation. She flexed the elbow and concluded that there was no serious damage, although the boy would probably have painful bruises there for two or three weeks.

"Looks like it just needs cleaning and bandaging. Come on, let's go inside out of the rain and I'll look at your knee as well," said Tanya. She put a hand on his back and pushed him gently towards the office. He tried walking a few steps, but almost fell whenever he put his weight on his damaged knee. Soon he started hopping, though that obviously hurt too.

"That's all, everyone," the teacher told the surrounding students. "Make sure you're all ready to go as soon as Tanya has cleaned up Ben's elbow and knee. Thanks, Tanya." Dan then saw the teacher go and speak quietly to the boy Ben had looked at. With the noise of the other students moving away, Dan only caught the teacher's final words, as he said more loudly: "Off you go now, Ali. Hurry up."

The boy left, a surly look on his face, and Dan wondered what it was all about. During the camp he had found Ben helpful and cooperative in organising and participating in the sports events. He made his way into the office to see how Ben's knee was.

In the office, Tanya asked Belinda to continue checking the invoice, since she was not partial to the sight of blood, then sat Ben down on a seat where Belinda couldn't see him. Starting with the elbow, Tanya cleaned up the oozing wound and applied a dressing and a small bandage.

"That's the best we can do for your elbow," she said. "Now show me your knee, Ben."

"It's not important," reiterated the boy.

"Why don't you let me be the judge of that?" sighed Tanya, rolling up his badly-torn trouser leg, which was covered with blood.

She gently wiped the wound with a wet cloth and cleaned it with swabs dipped in antiseptic, commenting, "Ouch, this doesn't look good. Dan, can you please take these swabs and get me the scissors from the kit?" She turned to Ben again and said, "I don't think you need to go straight to a hospital, Ben, but I really think this knee is bad enough that you should see a doctor today – or tomorrow at the latest."

"My dad can look at it when we get home. He's a doctor."

"That's even better. It really does look nasty – worse than I'd expect from a simple fall, so make sure someone checks it or you may end up with long-term damage."

"Okay, I'll tell Dad."

Tanya quickly finished dressing the knee, then stood up and said, "That's the best I can do at the moment, Ben. Can you walk enough to go and finish packing up now?"

Ben stood up and put his foot gingerly on the floor.

"That feels a bit better," he said. "Yes, I should be able to finish packing if one of the others will help me carry my bags. This won't stop me walking today. It's likely to be worse tomorrow." He walked slowly to the door.

Tanya smiled. "You're right. Can you let us know what happens with your knee? And your elbow too?"

"I'll try to remember. Thanks for fixing me up, Mrs Turner."

Tanya laughed. "Just call me Tanya, Ben. And I haven't *fixed you up*, that's for sure. I hope your dad can do better with that."

As Ben closed the door, Dan asked Tanya, "Is his knee really that bad?"

"I'm no doctor," answered his mother, "but it doesn't look good to me. And I'm amazed that he could do so much damage to his trousers and his knee in a simple fall like that."

"Perhaps he's just easily injured," suggested Dan.

Chapter 2

The Bracelet

Patchy rain continued as the rest of the luggage was packed and the teachers hurried the last students into the buses. The camp coordinator was checking the final bus when Belinda hurried out from the office and proudly handed him the completed camp invoice.

Cries of "Three cheers for Roses Gap" floated out of one of the buses, followed by three rousing cheers, and Dan couldn't help smiling and waving. The camp had been good fun and it was good to know that the students had enjoyed it too.

But how strange it had been to be part of the staff arranging a camp for students, some of whom were almost the same age as himself!

The buses edged away along the driveway and soon Dan heard them turning onto the road that led east towards the Western Highway.

Another splendid camp was over; success tasted good.

Best of all, this time there was no pressure to make immediate arrangements for another camp. Instead, six glorious, wonderful weeks of holiday stretched out in front of them!

"Hooray," cheered Dan as he looked around the parking area, so recently full of noisy students. "Holidays!"

"It's a nice feeling, isn't it?" smiled Nathan. "But let's straighten out one thing first."

"Oh no!" groaned Dan and Dave together.

Nathan laughed. "It's not that bad – we just need to go and check that leaking cold water hose."

Dan stopped suddenly. He shook his head and groaned, looking at Dave. "The bracelet!" he said, fishing it out of his pocket. "I forgot it."

"Where's it from?" asked Nathan.

"We found it under the dishwasher."

"It looks quite new. It can't have been there long."

"We think one of the students probably dropped it during the camp," said Dave.

Dan handed it to Nathan. "I intended to give it to the camp coordinator before they left, but with all the excitement over Ben's injury, I forgot about it."

Nathan examined it for a moment. "I guess you're right. I wonder who dropped it?" He gave it back to Dan. "How about you look after it for the time being."

"Okay," said Dan. "We've got to get it back to its owner, which would have been much easier if I hadn't forgotten it."

"True. Anyway, let's go to the camp kitchen. I want that dishwasher hose fixed."

In the kitchen, Dan and Dave were quite pleased that Nathan had to use a shifter to undo the wingnut on the cold water hose. After disconnecting both ends of the hose, he took it out to have a look.

"This didn't fail from old age," he said, puzzled. "It's a very clean split – almost as if someone cut it deliberately."

"Well, we did find a knife under the dishwasher," admitted Dan. "Over there." He pointed to a bench.

"But why would anyone cut a hose like that?" asked Nathan.

"Doesn't make any sense to me," answered Dave.

Nathan picked up the knife and held it against the clean cut in the water hose.

"Looks like it could fit, but I'm no forensic scientist."

"Can we get a new hose from Stawell?" asked Dan.

"Are you wondering if we might have to go to Horsham?" teased Nathan.

"Well, that would let us kill two birds with one stone and return the bracelet."

"Hmm," mused Nathan, frowning. "You found that bracelet under the dishwasher, didn't you?"

"Yes."

"And the knife was under there too?"

"Yes."

"It seems pretty clear what happened," said Nathan, shaking his head. "But why?"

"Some people just seem to like causing trouble," said Dan. "Craig and Brad taught me that."

"Suddenly, I'm not in so much of a hurry to get this bracelet back to its owner," said Nathan.

CR

Four months ago, when they decided to leave Melbourne to escape another round of lockdowns, their plan had been simply to cross the western margin and take a holiday in the Grampians, but that wasn't how it had worked out. Instead, the family had taken over the management of the Roses Gap campsite to help a couple they had never met.

None of them regretted the decision and they were all glad that their efforts had genuinely helped Steve and Sylvia, but now the tantalising picture of a camping holiday danced again before Dan's eyes.

His paternal grandfather had often said that hard work was its own reward, but Dan had never understood what he meant. Now he felt that he did understand: hard work had made him grow up, and he felt like a different person from the teenager who had walked out of his last exam just four months earlier, looking forward to a holiday followed by a few lazy years at university.

Hard work really did bring its own rewards, and so did helping others. He was also glad to have a growing knowledge and experience of Christianity – Alex had taught him a lot, and he was eager to learn more.

The magnificent start of a glorious holiday was right there in front of him, but there was one major problem: rain.

One of the teachers had said that March was normally one of the driest months in the Grampians, yet this year rain had fallen frequently and heavily since the very first day of the month.

The last two days had been the wettest of all, and the campsite was saturated all over, and boggy in various places.

The small lake in the campsite was full and overflowing, and the creek that ran down the valley was flowing rapidly, carrying far more water than Dan had seen at any time since their arrival. Every water tank on the site was full and the family's washing was hanging limply on the line, as it had done for three days.

And who wanted to go camping in the rain?

He remembered one particular camping holiday that wasn't a pleasant memory. The rain had begun as soon as they had set up the tent, and soon afterwards he was out with a small spade digging trenches. True, he hadn't been asked to do so, and maybe there wouldn't have been any trouble if he hadn't, but he remembered being out there in the rain while water dripped in large drops off the trees, the tent, the ropes and the annex. Most of it had seemed to drip down his neck!

Camping in the rain was not Dan's idea of fun.

True, he had enjoyed watching his carefully dug trenches carrying the unwanted water away from the tent, but he still had a fixed idea that rain and camping did not go well together.

If only the rain would stop! Didn't God control the rain? Should he pray about it? He didn't feel that he knew enough about God to be sure of the answer. And didn't the countryside need rain anyway? Throughout the summer, many campers had said that the Wimmera was facing a drought and needed rain badly. A wettish spring had been a help, but more rain was needed.

He decided that he should leave it up to God, although he knew what he wanted!

When Alex returned – rather wet – from cleaning the solar panels, Dan asked him about praying for dry weather and Alex smiled.

"If everybody prayed for what they wanted with the weather there'd be a real problem, wouldn't there? Imagine a family where the father wants cool weather for planting his crop, the mother wants hot weather to dry the curtains she's washed, one child wants gentle rain to keep him cool during a cross-country run and another child wants to see some snow for the first time. Then multiply that by thousands of families! Personally, I think it's probably best to leave the weather to God – most of the time, at least."

"Wasn't there a prophet in the Bible who asked for there to be no rain and it didn't rain for three and a half years?"

"Yes, that was Elijah. Another prophet, Samuel, once asked for rain at a time when it never normally rained in Israel."

"Was his prayer answered?"

"Yes."

Chapter 3

A Late Breakfast

Sometime during the night, the persistent rain finally stopped.

When Dan awoke rather late the following morning, he saw bright sunshine creeping around the edges of the curtains in his room. He rolled over onto his back and stretched out, revelling in the opportunity to stay in bed for a while.

Six weeks until the next camp, and today a lazy Saturday. He linked his hands behind his head and smiled to himself.

What a perfect day!

Over dinner the previous night, the family had discussed possibilities for the next six weeks.

Steve and Sylvia planned to stay at the campsite while some of the cabins were refurbished and a new demountable staff building was put in place. Since their return, Steve and Sylvia had been living in a cabin a little way from the rest of the camp buildings, which had suited them well with Sylvia's ongoing need for rest and quiet. Now, though, she'd improved enough that they planned to return to their ordinary living quarters after the Turners and Dave left. As a result, Steve had decided that having some staff quarters onsite made sense given the recent deterioration of many local roads. In the past, camp staff had commuted from Stawell and Horsham, but that was becoming increasingly difficult. He also hoped that the Turners would be willing to stay on a long-term basis, particularly if Sylvia became unwell again. Although she was no longer considered to be in danger, she was taking longer than expected to build up her strength.

Meanwhile, however, the Turners were free to pursue their own objectives. Nathan and Tanya had intended to find somewhere to camp, but the relentless, unseasonal rain had put a dampener on that idea. As a result, they had suggested waiting a few days to see if the weather might improve.

Belinda had kept quiet. Nobody had yet suggested that she should return to school, but she felt it best not to draw attention to herself in case her mother did so. She wasn't particularly worried about her father – he wasn't likely to think about it anyway, and if he did, she was sure he'd be easy to convince that a year of general education would be more valuable than having the whole family tied down somewhere in Stawell.

Dan wasn't worried about education at all. Not only had he missed the closing date for university applications, but the first semester had already begun. Dave was in the same situation, and together they were eager to go camping somewhere far from the madding crowd.

Neither, however, was eager to camp in the rain.

Dan lay in bed thinking of how much he had enjoyed their time in the Grampians. Life beyond the western margin had been even better than he could have imagined, and becoming a country lad was far more satisfying than the city life he had experienced until last November.

It was true that having no access to the internet and a mobile phone network had been frustrating at first, but he had got used to it. One thing he still missed, though, was weather reports, and he wondered what the forecast would have been for today.

Never mind – if he wanted to make his own forecast, all he had to do was get up and have a look outside! But for the moment, bed was too comfortable.

He also decided that he should pray before he got up. He had plenty to say thank you for and still found their freedom beyond the margin something to marvel at.

☙

In the living quarters behind the office that morning, their late breakfast was a light-hearted affair – when the Turners, Dave and Alex finally made it to the table.

Dan and Belinda had prepared toast and fried eggs and Dave had set out the cutlery, crockery, spreads and cereal on the table. Everyone looked refreshed from a long sleep and glad for a later start to the day.

"It's a very different breakfast from our first morning here," said Tanya. "Orange juice on our cereal!"

"It was pineapple juice, Mum," said Belinda.

"Ugh!" answered Tanya. "Even worse."

"And that was the morning we first met Brad Jessop," said Nathan.

"I suppose it was a profitable meeting, really," laughed Dave.

"It certainly led to a big reward," acknowledged Dan. "But I still think I'd prefer never to have met him. And as for Craig – I didn't know that there were such vicious people around."

"Well, he's dead and gone now, Dan," said Tanya, "so we don't need to worry about him anymore. I wonder if anyone misses him."

"And what was he like as a kid?" asked Belinda, soberly.

"Perhaps nobody fed him juicy porridge when he was young and that's what turned him bad," smiled Dan.

"People make lots of choices in life," said Alex. "It's not just one choice that makes us good or bad. It's a whole series of choices. Fergus told me some of Craig's history a few weeks ago. He started as a petty criminal and worked his way up – or down, I suppose – but he was always a criminal. And always violent, even at school."

"As you say, life is about choices," said Nathan, "and the choices we make show what we are. Brad Jessop is no good for society, but he's still very different from Craig."

"I'm sorry for Miranda Jessop," said Belinda. "At least she's doing her best to avoid following in her brother's path. I hope she succeeds."

"So do I," said Tanya.

"I think she will," said Alex, "but we'll have to wait and see – and that's just the same for all of us. As my grandfather used to say, 'life isn't over until it's over, and then it's too late to change'."

"As it is with Craig," observed Nathan. Everyone nodded.

Though dead, Craig had still managed to put a dampener on the company.

"How's the toast going, Dan?" asked Dave after a few moments. "I'm hungry."

"Some luscious toast coming up, Dave. Done to a turn and fit for a king." Dan took a piece out of the toaster, put it on a plate and spun it up into the air, catching it after it had made two lazy turns. "There," he said, "Spun to a turn – or two!"

"I wonder if we'll ever see Brad or Miranda again," mused Belinda.

"Brad won't be out of prison for twenty years or so," said Nathan. "I'm not sure whether it's one of the advantages of being separated from Melbourne, but his trial was very quick."

"The justice system out here has certainly sped up since the margins were drawn," said Alex.

Breakfast continued with all of them eating heartily and enjoying a relaxing time.

Finally, Nathan asked, "What are we all doing today? Are you doing any work for Steve this morning, Alex?"

"Yes, a few hours, and I must remember to measure up that leaking dishwasher hose. Then I'll be going back to Stawell and, come Monday, working in the bank for a while." He rolled his eyes as if working in the bank was much the same as going to prison. "Still, Dad is happy for me to work for Steve on a casual basis over the next six weeks whenever he needs me, so I can live in hope! I'll also get a replacement for the hose in Stawell."

"Hey, what are we going to do about worship meetings?" asked Dan. "I've been enjoying having them every week."

"I'm sorry, I hadn't really thought about you missing it," said Alex. "I was going to meet with some friends in Stawell tomorrow who I haven't been able to meet with while I've been here."

"Are these friends part of a church?" asked Dan, interested.

"Different ones go to different churches. We meet together because we're still learning by reading the Bible. Perhaps it'll become a church of its own some time. I'm not sure."

"So why do people from different churches meet together to talk about the Bible? Are they unhappy with their own churches?"

"I suppose so, to some extent. We've all become convinced that what the churches teach is not what we're reading in the Bible. So we're each trying to decide what to do about that."

"And are you doing the same?" enquired Dan.

"Not quite," Alex sighed. "You see, I've made up my mind not to join any church until I can find one that pays more attention to the Bible and less to either church history or the ideas of our modern society. I'm still looking."

"I agree with you about the Bible," said Dan, "but why do you feel that way?"

"My grandfather read his Bible all the time, and that convinced him to believe it above everything else. I've done the same."

"I'm trying to follow that path," agreed Dan, "and the Bible hasn't let me down yet."

"Maybe you just don't have enough life experience yet," interjected Belinda.

"But I've had people telling me the Bible is wrong all my life," objected Dan. "Almost everyone I meet tells me that, either directly or indirectly. But none of their arguments are convincing. Whereas the Bible's arguments are convincing: creation; right and wrong; foretelling the future; Jesus' resurrection; the popularity of evil and many other things. I'm no theologian, but the Bible makes sense."

"After our discussions over the summer, I'd have to say that I agree on that more than I used to," said Nathan.

"Same here," said Tanya. "You know I didn't think much of churches or Christianity itself, but I have to admit that actually reading the Bible has made me change my mind a bit."

"I'd like to meet your friends in Stawell if I could," said Dan. "But if you don't think I should, that's alright too."

"I'll see what I can arrange, but it could be difficult to get you there."

"That's true. I think it's too far to ride, so maybe I should just forget about it."

"Don't worry. I'll find a way. Are you going to be here when I leave?"

"I don't know. What are we doing today, anyone?"

"Your mother and I thought it would be a good idea to go for a walk. Since it's been raining so much, going to see creeks or waterfalls would be interesting."

"That would be great," agreed Belinda.

"Beehive Falls again?" asked Dan.

"You could do that," said Alex, "or you might like to go up the valley behind Troopers Creek Campground – where Fergus was camping when you first met him, Dan. There are quite a few nice waterfalls up that valley. Most of them aren't very big, but they're really good when they're flowing. And if you're determined to walk a long way, you can keep going up to the top of Mount Difficult."

"Is it?" asked Belinda.

Alex looked at her blankly. "What do you mean?"

"Is it Difficult?"

"No, not really, it's just quite a long walk for a day, particularly if you eat a big breakfast and don't start until lunch time!" laughed Alex.

"You might have a point," said Tanya.

"Why don't we go up to Beehive Falls again and maybe a bit beyond it?" Dan had a reason for asking.

"What do you have in mind, Danny-boy?" asked Belinda, a speculative look in her eye.

"Oh, nothing in particular," he answered, airily.

"Except for...?" persisted Belinda.

"Well... when we go camping, I thought it could be interesting to see what it's like to camp in a cave. Do you remember those caves we saw when we walked up past Beehive Falls, then crossed the valley and climbed up to the plateau? As you come out onto the plateau, if you look across the next valley you see a few caves, and one of them looked as it if might be a good place to stay. Since it's in a valley, I expect there's probably a creek, and if so, it should be flowing well after all the rain we've had."

"It could be worth going to see," said Nathan, "but I'm always a bit suspicious about caves and water. If they stay nice and dry all the time, how do they end up getting hollowed out into caves?"

"It could be the wind, couldn't it?" asked Belinda.

"I've never tried camping in a cave in the Grampians," said Alex, "but I've looked in a few, and most of them look as if they get wet inside."

"I'd still like to have a look at this one," said Dan, determined.

"Well, why not?" answered Tanya. "I'm not sure that camping in a cave would be much fun, but we can always have a look at it."

Chapter 4

Finding the Cave

Everyone agreed that their large and late breakfast should be enough to keep them going until they returned for an even later lunch, so as soon as they could, the Turners – including Dave, who was, after all, a Turner! – set off on foot for the Beehive Falls parking area.

"I'm glad the misleading signs and so-called honesty box are gone," said Dan as they arrived at the start of the walking track.

"And there's no Craig," added Dave. He had seen very little of Craig, but that had been more than enough!

The bright sunlight of the early morning had given way to a cool, cloudy afternoon and uniform grey clouds marched slowly east across the sky. Following the gravel path between encroaching walls of shrubbery up to Beehive Falls, Dan and Dave heard the roar of water from a distance and saw a cloud of spray obscuring much of the cliffs where they knew the falls were. As they came closer, Dan saw plenty of water plunging pell-mell over the cliff, as if eager to reach the invisible pool at its base. Luxuriant green ferns and contrasting orange rocks added vivid colour to the scene until all was lost behind the blanketing mist below. The path wound up the valley, crossing the creek that carried far more water than it had at their last visit. As they approached the pool at the base of the falls, clouds of drifting vapour surrounded them, almost as if they were in a cold rainforest.

The boys followed the steep track upward and quickly climbed above the spray. It wasn't long before they reached the top of the escarpment and were following the path along a ridge. Dan almost missed the turn-off to the old path, but saw it at the last moment and led Dave down and across the creek. Scrambling up a rocky slope, guided by occasional arrows, they climbed into a hanging valley and followed the steep path towards a tall cliff. Weaving between large boulders, they rounded a shoulder at the top of the valley and climbed an intersecting valley towards the plateau. Dan was eager to reach the plateau first, impatient to spot the cave he remembered.

Dave was experiencing the stark beauty of the climb for the first time, but he had little time to enjoy it as he hurried to keep up with Dan. As soon as they reached the sloping plateau, Dan scanned the valley to the left and quickly identified the cave.

"Look," he said, pointing it out to Dave. "Down there to the left."

Dave spotted it quickly and they studied the valley below them. With all of this rain, there must be a creek at the bottom, thought Dan, but he couldn't see it. It must be between them and the cave, but the valley must be deeper than it looked.

"Can you hear water falling?" asked Dave.

"Yes, I can. It wasn't like that the last time we were here. Where's it coming from? It sounds like a small waterfall."

"I think there are a few waterfalls along those cliffs. Just look along the rock walls and you can see water falling in a few places."

"You're right. It's more obvious when the falling water moves in the wind," said Dan.

The more they looked, the more small waterfalls they saw: streams or trickles of water that fell lazily onto rocks below, the wind producing a random pattering, splashing tune that echoed across the valley.

"If there are waterfalls, there has to be a creek at the bottom of that valley, Dave. Can you see it anywhere?"

"No. I thought the same thing, but I've been looking and haven't caught a glimpse of one yet."

Looking down into the valley, Dan could see that everything was thoroughly wet. Water oozed from patches of soil and moss where they covered the gnarly sandstone that sloped downwards, seeming to become steeper as it went. This rain would trigger plenty of growth while the weather stayed warm enough – before winter came to the Grampians.

Soon afterwards, Belinda arrived, walking by herself well ahead of Nathan and Tanya, who finally puffed their way up to join them as they continued to study the rock walls and temporary waterfalls opposite them.

"It's beautiful," breathed Tanya. Then as the sun shone briefly through a break in the clouds and lit up the scene, she pointed, "And look over there – a lovely fragment of rainbow near that waterfall. You can't compare this with being locked down in Melbourne!"

"No way. I'll take this, thanks," said Dan.

"Don't you miss the idea of going to university?" asked Tanya.

"Not at the moment," said Dan. "I'll let you know if it changes, but I'm hoping to learn some sports and climbing trainer skills from Alex during the year. Perhaps I can get some qualifications for that or learn more about managing a campsite. Those things seem more useful in the immediate future. And I couldn't get inside the margins to go to a university anyway."

"I'm sure you could go to Adelaide," Dave suggested.

"Mmm. Perhaps, but I still don't think I want it at the moment."

"And you, Belinda," said Nathan, "you're up here with us now, but you'll need to go to school in the next few months."

"I've already missed the first couple of months of school, Dad. It's not worth it now. Anyway, a year of education like this will be much more valuable than tying the whole family down somewhere in Stawell."

"Nice try, Belinda," smiled Nathan. "It rolls so smoothly off the tongue, doesn't it? But education is not something that's negotiable, and it's so much easier when you're younger. In fact, it's almost impossible later. At the moment, you've only finished Year 10, and that's not going to get you any sort of job that you'll enjoy."

Dan smirked at Belinda with a 'told you so' look. He had assured her that Dad wouldn't forget about her schooling and that he wouldn't be as much of a pushover as Belinda seemed to think.

"Both of you – and probably you too, Dave – need to give careful thought to education. It's easy to say that it doesn't matter now, but if you want a job you'll enjoy or to be able to support a family or buy a house, you'll find it hard without a good education. There are lots of jobs around that don't require so much education, but they're mostly not jobs you'd enjoy. Do you understand what I mean?"

"I guess you mean that if I like accounting work – and I think I do – then I'll need more than Year 10 to get a job in accounting." answered Belinda.

"Precisely," said Nathan. "And the same for you boys."

"I suppose so," said Dan, reluctantly. "But can I leave uni until next year?"

"I suppose so," said Nathan, mimicking Dan's grudging tone.

"Can I leave school until next year, Dad?" asked Belinda.

"No," said Nathan, firmly. He immediately held up his hands as Belinda bristled. "There, there. Calm down. You must do schooling this year, but you don't necessarily have to be in a school classroom to do it."

"I'm sure that's true," said Belinda, "but how do you convince a school of that? They seem to think they're the only possible way to get an education."

"Last week I talked to the headmaster at Stawell High School. If that school is anything to go by, I think the schools out here have changed a lot since they escaped from the Melbourne-centric stranglehold on education. He said they could give you some tests in the next few days to see what standard you were at and then test you again at the end of the year. If you could pass the Year 11 tests at the end of the year, they'd be willing to say you had completed the year successfully."

"So how am I going to do that?"

"The school also agreed to lend you some books for a nominal fee – and this time it is just nominal, unlike the 'nominal' fee we paid to cross the margin!"

"So I get to go camping somewhere with no power and then study at night in the pitch black?"

"No, our camping time will be a holiday. You won't have to look at any school books at all unless you want to.

But after those six weeks, you'll have to get on with learning. Mum and I will help you, and possibly even Dan. It's probably the best way to keep him up to scratch with the education he's already done."

"Hey, what about Dave?" asked Dan.

"That's up to him, but I'd say the same thing for everyone: if you don't use your knowledge and skills, you lose them. I'm concerned about the same thing myself."

"Okay, I'll try looking at some maths and science after we get back from camping, as long as we can get some books in Stawell. But now, can we go down to the creek and visit that cave?" asked Dan, pointing at the cave.

"Is it safe?" asked Tanya.

"As long as we're careful there shouldn't be any problem," answered Nathan.

"It's probably slippery," said Dan, "but none of it looks particularly steep or difficult."

"Then lead the way."

"And don't forget to look back to see where we've come from," said Nathan. "It would be easy to get lost in this sort of place, and who's going to find you out here nowadays?"

They left the path and made their way down towards the creek they couldn't see, working to the left in the direction of the cave. From time to time, Dan turned around to note landmarks for when they wanted to return to the path.

The side of the valley did get a little steeper as they descended, but walking down was easy. Soon they found a bubbling creek running between shrubs and bushes over boulders and sand bars. Although the creek had plenty of water flowing along, it wasn't hard to cross, walking from rock to rock. A sound of flowing water filled the valley, but it wasn't the roar of a surging torrent, just a persistent splashing gurgle as the water hurried through many rock pools and sudden drops. Often it disappeared into clefts or under boulders, only to reappear as it fell into small deep pools.

Soon they reached the cave, which lay a few metres above the far side of the creek. A cliff rose above the wide entrance and an easily scaled series of boulders led up to the lip of a cave as big as a medium-sized bus. Parts of the floor were level and covered with sand, while other parts appeared more like tables or chairs such as one might find in a caravan.

Dan climbed up first and called out, "Someone's had a fire here. And there's a steel can here too."

"It looks like it's meant to be a small portable stove," said Dave, coming up behind Dan. "You could sit a small saucepan on top."

"It's not only people who've used this cave," observed Belinda. "Look over there: droppings."

"Hmm," said Nathan, "Goat droppings, I'd say."

"This fire area looks good," said Dan. "You could light a fire here that would keep the whole cave warm."

"And keep the goats out," added Belinda.

They continued to examine the cave, finding evidence of damp areas where water had recently been running over the floor.

"That's why I'm suspicious of how dry caves are," said Nathan. "They look really nice in dry weather, but I suspect they'd let you down when you most needed their protection."

"I can just imagine it," said Dan, motioning with his hands. "We're sitting here happily in the cave and then it starts raining and we have to go outside to avoid all the water pouring in."

"It might not help much," laughed Nathan, "but I think you've got the idea roughly right."

"If we decide to camp here," asked Dan, "where would the sun be on a hot afternoon?"

"Surely it would be roughly where it is at the moment," suggested Dave.

"And down to the horizon towards the north west, I suppose," said Dan. "That means it would shine right into the cave. The burning sun in full strength. Not so nice."

"As long as the creek is there, you could sit in rock pools or just hide behind the boulders. There are some other caves around, too – perhaps they'd give better protection."

"There's one a little further downstream that I thought might make a good master bedroom," said Nathan. "It's not so tall and might give more shade."

"And there are quite a few smaller holes in the main cave that would make good cupboards," said Tanya.

"But they don't have any doors to keep out the goats," pointed out Belinda.

"If they did have doors, we might be able to catch some goats and keep them for milk or meat," suggested Dan.

"Goats in a cupboard? I don't think I'd like the smell," said Tanya, wrinkling her nose.

"And I can't imagine eating goat," said Nathan, wrinkling his in sympathy.

"What about goat milk?" asked Dave. "My mum used to get us to drink goat milk sometimes."

"You'd need to find a nanny goat for that – one which has had a kid recently," said Nathan.

"What does goat's milk taste like, Dave?" asked Dan.

"Horrible!"

"Ah. So it sounds as if we could do without a nanny goat."

"What about a pet kid?"

"How long would we be staying here?"

"That's a good question," chuckled Nathan. "I was thinking we might camp somewhere around here for a week and then go over to the Victoria Valley or somewhere like that."

"One week in which to make some cupboard doors and domesticate some goats? Perhaps not," laughed Dan.

They spent a relaxing hour exploring the cave and its surrounds and sitting comfortably on some natural seats that felt as if they were designed for the purpose.

"Hey, Dave," called Dan. "Do you want to follow the creek and see where it goes?"

"Sounds great," said Dave, and the pair set off, leaving the other three enjoying the faint sun that was again beginning to fight its way through the clouds.

The valley gradually narrowed until the creek was forced to hug the cliff on the right that climbed high above them. Suddenly, the creek disappeared into a crack in the rocks and as they walked on they could hear the water gurgling, but see nothing of it. Climbing over a rock beside the crack, they saw a valley spreading out some 30 or 40 metres below them. Hoping to see over the top of a waterfall, they made their way carefully beside the crack down to the edge of a cliff, but no waterfall fell away below them.

Instead, a ledge traversed the cliff that still rose on their right, and along that ledge, the crack continued, carrying its gurgling burden of water. Having crossed the cliff halfway towards the opposite wall of the valley, the crack suddenly opened out and the hidden creek poured over a large rock and leapt out into space, tumbling down into the rocky valley below.

Dan and Dave stopped and stared at the stunning view of a waterfall that appeared from the middle of a cliff in a way neither of them had ever seen before. Above and below the waterfall was an open expanse of cliff with nothing but the ledge leading to it from one side. It was as if someone had made secret piping for the waterfall.

This waterfall was well off the beaten track and was, in all likelihood, normally dry in summer. Dan wondered how many people had ever seen this incredible sight.

"Phew!" he said.

"Amazing, isn't it?" answered Dave.

"We should go and get the others to see this. I've never seen a waterfall like it!"

They hurried back to the cave and Dan called out excitedly, "You should see what we found! Come and have a look."

"What is it? A cupboard with a door?" asked Belinda, lazily.

"If you don't want to look, you don't have to," said Dan, huffily.

"But we think you'll regret it," said Dave.

"Oh, okay," said Belinda, standing up."

"Are you coming, Dad?" asked Dan. "Mum?"

"If it's really so good, I shouldn't miss it, I suppose," sighed Tanya, half asleep in the warm sunshine. She struggled to her feet and reached down a hand to help Nathan up.

But there was no response from Nathan – he was fast asleep, snoring gently.

Chapter 5

Sunday in Stawell

It was quite late in the afternoon by the time the Turners returned to the campsite. They had enjoyed a long, lazy afternoon in and around the cave they had discovered halfway up Briggs Bluff.

Nathan, in particular, had enjoyed his rest in the sunshine, relaxing completely for the first time since they had crossed the western margin.

The beauty and peaceful isolation of the surroundings had touched them all, and the location of their first week of camping was decided almost without discussion.

They found Alex still at the camp, finishing some routine maintenance for the cabins.

"Ah, you're back," he said with relief. "I was wondering if I'd have to find some way of contacting you about tomorrow."

"I'm sorry," said Dan. "It's not the end of the world if I can't get there."

"No, I think I can come and pick you up tomorrow afternoon if that suits you," said Alex.

"How about we take Dan there instead?" suggested Nathan. "Do your parents join the same group?"

"No, they go to a church in Stawell. They don't feel the same as I do about the Bible."

"What time do you meet with your friends?"

"We meet at two o'clock in the afternoon so that various ones can go to their churches beforehand."

"Okay. So where and when should we meet?"

"If you get to my parents' house by quarter to two, I can show you the way from there."

"Very well. We might go a bit earlier anyway. It shouldn't be too hot, so we could have a picnic in the park near the lake."

"Cato Park, you mean? Sounds ideal – I hope you enjoy it. Well, I'd better head off. I look forward to seeing you tomorrow."

"Is there anything I should do to prepare for your meeting?" asked Dan, as Alex wrote his parents' address on a piece of paper and gave it to Nathan.

"No, just bring your Bible – and a willingness to listen."

"No hymn book?"

"No. We don't sing in our get-togethers."

☙

Next morning dawned sunny and warm, and Nathan and Tanya decided that since they were going to Stawell, they might as well visit the church Alex's parents attended. The Turners left the Roses Gap Campsite at about nine o'clock and they saw no other cars until after they reached the

Western Highway. Although it was not busy, there were more cars than they were used to. As they drove into Stawell, Nathan commented, "There's more traffic on the highway today than we've seen since we came here. I wonder if times are changing again?"

"It would be good to get back to normal," said Tanya. Noticing Nathan and Belinda looking at her in shock, she added, "...in some ways."

"It would be nice to be able to get back to Melbourne and empty our old house," observed Nathan.

"Yes, I miss my little car," agreed Tanya.

"There were quite a few cars with South Australian number plates," said Dave, eager to change the subject from "getting back to normal". He was thoroughly enjoying life as it was.

"Most of them were travelling the other way," said Belinda. "Heading toward the border."

"Maybe they came to spy out the place and now they're going back to report what they found," laughed Dan as he turned towards the centre of Stawell.

"Yes," agreed Dave, laughing too. "SA might want to take over the parts of Victoria that the Victorian government doesn't want."

"It's hard to see why the Victorian government wouldn't want the Grampians," said Dan, "but I'm glad they don't or we couldn't have come here. The local newspapers say Victoria still has lockdowns and strict travel limitations. If we were part of Victoria, we couldn't even have travelled from Roses Gap to Stawell today!"

"I saw a car with no number plates at all," said Belinda. "I wonder what will happen with administrative things like that?"

"I believe that the requirements for vehicle registration are much the same," said Nathan, "it's just that now local councils collect the fees."

"Are they issuing new number plates too?" asked Dan. "Plates with BTWM on them?"

"And with a slogan like 'Where the fun starts' or 'Garden State' or something like that," suggested Belinda.

"Sorry to dampen your enthusiasm, kids," laughed Nathan, "but I believe they've decided to keep using 'Victoria'. They're convinced the separation won't last."

"Just as long as Victoria doesn't try pushing their draconian travel restrictions on us," said Dan.

"That's true," said Tanya, "but if people start ignoring laws and driving unsafe or unregistered cars, that's not so good either."

"And the people in that car with no number plates didn't look good to me," said Belinda. "They looked, um... threatening, dangerous. There were stickers on the windows and they were holding placards in a language I didn't know."

"Yes, I noticed that car too," said Nathan, quietly.

Dan drove to the church and parked nearby. As they made their way towards the entrance, Terry and Linda parked their car and climbed out, greeting the family warmly.

"Good morning, Nathan," smiled Terry. "We didn't expect to see you here. Are you coming to church?"

"Yes, Alex has shown us that we should have more to do with God and the Bible, so we thought we'd try your church."

"There's no doubt that Alex loves the Bible," said Linda, "but..." She stopped and looked at Terry. "It's just a pity he doesn't come to church with us any more."

"You know why he doesn't," said Terry. "And perhaps he's right."

"Well, let's go in," said Tanya. "I couldn't have imagined doing this a few months ago, but Alex has convinced me to give religion a fairer go than I've ever given it before."

They entered the church and spent the next hour in worship. A passage of scripture was read and the sermon encouraged the worshippers to be gentle with unbelievers and to avoid bigotry and self-righteousness.

It was a large church and Dan couldn't help noticing how many empty seats there were. The singing was a little thin, but when the service finished, the congregation welcomed the Turners warmly. Some even said that they recognised them from their photos in the local paper with reports about the capture of the gold robbers and NK2.

"I didn't realise you could become famous from one picture in a newspaper!" said Dan.

As they headed back to the car, they met a teenager on crutches making his way towards them along the footpath. He looked familiar, but Dan couldn't work out who it was.

"Ben," exclaimed Tanya, smiling at the boy. "How's your knee? I presume your Dad wasn't happy with it!"

"No, Mrs... Tanya, he wasn't. He sent me to the hospital here and they did some tinkering with it and told me not to put any weight on it for a month. So now I've got these," he said, holding out the crutches.

"Do they think it'll be alright after that?" asked Tanya.

"Yes, they say it should be fine, but how can I keep up with sport in the meantime?"

"Just be glad you haven't done any permanent damage," answered Tanya.

"What sports do you like?" asked Dan.

"Oh, several, but the one I really love is rowing. We live near the river in Horsham, so I can go rowing any time I want to."

"How come you're in Stawell, if you live in Horsham?" asked Dave.

"There wasn't any room in the hospital in Horsham, so Dad arranged for me to come to Stawell. I've been in the new wing they've just built for the hospital. The hospital has to grow because the population of Stawell is growing."

"How long will you need to use the crutches?" asked Dan.

"Four weeks," groaned Ben.

"Wow. That seems a long time for just scraping your knee."

Ben shrugged his shoulders but said nothing.

"It looked pretty bad to me, and having the doctors agree is balm to my professional feelings," smiled Tanya.

As she spoke, Nathan glanced back along the footpath and noticed a concerned-looking man hurrying towards them. He stepped back to allow him to pass, but instead, the man came right up to them. "Why are you obstructing my son? He was meant to come and meet me and you're stopping him. Can't you see that he has an injured leg?" The man had a slight accent which Dan couldn't place.

"Don't worry, Dad," soothed Ben. "They're not stopping me. Remember I told you about the people who helped me at the Roses Gap Camp? This lady is Mrs Tanya Turner, who cleaned up my knee and recommended that I see a doctor."

The transformation was instant. A smile lit up the man's face and he said, "An excellent diagnosis that was, too. Thank you, madam. If you hadn't said that to Ben, I'm sure he would have carried on as if nothing was wrong and his mother and I would have known nothing about it until some of the damage was permanent, so thank you."

"You're Ben's father, are you?" asked Nathan.

"Yes, I'm Ehud Cohen. I'm sorry I suggested you were causing trouble for Ben. I'm just a bit touchy, you see, because this is just the latest in a series of attacks on him, and this one could have been serious. I wanted to make sure that nothing worse happened to him."

Ehud smiled and absently reached up to his neck and rubbed a small star that hung from a fine chain around his neck. With a sudden shock, Dan recognised it as matching the one on the bracelet he had found under the dishwasher. He dropped his hand to his pocket. Yes, there it was – he had made sure it was before they left that morning, although he couldn't have said why. He was about to pull it out when his mother continued.

"Are you suggesting that Ben's injury was deliberate?"

"Yes," said Ehud, grimly. "He was pushed."

"Is this true, Ben? Why didn't you say so at the camp?"

"I didn't want to cause trouble, and... well, frankly, it's happened before. It just hasn't been so bad."

"Was it Ali who pushed you?" asked Dan.

Ben looked at him, open-mouthed. "What do you know about Ali?"

"Nothing – I just noticed that the teacher went and spoke to him after you went into the office to have your knee bandaged."

"I wonder if he knows that Ali did it?" mused Ben.

"What *did* he do?" asked Dave.

"Pushed and then tripped me," answered Ben

"Could it have been accidental?" asked Tanya. "I mean, could he have tripped you by accident then lost his balance as a result and pushed you when he was trying to save himself from falling?"

"I don't think so, Mrs... um... Tanya," answered Ben. "I was running past the end of the bus and he was standing there waiting for me. He's done it before at school. He pushed me sideways and tripped me as I was trying to regain my balance. I shouldn't say tripped, really: he kicked my legs out from under me so that I landed on my knee. And then he laughed."

"I don't understand," said Dan. "Why would he do that?"

"It's an ancient sickness," said Ehud, grimly. "It's highly infectious and there's no known cure."

"Oh, Dad, don't!" said Ben. "It's just that he's a bully."

"How long has he been bullying you?" asked Dan.

"About four years now."

"Does he bully others?"

"Not really, it's just me. And any kids who are friendly with me or support me."

"Do others help him?"

"Yes. His friends do. And he's gradually getting more people who support him."

"Don't the teachers do anything about it?"

"Not really. I've complained..."

"And so have I," interjected his father.

"...but they don't do anything to stop it. They say they will, but it never quite happens."

"That teacher did *talk* to Ali," said Dan, "but he didn't actually *do* anything. In fact, Ali didn't seem to pay any attention to what he said."

"He knows he doesn't have to listen to any of the teachers."

"Why not?"

"Well, the deputy headmaster doesn't like me, and he protects Ali and his friends. There's another teacher who does the same, although he's not so obvious about it."

"But that's ridiculous," said Belinda. "My school wasn't a great school, but they wouldn't allow bullying like that!"

"It's not limited to schools, miss," said Ehud. "Schools are often just training grounds for this sort of hatred."

"Anyway, Dad, this is the family that helps to manage the camp I went to last week. I don't know them well, but I think I know their names." Ben turned to the Turners with an awkward smile and introduced them one by one to his father. He got all the names right, including Dave. "And this is my father," he continued proudly to the Turners, "Doctor Ehud Cohen. He's one of the chief doctors at the Horsham hospital, and also has his own independent practice in Horsham."

"And I'm afraid I need to go back there now," said Ehud, apologetically. "I brought Ben here late on Friday evening because I thought it was urgent, and I knew that a good orthopaedic surgeon I know had been working at the hospital here during the week. He was kind enough to work on Ben's knee yesterday – he said it wasn't a big job as long as it was done immediately." Ehud turned and smiled at Tanya. "In fact, he was impressed that a nurse with no special orthopaedic training had been able to recognise the problem with Ben's knee. So thank you again."

"He also said that if I hadn't had that operation, I might never have been able to row much again," said Ben. "My knee would have gradually got worse and worse."

"And all because of a bully," said Belinda. "That's terrible. He should be expelled."

"No doubt," agreed Ehud, "but I must take Ben home now. Travel is a bit slower nowadays and Ben will have to sit sideways in the back with his leg across the seat – he's not allowed to even bend his knee for a week or so."

"Before you go," said Dan, pulling the bracelet out of his pocket and holding it out to Ben, "is this yours?"

Ben's face lit up. "My bracelet!" he said, taking it and showing it to his father. "Look, Dad. I told you I lost my birthday present at the camp. I was afraid it'd been stolen..."

"That's just another thing that you owe the Turners," said Ehud. "I'm glad you've got it back, but we really must go straight away."

Ben turned back to Dan and smiled. "Thanks, Dan. I'm so glad to have it back. Mum and Dad only gave it to me two weeks ago."

Chapter 6

Cato Park

As the Turners were saying goodbye to Ben and his father, Terry and Linda walked out of the church.

"Who was that young lad?" asked Linda, joining the Turners. "He looks a bit familiar."

"Ben Cohen, one of the students at the camp last week," answered Tanya. "He hurt his knee and had to come to the hospital here for an operation."

" 'Hurt his knee'," snorted Dan. "Had it hurt by someone, you mean."

"Well, yes, but I was glad to hear that the operation should make him able to keep going with his rowing."

"Ah..." said Linda, "*that's* why he looked familiar. He did very well in the state rowing competitions a few years ago and we saw him on the news a few times. We couldn't help noticing him because he came from Horsham. He was a very good rower for someone so young. Everyone was suggesting that he'd be able to go to the Olympics in a few years, but then came the margins."

"I never thought about that," said Dave. "Will they still hold the Olympics? And if they do, who will compete?"

"We don't get much international news now, but I saw a few weeks ago that they're planning to hold the Olympics next year, a year later than they should have been. As for who'll be competing, that's not clear yet. What with some nations avoiding all trade and others swapping blame for what caused the original problem or the later variants, I don't think there'll be any Olympics the way we knew them for a long time – if ever."

"So, what about Ben and kids like him?"

"Some of the states of Australia have talked about sending teams of their own. Others have said no-one can afford it anyway and we should wait until we can get Australia back together again."

"And without specialised Institutes of Sport, Australian sport might not be good enough," said Dan.

"We'll have to wait and see what happens," said Terry. "However, it seems very clear that Ben won't be going to the Olympics, even if Victoria does send some athletes. We're beyond the western margin."

"And it would take a long time to get to America at 25 kilometres per day!" laughed Belinda.

"Yes, maybe Ben could go to the Olympics by canoe. It would be good training," smiled Dan.

They all laughed, but it was sobering to think of everything that had changed in the world over the past few years.

❧

Linda led Tanya a little away from the rest of the group. "Alex said you were thinking of having a picnic lunch in Cato Park. Could we join you?"

Nathan and Tanya were both confident that Terry and Linda would make good friends if they only had time to get to know them, but both couples had been so busy since the Turners arrived that there had been little opportunity.

"I know Nathan would be very happy with that," answered Tanya, "and I'm sure the young ones would too."

"In that case, I'll go home and rustle up a quick picnic. I could even ask Alex if he'd like to come. He might be busy, though: he often spends his time studying the Bible while we're away at church. It's a pity he doesn't come with us, although we do understand his reasons."

"Is he becoming a Bible fanatic? He doesn't seem to be, but, well, you know – saying the churches don't follow the Bible and so on."

"I wouldn't call him a fanatic," said Linda, slowly. "Perhaps it's just that he's more committed to it than I am. Maybe he's right and I'm wrong, I don't know. But it does make things difficult at times."

"He's a lovely boy," said Tanya. "You've done a marvellous job bringing him up."

"Thanks. We did our best, but it was actually Terry's father who made the biggest impression on him – and that was through his attitude to the Bible."

"His grandparents died a couple of years ago, didn't they?" asked Tanya.

"Yes, of COVID-19. It was very sudden. Poor Alex found both of them dead when he went to see them one Sunday afternoon. I'd visited early on the Saturday and they seemed quite alright. Perhaps I didn't check them well enough, but they certainly weren't admitting that there was anything wrong. They never did like to admit to being sick."

"Poor you, to have such a horrid shock when you were doing your best to look after them."

"I've felt so guilty ever since, wondering if I should have been able to tell that they were seriously sick. Perhaps they'd have survived if they'd been in the hospital."

"I understand why you might feel like that, but you can only do your best. Death comes to us all eventually."

Linda sighed. "You're right, but it's horrible to think of them dying all alone when we were so near."

"They weren't alone. They had each other and probably preferred it that way. If they'd been taken to hospital, they'd have been separated and still might have died anyway."

Linda paused for a while, then nodded slowly. "I suppose so. Thanks, Tanya. Maybe they didn't think the situation was as bad as I felt it was."

"I'm sure they knew you loved them and would never have abandoned them."

"I hope you're right. Anyway, I'll go and get some lunch and see if Alex wants to come. He said Dan had asked about his meetings. Did any of the rest of you want to go with Alex? I think he'd be happy enough for any of you to come if you wanted to."

"I'm not sure. It may seem a bit strange, but we haven't talked about it. I still don't know what to make of it. Loving the Bible and yet not going to a church seems strange."

"Alex thinks it would be wrong – hypocrisy almost – to worship with people whose beliefs don't match what the Bible says."

"I suppose that makes sense, but don't all churches say that their beliefs come from the Bible?"

"Mostly, but some say that the church can interpret or add to the Bible in some cases – and Alex can't agree with that. He thinks truth matters and that religious truth only comes from the Bible."

"He's certainly made that point to us quite often over the last few months," said Tanya.

"I'm not surprised. He's convinced that a lot of church teachings don't come from the Bible but from human reasoning or pagan beliefs. He doesn't feel that he or anyone else has any right to change God's teachings in that way."

"Alex has really made me think about what I believe about God," said Tanya. "My parents were very much against religion because they had some very bad experiences, and I used that as an excuse to avoid thinking about it at all. Alex has made me realise that I've gone a fair way towards passing on the same bias to my children. Well, not Dan, but certainly Belinda. Dan's always been a bit different. He's willing to go his own way if he needs to, whether his friends agree or not, whereas Belinda has always wanted to keep her friends happy."

"Alex was always very popular at school – partly because he was so good at sport – but he wouldn't follow if he didn't like what his friends were doing."

"I suppose that's the sort of person we all dream of being!" said Tanya. "And the sort of person we want our children to be."

"Yes. We could only ever have one child, and Alex has been wonderful – but it's been tough at times recently with his attitude to the Bible and the churches. Yet really, he's just being honest."

"Have you ever been to one of Alex's meetings?"

"No. We nearly did once, but it didn't work out and then we never got around to it."

"Do you think the meetings are likely to be bad for Dan? Do you know the people Alex meets with?"

"I don't think they're likely to be bad in themselves, but they might have a bad result. I know some of the people and they come from several different churches, but they're all... all..."

"Are we going to the park soon, Mum?" called Dan. "I'm hungry."

"Of course you are," laughed Tanya. "You're awake!"

"Which is more than Belinda was in church," said Dan.

"I wasn't asleep," replied Belinda loftily, "I was thinking deep thoughts with my eyes closed."

"And snoring deep snores, with your mouth open."

"Children, children," said Tanya, laughing again. "It's not quite noon yet, but I suppose we could go to the park now if that suits Terry and Linda."

"Yes, I'll go and get some lunch. I should have known that we've been talking too long for a teenager's stomach, but it's really nice to get to know you better, Tanya. See you at the park."

Terry and Linda left, while the Turners drove to the park. Parking under the trees in the shady carpark, they crossed to a table near the playground and spread out their food and picnic equipment. They sat down and chatted as they waited for Terry and Linda.

After a few minutes, Dan and Dave took a ball out of the car and began throwing it, each doing his best to direct his throw so the other had a genuine opportunity to catch the ball, but without it being too easy. It was a game they both enjoyed, delivering both spectacular diving catches and equally spectacular failures where the would-be catcher ended up spreadeagled on the damp ground while the ball bounced mockingly away.

The park wasn't crowded, with only a few family groups spaced out across the wide grassy area around the lake. One larger group of men was gathered on the grass near the lake. They had their backs to the Turners and each appeared to be kneeling on his own little mat.

Dan took a spectacular catch and jumped to his feet determined to give Dave an even better catching opportunity. He threw the ball hard and low, but alas, his judgement was awry, upset by the excitement of the moment, and the ball was well out of Dave's reach as it bounded away towards the lake. Among the kneeling men it flew, striking one a sudden blow on the arm. It was not a heavy blow, but it was unexpected – and the reaction was equally so.

The man jerked in shock and, looking up, saw the ball ricochet away and roll into the lake.

"Who did that?" the man shouted, leaping to his feet and turning around.

"I'm sorry," called Dan. "It was an accident."

"You fool!" said the man, obviously furious. "You deserve..." Dan felt a thrill of fear as the man thrust his hand into his pocket and began awkwardly to pull a large black object from it. Was it a pistol?

One of the kneeling men hurried to his feet and stood between Dan and the unexpectedly angry man. He put a soothing hand on his companion's. "Hush, hush," he said quietly, "Put it away," then dropped into another language that Dan didn't understand. The irate man paused, but if looks could kill, the black scowl on his face would have left Dan cold on the grass.

Fortunately, however, even such an extreme of fury was harmless without action, and slowly, his friend convinced him to put his hand back into his pocket. Not until later did

Dan recall the friend's practised skill and wonder if calming was often needed.

As the friend paused, Dan recovered from his shock and repeated, "I'm sorry."

The scowl didn't lighten one iota, but the man's hand did come out of his pocket – empty, much to Dan's relief.

"Excuse my friend," said the conciliator. "You gave him a shock, interrupting his prayers like that."

"Prayers?" repeated Dan blankly. Could interrupting a prayer really trigger such potential violence?

"Yes, our prayers are very important to us, so we can be quite upset if they are disturbed."

Dan shook his head a little, but decided to apologise one more time – after all, he had never intended to interrupt anyone's prayers. "I'm sorry to cause trouble." He walked past the group to where the ball was bobbing on the water. Fortunately, a stick lay nearby and he was able to reach the ball and shepherd it back to land without getting wet. Picking it up, he retraced his steps, doing his best to wear an apologetic smile, although he still didn't understand how the interruption could possibly have been so important.

As he passed, the man, his scowl only a few shades lighter, pointed at Dan and growled, "I'll remember you."

It was a disconcerting incident, and Dan and Dave put the ball away.

Soon, Terry and Linda arrived with their picnic, announcing that Alex would come in his own car in a few minutes.

Lunch began quietly. Mid-way through, Dan was pleased to see the men pack up and leave. After that, he relaxed a little and was able to explain to Terry, Linda and Alex what had happened.

"So it was the guys between us and the lake?" asked Terry. "I've never seen any of them before."

"I hope we don't see them again!" said Dan.

"So do I," said Belinda. "To be honest, that bloke reminded me of Craig."

There was a sombre silence.

A few minutes before two o'clock, Alex said, "Dan, are you ready to go to Matthew's house? How about I take you in my car?"

"That sounds good," said Dan. "What do you think, Dad?"

"We need to meet you somewhere afterwards, Alex."

"Just go to Mum and Dad's house, if that suits, and I'll take Dan back there. Our meetings normally go for an hour or two, but it really depends on what we're reading. We also might have another new person joining us. You know him, Dan, but that's all I'll say for now. He may not come. Let's go."

"Could I come too?" asked Dave.

Alex looked pleased. "Of course, Dave. We'd be glad to have you join us."

Chapter 7

Discussions

The drive to the home where the group met was short. As Alex parked outside, he laughed and said, "Now, before we go in, one of the funny things about this group is the names of four of the men here. Matthew owns the house, then there's Mark, Luke and John. Yes, seriously, they do have the same names as the four gospels in the Bible. There are also six women in the group, but I won't overload you with their names at the moment – though you might be amused when you hear them too."

They walked up the path and the front door opened as they climbed the stairs to the porch. A smiling man welcomed them and Alex carried out introductions: "Dan and Dave, this is Matthew. Matthew, these are Dan and Dave Turner. Cousins, not brothers."

"Welcome, Dan and Dave," said Matthew. "Come in and meet the others."

As they walked along the hallway, they heard a growing murmur of voices until Matthew led them into a large lounge room where several people were already seated. Greetings were exchanged and Dan and Dave were introduced to Mark, Luke and John as well as six women: Sarah, Rebecca, Hannah, Mary, Felicity and Dana.

Alex smiled at Dan. "You see what I mean about the names?" he asked. "Of the twelve of us who often attend – including Eve who said she couldn't come today – nine have names straight out of the Bible, and mine's not far off. It's amazing."

A ripple of laughter spread across the room.

"For what it's worth," said Mark, "it's not because my name's Mark that I believe in the Bible!"

"The same for all of us," said Rebecca, "but I admit that my name does make me think of Rebecca in the Bible. She had amazing faith."

The others agreed with both sentiments.

Everyone found a seat and Luke was about to begin the more formal part of the gathering when there was a knock on the door.

Alex looked up and said mysteriously, "Sounds like he made it. I'll go and let him in, if that's okay, Matthew."

Matthew nodded and Alex stood up and left the room. In the sudden silence, they heard him open the door and say, "Welcome. Come in and join us."

"Thanks for the invitation," said a voice that Dan recognised immediately, but couldn't quite put a name to.

Alex led a man into the lounge room and said, "This is Fergus Norton, a relative of mine – and a policeman."

"Fergus!" said Dan in surprise. "I didn't expect to see you here."

"Nor I you, young man. Caught any criminals lately?"

Dan laughed and some of those in the room smiled, but one or two wore serious expressions. Dan was puzzled – it seemed Fergus wasn't as welcome as he might have been.

"Our famous policeman," said Mark.

"Not for much longer," answered Fergus, "but I didn't come here to hijack your discussions with my problems."

"Have a seat here," said Matthew, waving to a comfortable-looking chair in the corner. "I think we have a full house now, so let's start. Sarah and I are very glad to welcome you all here as people who love the Bible and want to understand it better. Let's start our time together with a prayer to God."

As Dan listened to the prayer, he couldn't help noticing how different it was from the euphonious prayers he had heard that morning in church. It was specific and down to earth, with much of the stark simplicity of the Lord's prayer. Which would God prefer to hear? he wondered. Should one pray in plain and simple terms that suited the moment, or would pre-prepared poetic essays please him more?

He would have to think about it later, he decided, realising he'd almost missed what Matthew said next.

"Over the last couple of weeks, Sarah and I have enjoyed reading from the book of Hebrews," said Matthew, "so today I thought we could look at Hebrews 11 in this class, a chapter that tells us all about faith."

After reading the chapter out loud, he made some comments. "Since this chapter is all about faithful people, the best part of it is that it starts by telling us exactly what faith is. The very first verse gives us a clear and simple definition: 'Now faith is the assurance of what we hope for and the certainty of what we do not see.' We're all used to the scientific approach of examining things to find out the facts, but faith is being sure of the facts *before* you can prove them! Next, the writer tells us that God commended people *because of their faith*. It's not that the Bible is against science, it's just that science only helps with things you can see or test – and faith is about things you can't see or test.

"Then in verse six we're told just how important faith is to God: 'without faith it is impossible to please him, for whoever would draw near to God *must* believe that he exists and that he rewards those who seek him.' Isn't that amazing? If you can't trust God in things you can't prove, you can't please him! Wow!

"So it's not the greatest scientists or the most convincing sceptics who please God – no, it's people who can believe without proof that please him.

"I think our society pretty well worships science nowadays. We believe science and scientists before we believe God. How foolish is that, when science for the last six thousand years has been busily trying to reverse-engineer what God took just six days to do?

"Then the writer goes on to tell us about the faith that drove these people, from Abel to Samuel and others.

"Faith trumps everything!"

"Can I interrupt?" asked John. Matthew nodded and John continued, "I don't think faith trumps *everything* – not quite. Look at 1 Corinthians 13:13."

"Can you read it for us, John?" asked Matthew, turning up the passage in his own Bible.

"Sure. It says, 'So now faith, hope, and love abide, these three; but the greatest of these is love.' "

"Ah, I see what you mean. Yes, you must be right – love is greater than faith. "

The discussion continued, led by Matthew that day, but with others interjecting from time to time or trying to answer the questions he posed. Dan enjoyed the detailed discussion of faith, but he particularly appreciated the level of Bible knowledge shown by the different members of the group. It was clear he still had much to learn! He and Dave both remained silent throughout.

So did Fergus.

Dan noticed that Fergus paid close attention to the speakers, and his face was often thoughtful as he weighed the points made.

After about an hour, Matthew summarised what he had presented, acknowledging the modifications suggested by others, and then concluded by saying that the class was open for anyone to ask any other questions or make any comments.

From then on, discussion was intense.

Dan was interested to hear the different attitudes people expressed towards faith. Some argued that faith was critical and therefore works were unimportant. Others argued that faith was important, but that if no visible works resulted, it wasn't genuine faith. Still others argued that God's grace was all that mattered, since everything needed for salvation came from God.

Dan wasn't completely sure for himself, but felt most satisfied with the idea that, while salvation definitely came from God, his free gift of salvation demanded a response. In short, salvation would only be given to people who responded with faith shown through works, as it had been by people like Moses and David – not to mention Jesus himself.

Dan began to see that some of those present based their conclusions on an interpretation of one or two verses which seemed to override the clear meaning of several other passages. Others seemed better at balancing concepts that were, at times, almost in conflict. To Dan, this approach made more sense and seemed more likely to end up with the meaning that God had intended. He was convinced that the good news of the gospel was simple at its heart, but that it had to be a balance of the concepts of grace, faith and works. Certainly salvation would never be available for anyone without God's grace, shown in forgiveness, but it also seemed obvious that God's grace had some strings attached. People truly could "fall from grace" if they did not pursue a godly life in faith.

The discussion continued for about half an hour, with all participants sharing their ideas openly, but gently. Many different parts of scripture that Dan had never heard of were referred to, and he wished he could find them more quickly in his paper Bible. In the end, he took out his phone and used it to find the passages more quickly.

Fergus was silent most of the time, but asked a couple of questions towards the end. Dan was interested to find that, while Fergus obviously knew the Bible to some extent, he had significant gaps in his knowledge.

When the discussion began to slow, Matthew wound it up, inviting everyone to stay for afternoon tea, then asking Alex to say a prayer.

Alex agreed and, once again, Dan felt encouraged by his prayer, which was clear and simple, praising God, thanking him and asking for his blessing on everyone who had attended.

After the prayer, Matthew and Sarah offered drinks and nibbles to everyone and the chatting continued for a while. Everyone seemed happy and far more enthusiastic than any church group Dan had ever met before.

He took the opportunity to talk to Fergus, interested to find out more about why he was there. For a moment or two, he had wondered if Fergus might be working on a job, but quickly dismissed the thought – attending a meeting like this would warn any suspect that the police were on his or her tail!

"What brings you here?" asked Dan.

"You may not remember, but when we were tracking down Craig and his gang, I said that I might not be doing my existing work for long. This is why. I've been wanting to spend more time looking at the Bible and my current job doesn't let me. I'm on extended leave at the moment, which is why I've been able to stay here, beyond the margin. I've also started having some doubts about the job, but that's another matter."

"Why are you interested in the Bible?"

Fergus smiled. "Why are *you* interested in the Bible?"

"Two reasons, really. Firstly, the Bible tells me about God as creator, and the world around me convinces me that there has to be a creator. Secondly, it tells me what God likes, and I find that I like the same things: goodness, love, mercy, justice, and so on." He paused, then smiled and added, "Or in some cases I'm *learning* to like those things. It's not always so easy."

"Well said," smiled Fergus. "I became a policeman because I liked justice. I confess that at the time I was a whole lot less interested in mercy – it seemed to me that if people wanted to be good, they would be."

"And do you feel differently now?"

"I started reading the Bible during the first lockdowns, for a mix of reasons. Sometimes it was being stuck at home with lots of spare time. But at other times law enforcement kept me very busy and I saw lots of distraught people missing their loved ones in a time of terrible trouble. It stirred my compassion and taught me more about mercy. And that has slowly brought me into a growing conflict with my job. I'm still working through that."

"How much leave do you have?"

"About another six weeks or so."

"What do you plan to do then?"

"I'm not sure yet. There's a lot of time to be spent in the Bible before then." Fergus smiled wryly. "Maybe by then I'll know what I should do – and I also hear that there may be problems brewing further west."

Chapter 8

Cave Camping

It was Monday morning and the Turners were packing their backpacks. Briggs Bluff loomed above them and the family planned to camp high above Beehive Falls until Friday morning. They would spend four nights in the cave, preparing meals as necessary and exploring the surrounding area. The rain had stopped, but the weather was still unexpectedly cool and Nathan suspected they might find the nights quite cold. Still, they all had good sleeping bags and they should be able to find firewood if necessary.

Sunday evening had been spent discussing what camping equipment they would need and how to divide up the load.

Dan and Dave felt that the most important thing was having sufficient food, while Belinda was more concerned about how they could maintain hygiene without toilets, showers and running water.

"There was lots of running water on Saturday," said Dan.

"Yes, but no toilet," responded Belinda. "And no shower blocks or change rooms."

"We could take the little shower tent and you could get changed in there," suggested Dan.

"That sounds good. Thanks for volunteering to carry it!" teased Belinda.

"But there's still no toilet," said Tanya.

"We'll need to find somewhere that's far enough away not to pollute the creek," said Nathan.

"Since I've nobly agreed to carry the shower tent," said Dan, "perhaps Belinda should carry the portable toilet from the camper-trailer."

"No, I don't think so," said Belinda. "But perhaps I should stay back at the campsite to look after it."

"Don't be a spoilsport," said Dan. "This trip is going to be good fun and we need the whole family there."

"And me?" asked Dave.

"You've been part of the family for so long now that I forget you weren't always. Your Dad and Mum are meant to be coming back at the end of April, aren't they?" asked Dan.

"Yes – at least, that was their latest suggestion. They sound like they're enjoying themselves in the high country, over beyond the northern margin. The mail system out here seems to work pretty well for something Victoria abandoned because it was too hard to maintain."

"It's amazing how much better many things work now," said Dan.

"And with far less conflict, too," observed Dave.

"Have you forgotten Craig so quickly?" asked Nathan.

"Don't count on peace or freedom lasting automatically," warned Tanya. "There are always people whose idea of freedom is the opportunity to oppress others."

"This conversation has become very serious all of a sudden," said Belinda.

"Well, I hope my Dad and Mum aren't meeting people like that!" said Dave. "And I'm glad Brad and Craig can't do their worst here any more."

The family – including Dave – set out mid-morning. Everything they needed while camping was packed in their backpacks and they were all glad they didn't need to carry water. They had a filter that was quite good at purifying water, but Nathan had decided to bring some chemical treatment tablets with them as well. In reality, the filter would probably do all they needed, but using the chemical treatment too would be an added safeguard.

They left the camp and walked along the Roses Gap Road until they came to the Beehive Falls carpark, then followed the now-familiar path towards the falls. It was an undulating track, sometimes close to the creek in the floor of the valley and at other times mounting the valley sides, giving views towards the cliff over which Beehive Falls cascaded. The warm sunlight shone through the trees and a cool breeze moved the branches. Many birds fluttered through the undergrowth while others soared above the trees, their raucous calls somehow imparting a wistful edge to the beauty of the morning. It was a calm, peaceful scene.

The packs were heavy and bulky, so no-one was in a hurry, but it still wasn't long before Dan and Dave left the others behind. As they approached Beehive Falls, Dan noticed that their sound was reduced, and when they reached the pool at the bottom, they found the quantity of water flowing over the cliff visibly reduced from two days before.

"Hey, we might run out of water before Friday," said Dan.

"Particularly if the weather gets hot," agreed Dave.

The pair continued climbing the steep path up the escarpment, and eventually reached the top. They sat down on a rock, packs on their backs, expecting the others to arrive in short order.

Their arrival took longer than Dan and Dave had expected, and all three were breathing heavily as they approached.

"Slowcoaches," said Dan.

"We've been here for ages," added Dave.

"Maybe we need to redistribute the load," panted Nathan. "I think I got all the heavy things in my backpack. Plus, I've been having to almost carry these two." He gestured to Tanya and Belinda with a breathless smile.

"I don't think I'm used to climbing with a pack," gasped Tanya.

"Since you two went on ahead, I had to stay with Mum and Dad to look after them – and provide moral support," said Belinda, trying to speak evenly despite breathing hard.

"So why are you last then?" mocked Dan.

"To make sure they don't feel left behind, of course."

"How kind of you! Anyway, why don't you three sit down and have a rest? It's a lovely morning and there's no hurry."

They sat for a few minutes in the shade while Nathan, Tanya and Belinda caught their breath. Then Dan made what was probably the most generous and selfless offer he had ever made.

"Would you three like to stay here while Dave and I take our backpacks up to the cave and empty them? Then we'll bring them back and we can split the load between the five packs."

"Oh, no..." groaned Dave, but his smile showed the complaint wasn't serious.

"I don't think we need..." said Nathan, then stopped as Tanya put her hand on his. "Well, perhaps we do." Another thought occurred to him: "We could leave Mum's and Belinda's packs near the creek a bit further on and all walk to the cave together. Then you two could come back and get the other two packs while we three stay at the cave and start setting things up."

"That could work," said Tanya, "...if you think you can make it up with your pack, dear."

"I don't think that'll be a problem," Nathan answered. "Although I may be a bit slower than the boys."

"I don't want to just give up, though," frowned Belinda.

"You've already got this far," said Dan, "and when we come down on Friday, you can carry your pack all the way down. That won't be easy."

Belinda protested a little longer, but finally agreed.

They found the old path and followed it down into the valley where it crossed the creek. Already, there was very little water left in it. A little way up from the creek, Tanya and Belinda took off their packs and stowed them in the shade of a large rock. Then they all set off up the steep slope, following the arrows as they scrambled up rocks.

With no pack to slow her down, Belinda found the going much easier and was soon walking at the front with Dan and Dave, jumping lightly from rock to rock while they laboured on with their heavy, awkward packs.

"The pack animals struggle on," said Dan dourly, making sure Belinda could hear him.

"While the pampered, carefree fraülein skips happily above," mourned Dave.

"Sorry," said Belinda, "but you did offer! I'll see if I can serve you some special morning tea when we arrive, since I know food is the subject closest to your hearts."

"Not quite," grinned Dan, "but pretty close."

They kept climbing, and quickly the valley with its drying creek dropped away below them. The vista expanded behind them and the boys stopped often – explaining that they were enjoying the view and that shortness of breath played no significant part in their sudden interest in the scenery.

The path continued to climb until eventually, breathing heavily, they reached the rim of the sloping plateau. Shrugging off their packs, the boys sat down to recover. Belinda was quite content to have a rest, too.

They sat looking down into the valley towards the cave that was their objective, but there wasn't much to see. Across the valley, a few small waterfalls still gushed over the edges of the cliffs opposite, but there was no question that there were far fewer than there had been just two days before. Their distant splashing still sounded like tinkling music, but it was no longer all-pervasive, and each individual rivulet had a sound of its own.

After a few minutes, Dan walked back to the edge of the plateau and looked down in search of his parents.

"No-one to be seen," he called back. "Oh, wait, Mum's down there...."

"Remember, don't be nasty to Dad," called Belinda. "It's not his fault he's not as young as he used to be. And I think he really did have the heaviest pack."

"I don't laugh at Dad," said Dan, turning to face her. "He's still stronger than me – but don't tell him I said so. And you're probably right about him having the heaviest pack."

"Of course I do," said Nathan from behind Dan, making him jump.

"Where did you appear from?" asked Dan, turning crimson.

"I just came up the path like you." He turned and pointed at a large rocky outcrop behind which Tanya had now disappeared. "Maybe I was hidden behind that rock when you looked."

Nathan and Dan waited as Tanya struggled up onto the plateau.

She was breathing heavily, but turned around immediately to admire the view. "It's beautiful," she breathed, "and such a delightful trail. I liked it last time, but it's even nicer this time."

"Shall Dave and I take our packs to the cave now?" asked Dan. "Then we can go down and get the other ones."

"Don't you think we should wait until after we've had morning tea?" asked Dave, sounding worried.

Tanya smiled. "Okay," she answered. "Once we get to the cave, we should be able to find some muesli bars in your backpacks."

"Let's go then," said Dan, swinging his pack up onto his back.

"I'll stay here with Mum for a few minutes while she has a rest," said Nathan.

"Don't worry, dear," said Tanya. "I can keep going now. It's all downhill, so it'll be easy enough."

Before long they had reached the cave. Dan untied the groundsheet from his pack, spread it out over the sandy floor and then sat his pack on it. Rummaging around inside, he found some muesli bars which he distributed to the others, except for Nathan who had gone to collect some water from the creek. Already he was setting up the filter, hanging the upper bag from a tree branch. The filtered water would collect in the lower bag and then Nathan would add the tablets for treating the water.

Taking a muesli bar for himself, Dan sat down on the groundsheet and looked out at the creek below and the valley beyond as it rose towards the plateau. It was a relaxing scene and he sighed and leaned back against the sandy wall of the cave.

"This is the life," he said.

"Until we have to go down and collect the other backpacks," said Dave.

"At least you know that we appreciate your help," said Belinda, sweetly. "And when you get back, we'll have a special lunch waiting for you."

"How long before the water is ready, Dad?" called Dan.

"The filter will finish enough water for you two in about two or three minutes. If you want to wait for the chemical treatment as well, add about another half an hour."

"I'm happy with the filter," said Dan. "What about you, Dave?"

"Fine with me. Those filters do a good job. Using the chemicals is just like having a belt *and* braces."

After finishing their muesli bars and enjoying the cold, filtered creek water, Dan and Dave set off back across the creek to collect the backpacks. Dan was already regretting his offer a little because the temperature was rising, and climbing the steep track again would be hard work. However, he was sure it was the best way to get the camping equipment up to the cave.

He and Dave had an easy time climbing down to the lower creek and they found the backpacks still partially in the shade. The return journey was gruelling, but at least these two backpacks were a little lighter than their own had been!

By the time they arrived back at the cave, they were glad to ease the packs off their shoulders and slump down on the floor while Belinda plied them with what she called "special filtered cloud juice".

Plenty had been done to organise the cave during their absence, and Nathan had even set up the shower tent on a flat section of rock right next to the creek, but out of sight of the cave.

Lunch was a wonderfully relaxed meal.

"You were right, Danny-boy," said Belinda. "This is the life."

"We're out in the wilds beyond the western margin," reflected Nathan. "The place everyone warned us about, telling us just how dangerous it all was."

"Yet here there aren't any of the new viruses or variants, and we have freedom to move. Freedom to enjoy life!" said Tanya.

"And God's creation," added Dan. "What a gift!"

❧

As the sun set over the hills behind the Roses Gap Camp, they were all ready for their first night sleeping in the wild. The weather had cooled quickly in the late afternoon and they were ready to light a fire as dusk fell.

Two beds had been set up for Dan and Dave at one end of the main cave, while Belinda's bed was at the other end. Nathan and Tanya would sleep in the small cave just a few metres along. Its sandy floor was enticing, but the low roof would punish anyone who forgot and stood up suddenly.

The meal was cooked on the small stove set up in a sheltered place in the middle of the cave. It wasn't a meal for a connoisseur, but what it lacked in class it made up for in quantity, and Dan and Dave in particular were well satisfied with their first cooked meal on the side of Briggs Bluff.

The moon having set a few hours before the sun, the night was going to be moonless until well past midnight, so the family intended to go to bed early and rise with the sun. They had lights and torches with them, but why run them flat when they could lie in bed and watch the stars wheeling slowly across the sky?

As they lay in bed, finding their so-called self-inflating mats quite firm on the sandy floor, Dan said, "It's good to have a roof over our heads in some ways, but it does limit our view of the stars."

"Didn't Banjo Patterson describe it as 'the wondrous glory of the everlasting stars'?" replied Dave.

"Clancy of the Overflow, wasn't it?" agreed Dan.

Dave probably nodded, but it couldn't be seen in the moonless dark.

Chapter 9

Waterfalls

Dan woke in the half-light of dawn after a satisfying night's sleep. True, he felt a little stiff after the previous day's climbing with heavy packs, and his hip felt as if he had been lying on a hard surface through his thin mattress, but it was a relaxing awakening. He stretched out and yawned, revelling in the comfortable knowledge that there was no work to be done and that their six weeks of holidays had finally, really, genuinely begun. Week after week of peaceful relaxation lay ahead, time spent in the wild enjoying God's creation.

Light quickly overcame the darkness and Dan delighted in the unspoiled landscape it revealed. After a while, the others began to stir and soon they were all up. Everyone agreed that their first night of 'cave-camping' had been unexpectedly comfortable, and that sleeping almost under the stars had been thoroughly satisfying.

"What are we doing today?" asked Dan as they took their time preparing breakfast.

"First things first," protested Dave in mock distress. "Breakfast before we go anywhere!"

"Well of course," said Dan, looking shocked. "Do you think I've gone mad?"

"No questions about that one!" said Belinda, promptly.

Dan did his best to look deeply offended.

Tanya smiled and enjoyed the light-hearted repartee. The events of the last four months had been completely unexpected, but the family did not regret any of it. Finishing the children's education would become a pressing problem sometime, but Nathan and Tanya were willing to take whatever could be obtained from the Stawell High School until the end of the year. After that, they'd have to review the results, but Tanya was confident of success.

Dan waited until breakfast was well underway before asking his question again: "Now that we've got one of the most critical parts of the day under control, what else are we doing today?"

"Well, there's still lunch and dinner to plan," grinned Dave.

"You two are hopeless," said Belinda. "Why can't you consider important things for once?"

"Like what?"

"Like where I should put my teddy during the day while we're camping here?"

"Oh, no!" groaned Dan. "Have you still got that thing? You dragged it all the way from Melbourne, and now you've dragged it up here – or got Dave and me to! I really thought you'd have grown up by now, Sis."

"I'm working on it. It would happen quicker if I had some better examples close to my age."

"Why don't we head up to the top of Briggs Bluff?" asked Nathan. "It's going to be much easier going up from here than from the carpark."

"True," said Dan, "but I had another thought too. We didn't go to the waterfalls near the Troopers Creek Campground and the amount of water in this creek keeps decreasing. Could we walk down there today rather than leaving it until another day?"

"That sounds like a good idea," said Tanya. "I'd like to see those waterfalls."

"Me too," said Nathan. "Then we can go up to the top of Briggs Bluff tomorrow."

"Should we pack up all our camping stuff and hide it somewhere?" asked Belinda.

"I think we'll pack things up a bit in case it rains or we get strong winds," said Tanya, "but I don't think we need to worry about hiding things. There's nobody here, and even if there were, they wouldn't be the type of person who'd steal our stuff."

After breakfast, they set off for the waterfalls walk, taking a picnic with them. Making their way back over to the old walking track, they continued along the plateau until they met the new path, which at that point was part of the Grampians Peaks Trail. Continuing along the path, they came to the first of a series of picturesque waterfalls and cascades that carried the cool, clear water from the peaks and high plateaus down to the surrounding plains.

"We keep going down, down, down," said Belinda as they passed the second waterfall. "But I know that sometime, we're going to turn around – and then it will be up, up, up."

"Not before we've eaten all the food we brought with us," said Dan. He and Dave were each carrying a half-full pack and looking forward to lunch, when most of the contents would be eaten.

Although the water flow was obviously decreasing, the waterfalls still presented shimmering ribbons of water, flickering in the sunlight. Water from the taller falls often drifted far to one side as the wind whipped the water into mist. Fleeting rainbows dyed the mist with delicate colours for anyone who waited patiently and watched.

Other entrancing sights could be seen as trails of droplets traversed the pools, drawing quickly-moving patterns across the surface. Ferns and sedges edged the water's path and glistened in the mist. It was a kaleidoscope of colour and movement. The observant might spot small fish darting backwards and forwards in the pools, while many intricate webs of hard-working spiders were picked out in tiny droplets. Beauty was all around them.

"Isn't it peaceful?" asked Nathan as they reached the base of what turned out to be the last waterfall. "We haven't met any people today and I haven't heard or seen any cars for two days."

"Shall we stop here and have lunch?" asked Dan hungrily, eager to get on with eating.

"It would be easier if we had a table to sit at," said Tanya. "Are there any tables at the Troopers Creek Campground?"

"Yes," admitted Dan, "but it's probably full of campers."

"Not likely," said Belinda. "Otherwise we'd have met hikers on the trail."

"Troopers Creek campground was where you met Fergus Norton, wasn't it?" asked Nathan.

"Yes, and I suppose it wasn't exactly crowded then," answered Dan. Reluctantly, he kept walking, and after a while they reached the campground, finding a table tucked away among the trees at which to eat their lunch. This time the campground was completely empty.

As they ate, the smells of the bush wafted by them on a gentle breeze. Attentive and persistent native birds did their best to convince the picnickers to share their food, receiving limited rewards from time to time.

"That sounds like a car," said Dave suddenly, tipping his head to one side.

Everyone stopped talking to listen. An approaching car was an unusual event.

"It sounds like more than one," said Nathan, cocking his head on one side to hear better.

The sound drew closer and closer, then they heard the crunching of gravel as if a car had turned into the campground. Soon a black four-wheel drive came into view, followed at varying intervals by several others.

Within the Troopers Creek Campground an almost circular track provided access to individual campsites. The table the Turners had chosen was in the most densely treed campsite. They weren't completely hidden from sight, but it was unlikely they would be noticed unless they did something to attract attention.

The first vehicle drove slowly around the loop, and it was clear that the men inside were scanning the campsites carefully as they passed. They stopped three-quarters of the way around, where there happened to be a signboard between them and the Turners.

Dan felt unexpectedly glad that this was the case, though he wasn't sure why.

A second car pulled up beside the first and the men in the two vehicles began talking, speaking loudly enough that the listening Turners could hear almost every word. Several voices joined the discussion, but none of the speakers were visible.

"This'd be a good place if we only need to camp for a short time," said the first voice.

"Sure, maybe for a month or so," answered another.

"But could we finish all the planning in that time, let alone doing the necessary training and getting the extra material we need?" A third voice.

"We don't have very long. A secret like this won't keep for long wherever we are." A fourth voice?

"True, but a remote, quiet place like this will help us keep the secret as long as possible." Was that a fifth voice or was it the first speaking again? Dan couldn't be sure.

"Look, we could use it if we had to, bro," said a different voice – no question this time. "But it'd be better to find somewhere with better facilities."

"Yes, a pity that campsite back there was occupied." Dan gave up trying to recognise the voices. Without being able to see the speakers, it was impossible.

"That would've been ideal. Good sleeping quarters, well set up for feeding a crowd, and probably enough sports equipment to make sure our men are all fit and ready."

"Too public and too close to Stawell. Also, too close to north-south traffic from Halls Gap."

"Comfortable, though."

"This campground would be good for the sort of training we want, including open areas for exercises. We don't want to let the men get soft."

"We might get a bit more intel when Saad gets back. He should be able to get a good view of the area from that mountain, whatever it was called."

"Briggs Bluff, I think," answered the first.

The Turners looked at each other. Was a friend of these men climbing Briggs Bluff right now? Their cave wasn't near the track, but there was no-one there to look after it and none of them was eager to have any associate of these men poking around their cave.

"We should send someone up that walking track. See what things look like around here."

"Good idea. Malik could do that and let us know if there's anything we need to be careful about."

By this time, a line of four-wheel drives was stopped behind the leading two. A few men had climbed out and were stretching or chatting.

"Hey, Malik," called a voice. "Come here."

A young man with dark hair and a darker beard walked towards the cars at the front, disappearing behind the signboard.

"Malik, we think this might be a possible site for us to set up. Have a look around, follow the tracks and see if there is anything that would cause us trouble: houses, settlements, people, that sort of thing."

"Oh no, no, no!" said a new voice, presumably that of young Malik, "I don't think this'd be a good place to stay at all. Have you heard of the GPT?"

"The what?"

"The Grampians Peaks Trail. It's a trail that goes from the north of the Grampians to the south, and this campsite is basically part of it. It may be a quiet place at the moment, but of all the quiet places you could choose, this one will have the most visitors passing through. And I've heard rumours that police officers hike the trail from end to end. In disguise."

"Are we on *that* track? Then I see what you mean – that was how NK2 was trapped. Perhaps we should move on."

"Good idea. You never know where the police might hide."

Immediately, the front car began to roll and the Turners watched as Malik walked back into sight and returned to his car. Slowly all of the cars moved on and after a minute or two, silence returned to the campsite.

"Phew!" breathed Belinda. "I didn't like the look of them!"

"I didn't like the sound of them, either," said Nathan.

"Did you notice the people in the rear car?" asked Dave. "They didn't get out at all. They just sat there, and they all seemed to be holding things. With the reflections off the windows, I couldn't see exactly what they were, but I think they were probably guns."

"I saw them," said Dan, "and I agree. They looked like rifles."

"Oh, no!" said Tanya. "Not again. That's what we saw on the way to Beaufort, and look what *that* led to!"

"Should we be getting back to our cave?" asked Dan worriedly. "I don't know who this Saad is, but I don't like the idea of him finding our cave."

"How many cars were there?" asked Nathan.

"Twelve," answered Belinda.

"With about four men in each, that makes forty-eight men," said Nathan.

"Forty-seven," corrected Belinda. "There were only three in the first car."

"And if four are armed, they may all be armed," said Dan.

"I thought this place was peaceful," said Tanya, "but maybe the people who warned us about what it was like beyond the margins were right!"

"Let's hurry back to the cave," said Belinda.

They quickly packed up their picnic things and hurried up the path past the waterfalls until they approached the junction with the new path from Beehive Falls.

Dan was in front, keeping a sharp eye open for anyone. Having passed the junction, he knew their path to the cave would follow Saad's probable route for about a kilometre.[1]

Just before reaching the point where their path to the cave would diverge from the track to Briggs Bluff, Dan saw a young man approaching from the direction of Briggs Bluff.

Dan thought quickly. Walking at his ordinary speed, he would reach the junction before he met the walker. Yet if he did so and followed the old path, he would divulge the secret of the old path that various arrows did their best to conceal, and in doing so, he might lead the young man to their cave. Alternatively, he could stop where he was and let the others catch up, allowing them to meet the young man in a better place.

Was it safe to meet this young man at all? As far as Dan could see, he was empty-handed but wore a backpack. What was in the backpack?

Dan walked a little way off the path and climbed onto a ridge of rock from which to get a better view of the surrounding scenery.

"What are you doing?" asked Dave, who was only a few metres behind.

Dan didn't answer, but gestured towards the approaching walker. After a quick look, Dave followed Dan off the path, facing in a direction that Dan guessed would allow him to see the walker out of the corner of his eye. Obviously Dave had his doubts too and wanted to keep an eye on the man.

Belinda, Tanya and Nathan were all in sight when the young man arrived.

"G'day," said Dan, smiling at the young man, who appeared to be a year or two older than him – though he would have preferred to ignore him completely.

---

[1] 0.6 mile

"Hello," he answered. There was no answering smile.

"Where are you coming from?" Dan tried to start a conversation to see if he could find any useful information.

"Top of Briggs Bluff. Looking around."

"It's a nice view, isn't it?" replied Dan. "Where are you from?"

"What does it matter to you?" replied the man truculently.

"I suppose it doesn't matter at all," answered Dan, "if you don't want to tell me."

"I don't. I don't like inquisitive people."

By this time, Belinda was approaching, with Nathan and Tanya close behind.

"Oh, isn't it a lovely day?" said Belinda, breezily. "We haven't met anyone on this path yet today. Where did you come from this morning?"

The young man looked irritated, but answered, "Near Horsham."

Belinda opened her eyes wide. "We didn't travel that far. Isn't that a long way to come by yourself?"

"I didn't come by myself. Look, I've got to hurry."

The young man walked off without a further word or a backward glance.

The Turners stood and watched him out of sight.

"Friendly," said Dave.

"Well done, Belinda," said Tanya. "You got him to answer Dan's question."

"Is *that* what you were doing?" said Dan. "I couldn't understand why you wanted to sound like a bouncy little dimwit, Sis."

Belinda looked at him pityingly. "It worked, Danny-boy."

"From Horsham. Hmm. I'm glad we don't have *him* as a neighbour."

They followed the old path back along the plateau and made their way down across the creek to the cave. Thankfully, none of their goods had been disturbed and there were no indications that anyone had visited while they were away.

That evening, there was plenty of discussion about the events of the day and many guesses as to who the men were and what they were doing in the Grampians.

Nathan summed it all up. "I didn't like the sound of them any more than I liked the look of them. They looked threatening and sounded dangerous. And as for going around the country with rifles…" He paused. "Maybe this is why the government decided they couldn't manage all of the state anymore."

Chapter 10

The Flag

Next morning after breakfast, the Turners set off to climb Briggs Bluff, retracing their steps of yesterday along the plateau, then following the Briggs Bluff track up to the higher plateau. They walked along it until they were almost directly above their cave, before making the short but steep climb to the summit.

"What's that up there?" asked Dan as he and Dave made their way up.

"It looks like a flag," answered Dave.

"There wasn't a flag there when we climbed up last time."

"I don't know," said Dave. "I've never been up here."

"And I've never seen a black flag in Australia before," said Dan.

"That's true. Most flags are colourful. I can see *some* white or yellow on it."

"Yes. It might be writing."

They climbed to the top, took off their backpacks and examined the flag, which was attached to a steel pipe.

"It looks as if someone drilled a hole in the rock and put the pipe in it," said Dave.

"How could you drill a hole like that?"

"And *who* would drill it?"

"I reckon it was that Saad bloke we met yesterday," said Dan, with a flash of inspiration.

"You could be right," said Dave. "I hadn't thought of that."

"So, what is this flag?"

"I've got no idea, but I don't like the look of it."

"What's the flag?" called Belinda as she approached.

"We don't know. Do you?" asked Dan.

"No. I think the script is Arabic, but I don't know what it says."

"But why would anyone put up a flag like that in the Grampians?" asked Dan in disgust.

"Is it a flag of a nation?" asked Dave.

"I don't think so. I know most of the flags of the world," said Belinda, "or at least, what they were when the pandemics began."

"Dan thinks it was put up by that Sad bloke we saw yesterday."

"'Saad'," corrected Dan absent-mindedly, then laughed. "Oh, perhaps you're right. He didn't look very happy, did he?"

"Was the pole already there?" asked Belinda. "I don't remember it."

"No, it wasn't here when we came last time," said Dan confidently. "He must have brought it up here with him."

"As well as the flag and something to drill the hole!" added Dave.

"He must have had some kind of battery-powered drill in his backpack," observed Dan.

Nathan and Tanya climbed the last few steps to the summit and Dan quickly explained their conclusions about the flag.

"That guy we met must have put the flag up here yesterday," he finished.

"I guess you must be right," said Nathan. "Time for another visit to the police in Stawell, I suppose. People can't just put up flagpoles in a National Park."

"I thought this wasn't a National Park anymore?" said Tanya.

"That's what most people thought," replied Nathan, "but it was announced during Brad Jessop's trial that the Grampians was still a National Park, but under shared local government jurisdiction."

"I'm glad to hear that," said Tanya. "National Parks are a wonderful idea."

"Yes they are, but what about this flag?" asked Belinda.

CR

After staring at the menacing flag for a little longer, they moved away and stood gazing in silence at the rolling plains that extended serenely to the distant horizon.

Dan was surprised to find that the presence of the black flag felt like a personal attack; a threat of violence; an open statement of someone's intent to dominate by force. Frowning, he turned and looked at it again, wondering if he was the only one who felt that way.

He saw his father looking at the flag, and for a moment their eyes met. Nathan pursed his lips and shook his head.

"I just can't leave it there!" he said. "That flag has got to go."

"I agree," said Tanya, "but is it safe to remove it, Nathan?"

"Those men were dangerous, and this Sad-man was one of them," remarked Belinda.

"It still has to go," chorused Dan and Dave.

"This is a national park," said Nathan. "It can't be taken over by this group of radicals any more than it could by Brad Jessop and NK2."

Nathan examined the flag and found that it was attached with zip-ties to loops welded onto the pipe. "Did we bring a knife with our picnic?" he asked.

"Of course," said Tanya. "I always bring a knife on a picnic."

Dan unzipped his pack, took out the knife and tested it against his thumb. "It's not very sharp," he observed.

"I'll feel safer if I do this myself – and not because someone else might cut themself," said Nathan, grasping the flag and holding out his hand for the knife.

The first tie was tough, but Nathan sawed at it for a while and finally managed to cut it. Two more ties still held the flag, but they were easier. Once they were cut, the flag came loose and Nathan let it fall to the ground.

"That's better," said Dave, and everyone agreed.

"I wonder where those men are now," said Tanya uneasily, looking around.

"I have no idea," said Nathan, "but I think we should take the flag and give it to the police next time we're in Stawell."

Dan grabbed the pole and shook it. "Can we get rid of this too?"

"Good idea," said Dave.

Dan pushed and pulled at it for a minute. "It's pretty well fixed in place. Come and help, Dave."

Together they did their best to bend or remove the pipe, but it wouldn't budge.

"No good," said Dave, giving up after a while.

Dan kept trying for a bit longer, but in the end, he gave up too.

"It's a strong pipe," he said, "and I think it's been glued in."

"Putting up a flagpole is illegal, but is somebody allowed to hang up a flag again if the pole is already there?" asked Belinda.

"We'll have to wait and see what the police say," answered Nathan, "but I hope not!"

Chapter 11

An Unexpected Visitor

The Turners were eating a late breakfast on Thursday morning when Steve appeared near the cave.

"Good morning," he called as he approached. "I'm glad you gave a good description of where the cave was or I'd never have found you."

"Why are you here?" asked Tanya in concern. "Is everything alright?"

"No, not really," said Steve, glumly.

"Would you like some breakfast?" asked Tanya. "We just made coffee – you can have a cup if you want."

"Oh, yes please. I had to leave in a hurry, so I didn't get any breakfast this morning."

"Have some toast too," said Dan, nobly, handing him a piece of buttered toast.

"Thanks," said Steve, taking the toast gratefully, then smiling. "And it's still hot! I appreciate the sacrifice, Dan."

"What's wrong, Steve?" asked Nathan.

"Sylvia had to go to the hospital for a checkup yesterday to make sure her treatment is working. As you know, she was gradually getting better, but that's turned around a bit in the last week or so and she's been feeling exhausted all over again.

"Anyway, when they examined her they decided to keep her in hospital in Stawell until Monday, so I wanted to tell you that I won't be at the campsite when you get back tomorrow."

Nathan looked as if he was about to say something, but Tanya said quickly, "You could have just left us a note explaining things."

"I know, but there was something else I wanted you to know. On Tuesday, about a dozen big four-wheel drives – mostly black – came into the campsite. They were full of men and I didn't like the look of them. They said they were looking for a place to hold a conference of about 100 to 150 people in two weeks' time. I said no because we're going to be busy with new work and you being away and so on."

"How did they respond?" asked Nathan.

"They were arrogant and aggressive. Quite threatening too, but I told them the site was not available in two weeks' time and that was that."

"Did they accept that?"

"Yes, grudgingly. Then they left, but a bit later one car came back and they tried to convince me to change my mind. They offered to pay a large bonus if I let them run their camp, but by then I'd decided I didn't want to have anything to do with them, bonus or no bonus. I told them the camp still wasn't available."

"At least it was only one car."

"True, but it was still three men, and they weren't friendly. In the end, I told them to go because I was too busy to spend any more time on them."

"Did they leave then?"

"Yes, after a while."

"Good," said Nathan. "We saw those cars on Tuesday too, at the Troopers Creek Campground. Twelve cars drove in, with four men in each car except the first, which I'd guess was the one that came back on its own to visit you, since there were only three men in it. The fourth man was busy climbing Briggs Bluff and planting this at the top." Nathan fetched the black flag from the back of the cave and held it up for Steve to inspect.

"Arabic," said Steve. "That would fit. Dangerous, too."

"We took the flag down," said Dave, unnecessarily.

"None of us were happy with leaving it there," added Tanya.

"I'm glad," said Steve. "I can't read Arabic, but I've heard translations of the Arabic on a few flags over the years and none of them were good news."

"Did any of the men come back again?" asked Dan.

"No. I think I finally convinced them they couldn't have a camp there."

"I'm glad," said Nathan.

"There were no signs that they came back yesterday when I had to go to Stawell for Sylvia's checkup. I'd have preferred to stay with her when she was admitted, except that I wanted to check that those fellas weren't causing trouble. I needed to tell you about it, too."

"Do you want us to go back and look after the place?"

"No, I don't think there's any need. If you can just check it out tomorrow afternoon, that'd be great. I'll be staying in Stawell from tonight onwards."

Having explained the situation, Steve was eager to leave immediately, and the Turners wished him well as he left.

"Well!" said Nathan once Steve was out of sight. "This latest group of troublemakers is at least as bad as Brad Jessop. Too many people don't seem to be content unless they can run things exactly how they want them."

"You know, I think we should go back to the campsite, dear," said Tanya, quietly.

"Just imagine if those men come back," breathed Belinda.

"I'm convinced they wouldn't leave everything as they found it," said Dan. "I know Brad Jessop tried to steal everything from the camp, but I reckon these blokes would just take over the camp altogether if they knew there was no-one there."

"We should've suggested that Steve go to the police," said Dave.

"Good point," agreed Nathan. "I hope he'll do so anyway, but with Sylvia not well, it might not occur to him."

"It's a pity to abandon our cave so soon," said Dan, "but things might not turn out very well for Steve if we don't go back to the campsite."

"I think we all agree," said Nathan, looking around at the others for confirmation. Everyone nodded. "There's one other matter I was about to mention to Steve: remember, we need to go to Stawell tomorrow anyway so Belinda can do her tests at the High School."

"Oh no," groaned Belinda.

"You hoped I'd forgotten, didn't you?" asked Nathan.

"Not exactly," mumbled Belinda.

"Just approximately," laughed Dan.

"I'm not sure what that would mean," said Nathan, "but I suppose we'll have to pack up and leave as soon as possible."

It was disappointing to have to pack up early, but they hurriedly stuffed all their equipment into the backpacks ready to leave.

"It's a pity to carry all this food down again," grumbled Dan. "It was heavy carrying it up here, and now we're just taking it back down again. Wouldn't it be better to eat some of it now?"

"You'd end up too full to move," said Belinda.

"It's never happened yet," objected Dan.

"And we don't want it to happen now," said Tanya. "I hope the camping food will be useful for us next week. Can you stave off your starvation until we get back to the camp, Dan?"

"Probably, if I must. But I can't guarantee it."

"Not exactly," grinned Dave.

"Perhaps we can camp here again some other time," said Tanya. "It's a delightful place to stay, even without power and water."

Soon they were ready to leave. They climbed out of the valley and followed the path over the edge of the plateau.

Scrambling down the steep path towards Beehive Falls was awkward with heavy packs, but it wasn't long before they were making their way down the escarpment towards the falls. After that, the path was easier, but they were all looking forward to a rest as they made their way along the camp driveway.

"Looks as if Steve is still here," said Belinda, seeing a four-wheel drive parked near the office.

"No, I don't think so," frowned Dan. "That isn't Steve and Sylvia's car, although it looks quite a lot like it."

"You're right," said Dave excitedly. "I think it's one of the cars that mob were driving on Tuesday. They're not the only people with dark tinted windows, but all of their vehicles had them."

"Here we go again," sighed Belinda, shaking her head.

They walked over to the car and peered inside.

"Empty," said Dan.

"I wonder where they are, then?" asked Nathan.

"Let's look around," said Dave.

"But stick together," said Nathan, grimly. "We don't know how many of them there are or how they'll react. Let's look around the cabins, bunkhouses and mess halls first. Then we'll look at the equipment sheds and the outdoor equipment."

A few minutes later, they spotted four men at the high ropes course, strolling around as if they owned the place.

"Hey there," called Nathan. "Are you looking for someone?"

The four men turned around in surprise and Dan's blood ran cold as one of them quickly put his hand in his pocket.

Dan had little doubt what that hand now held.

However, the man stood still and his hand remained in his pocket.

Scanning the other men, Dan recognised Saad, whom they had met on the Briggs Bluff track. There was no sign of recognition in the man's face as he glanced at Dan, but when he saw Belinda standing behind Dan, he obviously recognised her and pursed his lips.

"Ah, yes," replied the biggest of the men, with the blackest, bushiest beard. "I am Ahmed. We talked to Steve few day ago. We come back to ask more questions." He spoke with a heavy accent and it was clear English was not his first language.

"You were asking about arranging a camp here, I believe," responded Nathan, glad that Steve had filled them in. "It was a pity that the dates won't suit." It wasn't really a pity, but urbane words can often avoid conflict.

"Yes. Pity. But we modify our requirements now. We hold this camp two week later. OK?"

Nathan appeared to consider the suggestion for a few moments, then replied, "No, I'm afraid that won't work either. By that time there will be extensive work being done on the living quarters and shared facilities, and it won't finish until just before the next camp we have booked, which starts in about six weeks' time. I'm sorry, but it just can't fit in."

Seeing the man's frown, Nathan could understand why Steve had called this group arrogant and threatening. Some people might frown in disappointment, but this man frowned in anger at having his plans frustrated.

"We adjust our plan to accommodate you couldn't have the camp in two week time, so what the problem?" he snapped.

"The campsite is not available in four weeks' time either," said Nathan firmly, "and I'm sure Steve wouldn't have suggested that it was available then."

"This just unfair," replied the leader, angrily. "If I were a Christian you were agree what I ask."

"Are you serious?" asked Nathan. "How could you being a Christian change the bookings people have already made, or the arrangements already made for maintenance and construction work? The only thing that might be different if you were a Christian is that you might not complain!"

"This country, Christians get everything they want. Muslims are oppressed. Forced to fight for everything."

"If your complaints about the rest of Australia are as ridiculous as your claim about what we're doing here, then why would anyone ever listen to what you say?"

"Is true. Australians hate Muslims. Discriminate against."

"Rubbish. This campsite is not available over the next six weeks to you or anyone else."

"What if we take over anyway?" snarled Ahmed.

"Then you'd be doing just what you claim is done to you. Perhaps you expect persecution because that's how you would treat minorities if you were in the majority. How were Christians treated in the country you came from?"

"Christians are infidels!"

"It seems I was right," said Nathan, smoothly. "Anyway, the campsite is not available, Ahmed. That's the end of it – there's no point in any further discussion."

"You..." Ahmed shook his fist angrily at Nathan, his face tight. It was clear that he was struggling to control himself – or deciding whether to bother trying!

"And we will be letting the police know about events around here," interrupted Nathan, looking down at him. He was significantly taller than Ahmed, but he had the feeling that this man was used to getting his own way and would resort to violence if he believed it would help.

Ahmed looked as if he were about to attack Nathan, when suddenly he stopped and turned around. He said something over his shoulder in another language to his accomplices as he marched off. They followed him harmlessly enough, but the looks on their faces were not encouraging.

The Turners walked back towards the parking area and watched the car accelerate away, spraying gravel across the carpark.

"That was close," said Tanya.

"It was scary," said Belinda.

"Five against four," said Dave, "but with at least one of the four armed. I think we were lucky it turned out the way it did."

"That was pretty brave, Dad," said Dan.

"I felt as if I had to stand up to him to help Steve," said Nathan, "but are you serious about one of them being armed, Dave? How do you know?"

"When they first saw us, one of them suddenly put his hand into his pocket. The only reason I can think of for doing that would be to get a weapon. As it happened, he just left his hand there."

"I noticed the same thing," chipped in Dan. "He still had his hand in his pocket when he walked off."

"I wonder if the others were armed too?" asked Belinda.

"So now we know why people talk about Islamophobia," joked Nathan. "If that's Islam, it's good reason to fear!"

"Everything turned out well enough this time," said Tanya. "But I agree with you about telling the police. We should do that as soon as we can."

"Today's Thursday," said Nathan. "We'd better stay here this afternoon just in case those troublemakers return. Tomorrow it's probably okay for us to go to Stawell to see the police and take Belinda for her tests."

"And we should start getting ready for our camping trip," said Dan.

"Maybe," said Nathan, "but if Sylvia isn't well, we may have to stay here to supervise the construction work over the next few weeks. Steve might not be here to look after it."

Dan sighed. "I suppose you're right," he said.

Chapter 12

A Simple Mistake

No unwanted visitors came to the campsite for the rest of Thursday, so when Friday dawned clear and warm, the Turners planned to drive to Stawell.

"Nothing we plan seems to work out as we expect nowadays," complained Dan at breakfast time.

"And we've done pretty well from that, haven't we?" asked Belinda.

"I suppose so," admitted Dan, "but it would be nice to be able to have some sort of a holiday."

"Didn't you enjoy our time up on Briggs Bluff?" asked Tanya.

"Of course – I just wanted it to be longer."

Nathan's expression was serious as he said, "We all did, Dan, but you know that if we hadn't come back until today, these people would probably have already taken over the campsite."

"And what would they have done when we turned up?" asked Tanya.

"We could've been in trouble, dear," answered Nathan.

"Then we'd better not stay in Stawell for long," said Belinda, agitated. "What if they come back while we're away?"

"I don't *think* they're likely to," said Nathan, cautiously, "and we won't be away all day.".

"We need to tell Steve and the police about it all as soon as possible," said Dan.

"I'd like to see Sylvia, too," added Tanya. "I hope she hasn't had a relapse."

"And Belinda needs to do those tests at the High School," finished Nathan, smiling at her.

❧

Not long after breakfast, they were ready to leave for Stawell.

"I wish we had my little runabout," said Tanya, as she climbed up into their big four-wheel drive. "It would be ideal for trips like this – and save us a lot of money in fuel."

"I'm not so sure," answered Nathan. "With all the rain we've had, there could be damage to culverts, or even the road. There might be fallen branches or even complete trees to drive around, too. Not to mention kangaroos and emus. I think we're safer in a bigger car around here."

"You might be right," said Tanya, "but I'd still like to have my zippy little car again. Our agreement when we sold the house was for the new owners to let us store things there for twelve months. Four months have gone, and the Victorian government is showing no sign of relaxing the 25-km travel restriction. In Ballarat, they said the restrictions would last for at least six months *after* everything was under control, and we haven't heard anything yet that suggests the government thinks things are under control."

"No," sighed Nathan. "It's a bit of a worry, really."

"Come on, Dad, you always tell us not to worry," laughed Dan.

"That's true, but... well.... Oh, I suppose we're not running out of time yet."

They had all climbed into the car as they talked, and Nathan started the engine. He was about to drive off when Dan called out, "Hey, I forgot to lock the side door of the office. I'm too used to leaving things unlocked around here. Should I go and lock it?" He put his hand on the inside door handle. It moved a little under his hand, but he was too preoccupied to pay attention.

"It won't matter if we leave one door..." began Nathan, eager to leave, then he stopped and pursed his lips. "No, on second thoughts, let's make sure absolutely everything is locked up."

"I'll go and lock it then." Dan pushed the door open and jumped out.

Afterwards, he wasn't sure what went wrong, but as he landed, his foot twisted and gave way underneath him. Finding himself falling, he grabbed the door handle, but it came off in his hand. Losing his balance completely, he fell against the door, then slid, feeling a stab of pain as the side of his head struck its metal corner.

Dave gasped and Belinda squealed as they saw Dan falling, but there was nothing either of them could do.

Dan landed hard on his left hand on the gravel and lay shocked for a few seconds.

Nathan was out of the car and running around the front while Tanya was still opening her door. Belinda leaned over from where she had been sitting next to Dan, reaching out her hand and looking almost about to fall on top of him.

Dan groaned and started to roll over. Belinda immediately blinked and sat up inside the car again. Blood? Others could sort out Dan's accident.

Nathan knelt beside Dan and put his hand on his back. "Are you okay, Dan?"

Tanya peered over Nathan's shoulder. "Oh, son, your head!"

Dan reached up his hand and touched his right temple, where blood was flowing freely from a gash. "It's bleeding, but it doesn't feel too bad. It's my left arm that feels worst."

"It looks like we won't be going to Stawell just yet," said Nathan. "Let's go inside and see if Nurse Mum can patch you up."

"How's your hand?" asked Dave.

"The gravel's sharp, but I don't think it's too bad." Dan rolled up his hand into a fist, winced and loosened it, looking at the lacerations from the gravel. "Wow, I've made a real mess of myself, haven't I? That was pretty stupid."

Tanya looked quickly, then said, "Let's go inside and clean it up."

"Look, here's the door handle," said Dave, picking it up from the gravel. "No wonder you fell."

"That didn't help, but I was already falling – that's why I grabbed it," said Dan.

Dan made his way into the house. In the dining area, he sank onto the couch in the corner and lay back with a sigh. Tanya immediately got some warm water and began to bathe his cuts. When Belinda entered the room a little later, keeping her eyes averted from Dan's wounds, Tanya asked her to bring the first aid kit from the office.

Tanya gently cleaned the cut across Dan's temple. "It actually doesn't look too bad," she said, "but you might get a black eye from it."

Belinda handed the first aid kit to her mother.

"And there's no-one from school to tease you about getting into a fight!" said Dave.

Tanya applied some band-aids to Dan's temple. He was obviously beginning to feel a little better, but when she reached for his hand, he winced and pulled it away. "I'll do it," he said, getting up and going over to the sink.

"Oh, what a stupid thing to do," he grumbled. "Can't even get out of a car properly." He began to clean the heel of his left hand, washing off both the darkening blood and the gravel caught in the flesh. Tanya was keeping a close eye on him and noticed his frequent winces and the extreme care with which he moved.

"Is your arm alright, Dan?" she asked after a while.

"I'm not sure," he answered. "I'm no doctor."

"Can you move your arm? Your wrist? Your hand?"

"You saw me clench my hand earlier," he said. "But I don't think I want to do it again. Maybe I *have* done something to my arm."

"You mean, broken it?" asked Dave.

"Mmm," said Dan, "perhaps. Oh, I don't know."

"I can examine it if you like," said Tanya, "but I'm no doctor either. Would you like me to?"

"No thanks," said Dan. "I think it would be good to see a doctor." It was sometimes handy to have a mother who was a nurse, but Dan always preferred to see a doctor if possible.

"It sounds as if Danny-boy needs a lie down," said Belinda. "Perhaps it would be best if we stayed here instead of going to Stawell this afternoon."

"That's very kind and thoughtful of you, Belinda," said Nathan, "but you still need to do your tests at the school this afternoon."

"Nice try, sis," said Dan. "But maybe it would be best for me to stay here and rest my arm."

"I don't think so," said Tanya. "If you *have* broken it, it will keep getting worse the longer we leave it. You'll probably find it least uncomfortable if we go to Stawell as soon as possible."

"How will it feel bouncing around in the car?" asked Nathan.

"Ooh, don't talk about bouncing!" groaned Dan.

"Don't worry, I'll drive as gently as I can," soothed Nathan. "Are you going to take your mother's advice?"

"It's already looking more swollen," warned Tanya.

"I suppose I'd better come then."

"Well, let's try leaving all over again," said Nathan. "Let's make sure all the doors are locked, and can you all please climb into the car very carefully?"

Dan walked out to the car while everyone else checked the doors. He clambered in with difficulty, and soon they were ready once more to leave.

Chapter 13

Stawell Hospital

True to his word, Nathan drove as gently as possible, but by the time they arrived in Stawell, Dan's injured arm was even more swollen. He cradled it with his other arm, doing his best to absorb any shocks from the movement of the car, but even so, he was looking a little grey from the pain.

They drove straight to the hospital, hoping to find a doctor who could see Dan quickly. The latest plan was for Belinda and Dave to walk to the High School, where Belinda could do her tests. If no-one came to pick them up by the time she finished, they would walk back to the hospital.

Nathan wanted to leave his options open. He would wait in emergency with Dan and Tanya for a while, but if they had to wait too long, he would try to find Steve and Sylvia and then go to the police station.

Stopping at the door of the Urgent Care Centre, he dropped off Dan and Tanya. Dave and Belinda also climbed out and headed off to the school.

Tanya walked in with Dan to the triage nurse, who waved them towards a box of masks. Masks fitted, Dan described the accident to her and she looked briefly at his head and arm, before telling them to sit and wait for a doctor.

Having parked in the spacious parking area, Nathan joined them, and the three sat and waited.

And waited. New patients came in from time to time, while others kept coming and going through the doors that led further into the hospital. Whenever a doctor appeared, Dan's hopes rose, but none of them came to see him.

Nathan was starting to fidget and wonder if he should go and find Steve when Dan heard his name called. A woman was standing at the door and beckoning to him. He stood and walked towards the door, grateful when Nathan and Tanya stood and followed him.

From then on, action was swift. An X-ray confirmed a minor break and his lower arm was soon encased in a short cast.

Dan was pleased to have the arm supported in a sling. It was already feeling a little better – as long as he didn't move it much.

"Well, you were wanting a holiday, son," said Nathan as they returned to the waiting room on their way out of the emergency department. "You sure won't be able to work for a while now, but you might not be able to help us holiday much either."

They walked across to the main entrance and asked the girl at the reception desk about Sylvia. She gave them directions to Sylvia's room, adding, "She's looking much better, but make sure you all keep your masks on."

Following her instructions, they soon found Sylvia's room.

Steve was in an armchair while Sylvia sat up in bed. She looked tired and pale, but improved over Steve's description of her condition two days before.

"You're looking better," said Tanya at once, and Sylvia responded with a tired smile.

"Welcome," said Steve, standing up to greet them. "We didn't expect to see you here."

"I'm not surprised," said Nathan, "but we went back to the campsite after you visited us at the cave yesterday. And then we wanted to come and see you both today."

Steve noticed Dan's sling and cast. "What happened to you, Dan?"

"Embarrassingly enough, I fell over when jumping out of the car this morning."

"Oh, so it's brand new! How long will you have to wear the cast?"

"It's not a bad break, so they say only about three weeks."

"That's not too bad, then."

"I suppose not."

"Sylvia looks as if she'd find it too tiring having all of us here," interjected Tanya. "Can I suggest that you two go and have a chat with Steve while I stay and talk to Sylvia?"

"That sounds good," said Steve, and Sylvia smiled that tired smile once again.

Steve patted her hand and led the others out of the room, leaving Tanya and Sylvia alone. They made their way towards the entrance and met Dave and Belinda walking in the front door.

"Ah, perfect timing," said Nathan.

Belinda smiled and hurried towards them.

"How did you go with the tests?" asked Nathan.

"They were easy," she answered. "After all you said I was a bit worried that I might've forgotten everything I ever knew in the last four months, but I think I've learnt more than I've forgotten. Doing that accounting work with Mum has helped my maths."

"I'm glad to hear it. I'll have to chase things up with the headmaster in a few days. Another thing to fit in somehow. Now let's go outside."

Once they were out in the carpark, Nathan began to tell Steve about the previous day's events.

"You mean, they were already there when you got back from Briggs Bluff?" asked Steve when Nathan described discovering the unwanted visitors.

"Yes. I don't think they'd been there long. I'm not sure what they'd have done if we hadn't returned early."

"It doesn't bear thinking about," groaned Steve. "Oh, no. What should I do? I can't leave Sylvia now."

"Let me tell you the rest of it before we talk any more about that," said Nathan.

Dan and Dave helped Nathan describe the events of the previous afternoon and the unpleasant behaviour of the four visitors.

"You really think they were armed?" asked Steve when they finished.

"Oh, yes," said Dan and Dave together.

"In fact, I'm almost certain," added Dan.

"Well, that's worse than I thought – though not much, to be honest."

"Are you happy with us reporting all this to the police?" asked Nathan.

"Of course."

"At first, I was just going to tell them about the flag we found – and I'll still mention that – but this sort of intimidation should be reported too."

"Are you going to mention their claims that Muslims are always being picked on?"

"Do you think I should?"

"Yes. There have been some problems recently in Horsham and the police might like to know of a possible connection."

"What sort of problems?"

"The police could tell you more, but some Muslim extremists in the town have been causing trouble – and blaming other people for it."

"Trouble like we had, or more serious?"

"So far, I believe it's been more threats than action; more spreading hatred than actual violence."

As they talked, a car parked nearby and Dan saw a teenager climbing out awkwardly. It was Ben, and his father Ehud was hurrying around from the driver's side to help him.

"Hi, Ben!" called Dan.

Ben didn't hear him at first and continued taking a pair of crutches out of the car.

"Hi Ben," called Dan again, then added, "How's your knee?"

Ben heard this time and turned. Recognising them, he waved, then used his crutches to hurry across the carpark. He looked much more proficient than he had the previous weekend. Ehud followed.

"Hi Dan and Dave, Nathan and Steve – and Belinda too. It's good to see you all."

"Dan asked how your knee was," prompted Ehud.

"It's much better. I've come to have the stitches taken out. But what happened to your arm? Not to mention the side of your head."

"If you must know, I fell over in the camp carpark, right near where you did," said Dan.

"It must be a dangerous carpark," said Dave, solemnly.

"Is it a bad break?" asked Ben.

"No. They nearly used a splint, but in the end they decided a cast would make me remember it more and be more careful."

"It seems a little late for a formal greeting," said Ehud, "but good afternoon anyway. It's good to see you Nathan, Dan, Dave, and Belinda as well." He looked across at Steve, and it was obvious that he knew him, but his manner seemed to Dan a little reserved. "Hello, Mr Jones."

"Just call me Steve, Doctor Cohen."

"As long as you call me Ehud, Steve."

"Very well."

"Have you been to school, Ben?" asked Dan.

"Yes, Dad was able to take me to school each day."

"And that caused more trouble," said Ehud, shortly.

"There's no need to talk about that, Dad," said Ben.

"Yes, there is. The Turners need to understand a bit more of what's going on."

"Oh, I suppose so."

"As I say, me taking Ben to school caused more trouble. People who know me by sight spotted me dropping him off and saw him as another way to get at me."

"What do you mean, 'Get at you'?" asked Nathan.

"There are some people in Horsham who hate me," said Ehud simply. "They've been looking for opportunities to cause trouble, and when they discovered my relationship with Ben, they found one."

"Do they hate you because of your medical work?"

"Yes and no. They hate me because of my parents, and they are jealous of the fact that my father was a lawyer, my mother was a doctor, I am a doctor, and several other family members are doctors, lawyers, optometrists, surgeons and so on. They think it's unfair that we have those jobs when they can't."

"But surely there's nothing stopping them becoming doctors or lawyers if they want to? It's not as if anyone will stop them from entering the courses if they can get good enough marks!"

"They can't. And that's another reason why they hate us. We worked hard to get our education, and slaved our guts out to get our jobs, too, but these people don't believe any of that. They say we were given special treatment to make it easy for us, while they are discriminated against to stop them getting those jobs. It's all ridiculous, but they're very serious about it."

"We met some people like that yesterday," acknowledged Nathan. "Anyway, what did these people do?"

"They saw the opportunity to get at me through Ben and encouraged others to pick on him. I think you know he was already being bullied – well, these are just a few more people who want to join in."

"Why?" asked Dan. "It doesn't make sense."

"We're Jews," answered Ehud. "Plenty of people hate all Jews."

"But wasn't Jesus a Jew?" blurted out Dan.

"Yes, although he wasn't always so friendly to the Jews either."

"I thought it was the other way around," said Dan. "Wasn't it the Jews who persecuted Jesus and his followers?"

"For a while, maybe – although it was the Romans who killed him, of course. But once the Christian church got more powerful, they persecuted the Jews at every opportunity."

"I didn't know that," said Dan.

"It wasn't *all* Christians, of course, but it was enough that my people were persecuted all over the world. Everywhere they went, they met hatred and hostility."

"Wasn't that what the Bible predicted?" asked Dan.

Ehud looked at him. "It's my turn to say that I don't know. When I was young, my parents taught me that if the God of Israel was real, then he must be cruel to allow our people to suffer so much – so I've never learned much about him."

"So that would become a vicious circle. An endlessly repeating prophecy," said Dan, thoughtfully.

"What do you mean?" asked Ben.

"Well, if God punishes Israel for not obeying him, and then you don't worship him because he punishes you, the suffering will go on forever!"

"Hmm, I've never thought of it quite that way," mused Ehud. "Something to think about, but right now I've got to take Ben into the hospital to get those stitches taken out. Will you still be here for a while, Nathan?"

"Sure."

Ehud and Ben went into the hospital while the others continued their discussions, the Turners reporting more of their confrontation at the campsite.

After a few minutes, Ehud returned alone.

"How do you think Ben's knee is going?" asked Belinda.

"It's healing well. It looks like he won't need the crutches after another week or so. But there's some other news that isn't so good. Can I tell you all? Steve might already know it."

"I don't think so," frowned Steve.

"Then you'll probably hear soon enough," said Ehud. "History shows that these things tend to spread. Anyway, yesterday, our house was attacked by some youths. At the start, they were just throwing stones."

"Has that ever happened to you before?" asked Dan, shocked that such a thing could happen in Australia.

"No. Never. It was bad enough that Ben has been being bullied, but this was a big step worse."

"Do you know who the youths were?"

"No. We called the police and when they arrived, the youths ran away. However, the real problem happened after the police left. By then, it was getting dark, and once it was properly dark, someone came and threw a petrol bomb at the house."

"At your house?" asked Belinda, shock in her voice. "While you were inside?"

"Yes," answered Ehud. "We heard them shouting at us and were on the alert. Actually, it was good that we *were* there because we were able to go outside straight away and put out the fire, but it did do some damage. We called the police again and they came back, but they couldn't find anyone."

"What were they shouting?" asked Dave.

"It's probably better not to say," said Ehud.

"I could probably guess," said Steve.

Ehud nodded. "I'm sure you could. Anyway, they found some graffiti on the garage door, and that gave a few more clues because some of it was in Arabic."

"Arabic!" said Dan in surprise. "We saw some on a flag in the Grampians."

"Well, there aren't very many people in Horsham who write Arabic," said Ehud.

"Do you?" asked Belinda.

"No. English and Hebrew, but not Arabic."

"Is there anything you can do about it?"

"I have some ideas, but at the moment I'm worried about Ben. I was already worried about him at school, but now I'm worried about his safety at home too. I want him to go somewhere else for a while."

"Is your wife safe today with you away?"

"I left her with her parents."

"That sounds wise," said Nathan.

"What I was wondering was whether he could stay with you for a while at the campsite in Roses Gap," continued Ehud.

"Oooh," said Nathan, grimacing. "I'm afraid that might not be a good idea for his safety at the moment. Some men came during the week wanting to book the campsite. They've been very... let's say overbearing and arrogant. Yesterday they came again and were quite threatening.

"We found a black flag at the top of Briggs Bluff with Arabic writing on it. It was put there by one of the men who came to the camp yesterday. And they were complaining about how hard it is for Muslims to get anything in this country because of favouritism towards Christians.

"So we're worried that these people could be connected with your problem," finished Nathan, "which means it might not be safe to have Ben at Roses Gap in case they turn up again. We don't expect them to, but you never know. They've already come to the campsite twice, and they don't like taking no for an answer."

"Maybe you're right, but I don't know of any better way to get Ben out of harm's way."

"We've been planning to go camping for a few weeks," said Nathan, "but the main complication is looking after the campsite while Steve and Sylvia are stuck here in Stawell."

Ehud looked at Steve with concern. "What's wrong?" he asked. "I've been so full of my own problems that it didn't even occur to me that there must be something wrong or I wouldn't have met you in a hospital carpark. I'm sorry."

"Sylvia has cancer. She went to Melbourne for treatment and they're convinced that the treatment has been successful. Until a few days ago, she was gradually growing stronger, but then she started feeling sick and getting weaker. She's had some vomiting too. Naturally, we're worried, although the doctors here are convinced it's nothing to do with the cancer."

"I understand your concern, but, on the face of it, there could be quite a few reasons why she could be feeling like that even if her cancer is still in remission."

"If they can sort out the problem, we could go back to the campsite and supervise the improvement works that are beginning...." Steve stopped and thought for a few moments before looking a little concerned and concluding, "next week."

"Would you like me to go in and talk to the doctors here? I know most of them anyway. I wouldn't interfere in the case at all, but I may be able to get some information that could reassure you."

Steve looked pitifully grateful. "I really would appreciate it," he said.

"I'll go in now," said Ehud, and walked away.

Chapter 14

The Ambulance

As Ehud walked away, the others looked at each other: things seemed to be happening so quickly!

Steve looked anxious, but also a little hopeful that something positive might come out of this chance meeting.

Nathan looked thoughtful. This request to look after Ben was an unexpected complication.

Dan and Dave exchanged glances. They knew little of Ben, but they liked what they knew.

Belinda kept her own counsel.

Gradually, conversation restarted, but as Dan and Dave compared ideas about where they'd like to camp if camping was possible, Dan saw three people come out of the front door of the hospital and walk towards them. One looked like a maintenance worker, while the other two wore fluorescent orange vests over nurses' uniforms. They walked towards the group and one of the nurses asked, "Do you know whose car that is?"

She pointed to the Turners' car, which Nathan had parked in the middle of a mostly empty section of the carpark.

"Yes, that's mine," answered Nathan.

"Could you move it please? Find a place to park over there where the parking areas have solid white lines around them. Don't park in any of the places with dashed lines like these." She pointed to the intermittent lines that marked places in the area where their car was parked. "This part of the carpark doubles as a helipad and we have a patient arriving in a few minutes."

"Sure," said Nathan. He climbed into the car and moved it to another part of the carpark.

"Does this happen often?" Belinda asked the nurse.

"No, not at the moment. We used to need helicopters to take the more serious patients to Melbourne, but we don't do that anymore. With our latest upgrades to Emergency, Stawell Hospital now looks after such patients from across the region. It won't be long before we're the biggest hospital beyond the western margin," she concluded proudly.

"What's wrong with the patient?" asked Belinda.

"Ah, I don't think I can say..." hesitated the nurse. "It's an unusual case and we're... well, we're not even sure he'll still be alive when he arrives." She looked excited, as if she longed to describe the case in detail but had been told not to.

The maintenance man was checking the parking area, making sure there was no loose rubbish that could be dangerous when the helicopter's downwash played over the area.

"Where is the helicopter based?" Dan asked him.

"Horsham."

"And where does all the fuel come from?" asked Dave.

"Melbourne, mostly."

"With the convoys?"

"Mmm. They go as far as Horsham, now."

"Is Melbourne deciding it needs the rest of Victoria again?" asked Dan with irony.

"P'raps."

Nathan returned after parking the car and said to Dan, "Now I understand some of the things that didn't make sense about this carpark: those dashed lines, and the thick lines across some of the parking areas, which I now see is a big 'H' in the middle of the carpark. Not to mention the fact that nobody else was parked anywhere near the helipad."

"I suppose all the locals know about the helicopter – although the nurse said it doesn't come here very often anymore."

"I guess so."

More staff came out of the hospital and spread out around the helipad to make sure the helicopter could land safely and they could care for its passenger immediately.

Dan heard a faint noise and soon recognised it as the sound of a distant helicopter approaching from the northwest. Soon he could see the red- and white-painted helicopter as a wheeled stretcher was brought from the hospital to wait near the landing area. Dan was impressed by efficient preparations going on around him. It helped him to ignore the ache in his arm. He was pleased that they had accepted his mother's assessment of his head wound as being nothing significant, and left her band-aids in place. Yet it still hurt if he touched it and felt quite puffy.

Suddenly, a police car drove up the ramp into the carpark and was waved to a safe place by one of the staff. When four men climbed out of the car, Dan was surprised to recognise one of them as Fergus Norton!

The four moved across to where the stretcher was waiting. Still more people hurried out from the hospital as the helicopter made its final approach, hovered for a moment over the large painted 'H' and began to descend.

Was this normal? Dan wondered. It seemed a lot of staff to care for one patient! And why were the police present? Above all, why was Fergus there? Fergus himself had been scanning the carpark, and at that moment their eyes met. Dan raised a finger in greeting and Fergus acknowledged it. He was dressed in a dark uniform and what Dan guessed to be a bullet-proof vest.

The number of medical staff gathering near the stretcher continued to grow and Dan observed Fergus speaking to some of them. They looked as if they might be doctors, and Dan noticed with surprise that one of them was Ehud Cohen. What was he doing there?

This was becoming stranger and stranger.

Dan could feel the wind from the rotor as the helicopter descended slowly, but in just a few moments, its skids landed gently on the bitumen. At once, the rotor began to slow and the swirling wind quickly decreased.

Dan looked back towards the stretcher and noted that none of the police were there anymore. He tucked the fact away in his mind and looked back at the helicopter. Although the rotor was still turning, its door was opening and medical staff on the ground were making their way towards the helicopter, taking the stretcher with them.

A man climbed out of the helicopter and met the approaching staff. Dan could see them talking, but the high-pitched whine of the helicopter engine made it impossible to hear anything of the conversation. After a few moments, the man from the helicopter turned and gave a signal to the watching pilot, who immediately shut down the engine. The noise level quickly dropped, although the rotor continued to turn for some time.

The stretcher was placed a short distance from the door of the helicopter and the staff crowded around the door as another man climbed out of the helicopter.

Dan gasped. It was Ahmed, who had confronted them at the campsite. He exchanged looks with Dave and saw Belinda staring wide-eyed.

"Excuse me please, sir." Dan could just hear one of the staff speaking to Ahmed. "We need to get to the patient, sir. Can you please stand over there?" He pointed to a place a few metres away where Ahmed would be out of the way but able to see what was going on.

"No. I'm not leaving my son. May Allah have mercy on him."

"If you remain in the way, we won't be able to help your son," replied the attendant. "It is best for your son if you stand over there."

Ahmed grumbled in some other language and moved a very short distance away. He was still in the way and continued to remonstrate with the nurses whenever they touched the patient.

Working around him, the two medicos on the helicopter gently unloaded a stretcher from the helicopter and stood it on the asphalt next to the hospital's stretcher.

The medical staff were obviously examining the patient and discussing his condition. Dan wondered why they didn't immediately transfer him to the hospital stretcher and whisk him away into the hospital. Instead, two nurses hurried back into the hospital and returned with more equipment and supplies.

"Why don't they take him inside?" asked Dave.

"I'm no doctor," answered Nathan, "but I guess they want to stabilise him before they move him. They're probably afraid he'll die if they take him in straight away."

"He must be very sick," said Belinda.

Ehud was leaning over the stretcher, working quickly and issuing abrupt instructions to the assisting nurses. At times, he seemed to be giving orders to two others whom Dan guessed to be doctors. This was obviously a critical situation and it was clear the staff depended on Ehud to achieve the best result.

Ahmed continued to hover nearby, not only continuing his requests for Allah's care, but also criticising the staff for leaving his son in the carpark instead of taking him inside.

It was obvious that he did not understand the urgency of the situation, and none of the staff had time to explain.

When he began to complain that the hospital was discriminating against his son because he was a Muslim, however, the police took action, all four of them approaching Ahmed. He was facing the helicopter and only became aware of their presence when one took him gently by the arm. He pulled away and Dan saw his hand move towards his pocket, just as his associate's had at Roses Gap. Fortunately for everyone, he thought better of it when he turned and saw four policemen.

"Come with us, please, sir," said the policeman holding his arm.

"The doctors are looking after your son," said Fergus, "so it is better for you to leave them to get on with their work uninterrupted. They're trying to save your son's life."

"You aren't going to take me away," answered Ahmed belligerently.

"Yes, we are, sir. And if you don't cooperate, we will arrest you for disturbing the peace and threatening medical staff," said another of the policeman. Dan recognised him as Les, the policeman who had helped with the capture of Brad Jessop and his men.

Ahmed looked mutinous, but reluctantly obeyed the insistent pressure on his arm and walked with the police to stand near their car.

As they moved away, Dan heard Les ask Ahmed, "How did your son get hit by a bullet?"

He turned, eyebrows raised, and looked at Dave, who responded in kind. No wonder the nurse had wished she could talk about it!

The medical team working on the critically ill patient paid no attention to these events. Dan wondered if they had simply been too busy to notice.

Chapter 15

Enquiries

The bustle in the carpark gradually calmed down as the helicopter sat silent and unmoving and most of the hospital support staff returned to their work.

However, the feverish speed with which the small team of doctors and nurses worked on their patient didn't seem to slow. Oblivious to their surroundings, they seemed to be swabbing, connecting tubes, attaching wires, wiping away blood, bandaging and monitoring all at once.

The pilot sat waiting, unwilling to disturb them by moving his machine.

Steve was eager to return to Sylvia, so he and Nathan soon made their way to the main hospital entrance, leaving Dan, Dave and Belinda waiting in the carpark.

Some time later, some of the team surrounding the stretcher stepped back a little. A man slowly and gently began to push the mobile stretcher towards the emergency department door. The doctors and nurses still looked subdued, but some wore tentative smiles and exchanged signals that suggested their patient was, at the very least, still alive.

Dan, Dave and Belinda followed at a distance as the stretcher was wheeled into the emergency department en route to intensive care.

Ahmed was allowed to follow the stretcher into the hospital, with the police in close attendance. As they approached the door, Les, the senior policeman, told him sternly that he would not be allowed into the intensive care area and must be on his best behaviour while in the hospital. He must also report to the police station before leaving Stawell. "Those medicos gave you special treatment this afternoon by allowing you to travel in the helicopter," he said seriously, "and you treated them badly in return. You need to pull up your socks, sir."

Ahmed looked baffled.

"You need to behave better," explained Les. "In this town, we expect everyone to contribute to society, not go around causing trouble. So, make sure you come to the station before you leave town. Understand?"

"You are pick on me because..."

Les held up a hand and spoke peremptorily. "Stop complaining immediately, sir, or we'll take you to the station right now."

Ahmed subsided and went inside to sit in the waiting area. He still looked angry and Dan wondered how long he would keep his temper under control.

The entry to the emergency department was beside the main entrance to the hospital and Dan, Dave and Belinda went to wait for their parents between the two entrances. Les, Fergus and the other policemen were also standing nearby as they watched Ahmed through the emergency department door.

"Were you praying for that patient, Danny-boy?" asked Belinda, curiously.

"Of course I was," answered Dan.

"And you, Dave?"

"Yes."

"Even though Ahmed, who they say is his father, was part of that carload that threatened us? Even though he's been shot somehow?"

"Innocent people have been shot before now," said Dan.

"But he isn't innocent, you know that."

"I think you're probably right, and that's part of why I prayed for him. Wouldn't it be better if he turned his life around? And he can't do that if he's dead!"

"I suppose not. Anyway, I guess your prayers must be working, because he isn't dead."

Ahmed seemed to be on his best behaviour, and as the Turners continued their conversation, three of the four policemen walked across to the main entrance and made their way to the receptionist's window. Fergus remained outside and approached Dan, Dave and Belinda.

"Hi, Fergus," said Dan. "I didn't expect to see you here."

"Nor did I expect to meet you three, particularly with that cast on your arm, Dan. What happened?"

"A minor accident. I fell over."

"And hit your head and scraped your hand as well?"

"Yes."

Fergus raised his eyebrows. "Quite a comprehensive minor accident from the sound of it," he said.

"Bad enough to need people to pray for him," said Belinda.

"You don't need to sneer," answered Dan, defensively.

"I wasn't," protested Belinda. "I'm just wondering where prayer fits in."

Fergus turned to Belinda. "I heard your questions earlier while I was keeping an eye on Ahmed, Belinda. What do *you* think about prayer?"

"I think it's hard to prove that prayer works..." she answered carefully.

"...And hard to prove it doesn't?"

"Yes. I suppose it has to come back to the idea of faith."

"I think you're right, but there must also be absolute truth about it. In any given situation, prayer must either work or not."

"Of course," said Dan. "And I'm convinced that God answered my prayer about that patient this afternoon. And..." he grinned and paused for effect, "nobody can prove that he didn't!"

"Well said, Dan," smiled Fergus. "Now, can I ask you all a few quick questions?"

"Sure," said Dan. "Ask away. It's been an exciting afternoon."

"Yes. It's not often that someone gets shot around here."

"How did he get shot?" asked Belinda.

"We don't have any answers yet, but guns are dangerous things," said Fergus. "I'm here to talk to the older man. Are you busy?"

They shook their heads and Fergus asked, "What brought you here today?"

"We came to visit Steve and Sylvia," answered Belinda, adding cheekily, "and to patch up poor little Danny-boy!"

"Why are they here?" asked Fergus, prudently ignoring this gibe. "I thought they were back at Roses Gap with Sylvia recovering from her treatment."

"She hasn't been so well in the last week, so Steve brought her here to get checked out. They decided to keep her in, but he doesn't know why. They keep assuring him that it's nothing to do with the cancer."

"In fact, Dr Ehud Cohen was going to talk to the doctors for Steve to find out what they thought about her case," said Dan. "He went to do that just before the helicopter arrived."

"Ehud Cohen is the main doctor who was working on the lad who got shot, isn't he?" All three nodded, and Fergus added cryptically, "Ironic, really."

Dan didn't know what he meant, so he continued his explanations. "Once the excitement with the helicopter was over, Dad and Steve hurried back to Sylvia. Mum had stayed with her after we visited earlier. We're waiting for them to come back."

"Well, while you're waiting, have any of you met the man accompanying the patient before? Or the patient himself?"

"Yes, we've seen the excitable bloke before," said Dan. "He came to the campsite yesterday and demanded that we let him book the site for a camp in four weeks' time. He'd already tried to book it with Steve for two weeks' time and been refused. When Dad refused the second time, he became quite aggressive."

"His name is Ahmed," added Dave.

"And he's a Muslim," said Belinda, "though I don't know much about what that means."

"I'll give you a one-minute summary," answered Fergus. "Muslims believe in one God, Allah, who is said to be the same God as Jews and Christians worship. They also believe in a prophet called Mohammad whom they believe to be greater than all other prophets. They believe in special books like the Jews and Christians do, but different ones. Simply put, Jews accept the Old Testament of the Bible, Christians accept both the Old and New Testaments, and Muslims believe primarily in another book, the Koran, but also in the Bible, particularly the books of Moses, the Psalms and the gospels – although they believe many parts have been corrupted."

"Okay," said Belinda.

"Can we go into the emergency department now? I'd like to keep an eye on Ahmed and he's just moved to a different part of the room where I can't see him," said Fergus. As the door into the emergency department opened in front of them, Fergus continued, "That's a very simplified summary. Behaviour and beliefs vary as much among Muslims as they do among Christians."

"I suppose that shouldn't be a surprise," said Dan.

"Not really. We're all people. However, the greatest problem with Muslims is the violent extremists among them."

"Why is that?" asked Belinda, looking puzzled.

"Ah, there he is," said Fergus, spotting Ahmed and turning towards him. "We can talk about the reason some other time, but the fact is that while there are some violent extremists among Jews and Christians, you'll meet a much higher concentration of them among those who call themselves Muslims."

Fergus' words were delivered calmly and steadily as they entered the waiting room, but Ahmed's response to his words was anything but calm and steady!

"Why you say Muslims all violent extremists?" he shouted, jumping to his feet and advancing threateningly towards Fergus.

A hush fell over the emergency department as the triage nurses and the few waiting patients turned to see what was going on.

"I didn't," replied Fergus evenly.

"Muslims are opp-a-ressed in so much of world that they must have resist," retorted Ahmed, a little more calmly. The nurses cautiously resumed their work, while the patients continued to watch and listen.

"Well, they aren't oppressed in Australia, so if that's the only reason for having extremists, then there is no reason for any here," retorted Fergus.

"Good Muslims keep Allah's laws," insisted Ahmed, "so must be conflict with infidels."

"Stay within the laws of Australia and you can keep Allah's laws as much as you like."

"Australia's laws favour Christians," complained Ahmed.

Dan was tempted to argue that many Australian laws didn't suit Christians any more than they suited Muslims, but he managed to hold his tongue.

"Anyway, sir," said Fergus, holding up his hand to stop Ahmed, who was about to start again, "I didn't come to talk about Islam, I came to talk about your son and how he was injured. You sit down there, while I find a place for us to talk."

Fergus pressed Ahmed to sit down, then walked across to the triage nurse and said, "I need a room to interview this man."

"You could use the second staff room. It won't be in use now, and the door is just over there." The nurse leaned forward and added quietly, "Do you need any support, sir? He seems very... ah...excitable, and, after all, his son was *shot*. It could be dangerous."

"Three more policemen will be coming soon. When they arrive, send them to join me in the staff room," answered Fergus. "In the meantime, I'll talk to Ahmed."

Fergus thanked Dan, Dave and Belinda for their help and suggested that they look for their parents, then led Ahmed into the second staff room.

Chapter 16

Some Answers

Dan, Dave and Belinda made their way back to the main entrance then headed towards Sylvia's room in search of Nathan and Tanya. As they turned the final corner and approached her room, they saw Ben holding his crutches and leaning against the wall next to the door. He greeted them quietly.

"We make a good pair, Ben," said Dan wryly, pointing his cast toward Ben's crutches.

Looking in through the door, he saw that the room already seemed full of people. Sylvia was in bed with Tanya in a chair nearby, while Steve and Nathan were welcoming Ehud, who seemed to have just arrived. Dan gave Tanya a quick wave, to let her know they were there.

Ehud got straight down to business. "The doctors say that you are well, Sylvia, except for a grumbling appendix," he said. "They are very confident that there is no danger from the cancer at the moment."

"That's wonderful news," smiled Steve, turning to Sylvia and taking her hand. She gave a wan smile in return.

"I'm sorry that we didn't communicate the situation to you very well," said Ehud.

"It certainly wasn't your fault," said Steve, "but knowing that will make it much easier for us all."

"What do doctors suggest for the grumbling appendix?" asked Nathan.

"From their examination, they believe it will get slowly better over the next few days. You may need it removed at some time in the future, Sylvia, but not now."

"And that means we can go home!" rejoiced Steve. "Thank you."

Ehud smiled and held up his hand. "The doctors want you to stay in for one more night just to make sure, but all being well, you should be able to leave tomorrow morning."

Nathan reached his hand to Tanya. "We're glad to hear such good news, but now, we should leave you two so that you can get some rest, Sylvia."

"That's a good idea," said Ehud.

They all left the room and returned to the main entrance, walking slowly so that Ben could easily keep up on his crutches.

"If Steve and Sylvia return to Roses Gap, we're free to go camping with our camper-trailer," said Nathan to Tanya as they stopped outside the doors.

"Hooray!" said Dan.

"Which brings me back to the question I asked," said Ehud. "What do you think?"

"Tanya and I and the children need to discuss it," answered Nathan, taking the hint from Ehud and not mentioning anything specific about what the question was. Ben was looking tired and had found a nearby pillar to lean against.

Ehud glanced towards Ben and looked a little worried as he fingered his necklace. "We saw you here in Stawell last Sunday. Will you be here this Sunday?"

"We can make sure we are," smiled Nathan.

"I have to come back on Sunday to check on that young lad who's been shot. Given the work we did on him, I'm content to leave him with the doctors here for now. I don't expect any problems, but I'd like to make sure. Ben will come with me."

Ben heard the last statement and responded, "Do I have to, Dad? I'm sick of travelling back and forth from Horsham."

"I can't leave you there for such a long time by yourself," said Ehud. "And we may even stay around Stawell for a few days, so you'll need to bring some clothes with you."

Dan smiled to himself. If Ben were to come camping with them, he would need some clothes, and Ehud had chosen a clever way of making sure he had them with him. He wondered a little whether Ben would be safe in Horsham for two days until Sunday, but decided that if his father was satisfied, it must be alright.

"You were very generous in looking after that lad," said Nathan. "I was impressed."

"Well, hatred doesn't help anyone. And if I'm going to complain about people showing hatred towards me, I have to make sure I don't show hatred towards others."

"I agree, although I've never experienced much hatred myself," said Nathan,

"Did you find out how he was shot?" asked Dan.

"No. He wasn't conscious at all, so I couldn't ask him," answered Ehud. "For a while, I thought he might be coming around, but in the end, I only saw a few flutterings of his eyelids."

Nathan looked at Dan and inclined his head. Slightly puzzled, Dan followed the instruction and moved away with Nathan while the others continued chatting.

Once they were out of earshot, Nathan said quietly, "I'm a bit worried about Ben staying in Horsham. I wouldn't think twice about it except that Ehud is worried and he doesn't seem to me to be a man who worries without reason. So could you ask if Ben can come and stay with us tonight and Saturday? Then he's safe for the weekend even if we decide that we can't take him with us next week, and I really do want to talk to your Mum before we agree to that. I'm concerned about a few aspects."

"Sure, I can do that, though Ben will probably think it's a bit strange. We don't know him very well."

"Something about rowing? Uni? Religion?"

"Hmm, I'm not sure. Let's see what happens when we ask," said Dan.

They returned to the others, who were talking about NK2 in response to a question from Ben.

"Yes, Craig was NK2," Belinda was saying. "He was a horrible man!"

"He thought he was very clever with a double deception, but it didn't work," said Dave.

"I don't have heaps of experience with criminals," laughed Dan, "but all the ones I've seen seem to be a bit more confident than they are competent."

"You mean, they're stupid?" asked Ben.

"Not necessarily *stupid*, but not as brilliant as they think they are."

"And Craig loved violence, too," added Belinda. "He enjoyed it for its own sake. He wasn't violent just because he thought it was necessary to get what he wanted. He *enjoyed* it."

Hey, Ben," said Dan, "if you have to be back in Stawell on Sunday, how'd you like to come and stay with us in Roses Gap until then?"

"That'd be great," said Ben, surprised but enthusiastic. "Would that be alright, Dad?"

Ehud smiled. "It would be fine with me and I'm sure your mother would agree, but what about Mr Turner? Nathan, would that suit you? If you're getting ready to go camping, I'm sure you'll be very busy."

"That would be perfectly okay with us," said Nathan. "It sounds as if we're all happy with it, Ben, so let's fly with it."

"I know Ben won't have any spare clothes, but I'm sure some of mine or Dave's will fit him," said Dan.

"I don't mind wearing the same clothes anyway," laughed Ben.

"Your stitches were taken out earlier today weren't they, Ben?" asked Dan. "Is everything alright? Do you need any special medical treatment or dressings or anything?"

"No, it's all good," said Ben, reaching down and rubbing his knee gently.

Dan noticed the leather bracelet with its metal star on Ben's wrist and remembered where he had found it at the end of the camp. He must ask Ben this weekend how that bracelet had ended up under the dishwasher.

"That's settled, then," said Ehud, flashing a smile of thanks to Nathan.

Dan saw Ben cast a questioning look at his father and wondered if he had noticed Ehud's extra smile.

Chapter 17

Education Plans

Ben had had plenty of travel and activity that day and still found using crutches tiring, so he went to bed shortly after the evening meal. Tanya had arranged for him to use the same cabin as he had used during the school camp the previous week.

Soon afterwards, Nathan and Tanya called Dan, Dave and Belinda into the kitchen to discuss Ehud's request about Ben.

"Your mother – ah, I should say your aunt, Dave – and I have talked about it and we're happy for Ben to come camping with us as long as you three are happy too," said Nathan.

"I'm fine with it," said Dan.

"Me too," agreed Belinda.

"And me," echoed Dave.

"Good! That's settled then," said Nathan. "I think he needs our help at the moment."

"Well, we're planning to camp with the camper-trailer for four weeks," said Tanya. "I'm sure we'll have enough food for two weeks, but we'll probably have to top up after that if we have six of us."

"Our solar panels should keep the fridge going and provide a little light at night," added Nathan, "but we'll mostly go to bed when it gets dark. Now, I've been thinking a bit more about education since we'll have Ben with us."

"Oh, no!" groaned Dan. "You said no schoolwork while we were camping."

"True, and you can hold on to that assurance if you want."

"But..." prompted Dan.

"Firstly, I think we'll have to do some schooling with Ben, and it doesn't seem very fair to make him study while the rest of you laugh at him."

"We wouldn't," protested Belinda.

"I'm sure you wouldn't, but I think you get the picture."

"Is there a 'secondly', Dad?" asked Dan.

"There is. Secondly, I've been thinking about how much you'll need to study for the rest of the year. You'll find it easier to do some now if you want to be able to help with the camps at Roses Gap during the rest of the year."

"I do," said Dan, slowly. "But..."

"It does sound fairer for Ben," mused Belinda. "Although I agree with Danny-boy's 'But...' "

"The decision is up to you three," said Tanya.

"But you'll need to come to one agreed answer together," said Nathan. "So, what do you choose: to study or not to study, that is the question?"

Dan and Dave exchanged glances. Dan frowned. Dave screwed up his face.

Dan sighed. "I'm willing to study when Ben has to."

"I suppose so," said Dave.

"If you two are in, I am too," said Belinda.

"Good choice," said Nathan. "It really will be fairer for Ben too, now that we've decided he's coming with us. I'll talk to him tomorrow and confirm things with his Dad on Sunday."

"The Stawell library is open on Sunday afternoons, so we'll get some books on various subjects then. We'll start with three or four each, and if you run out of your own, you can swap with each other."

Chapter 18

Breakfast with Ben

It was a warm night, and Saturday dawned with the promise of a warmer day than they'd had for two or three weeks.

When Dan woke up, his arm ached. The unfamiliarity and awkwardness of having it in a cast had woken him plenty of times during the night, but at least the cast seemed to protect it from painful movement and it really wasn't *too* bad.

Since his injuries made getting ready take longer than usual, Belinda was waiting for him when he finally reached the kitchen, but she avoided the clever comments she would normally have made. As they began preparing breakfast as usual, Dan soon discovered how difficult it was to cook one-handed.

"I can't crack eggs *and* open them with the same hand," he grumbled as his first attempt ended up with his thumb in the middle of the egg and a puddle on the bench.

"Can't you use your left hand to help?" asked Belinda.

"I'd get egg all over my cast if I tried. And all over the floor, probably."

"Do you want me to drop them into the pan?"

"Yes, please."

She did so and Dan began frying the eggs.

Dave had gone out to fetch Ben, and they entered the kitchen as Dan was frying bacon.

"Hey, Ben," he asked, "how's your leg this morning?"

"It's fine. Better than yesterday. And what about your arm?" He looked closely at Dan and continued, "And your head?"

"He'll soon have at least one black eye, I reckon," said Belinda. "See how that bruise is spreading artistically from his temple?"

"Is it really?" asked Dan, touching gently around his eye. "That explains why it all feels a bit strange."

"Don't worry, it doesn't look too bad," said Dave.

Dan looked back at the bacon sizzling away in the frying pan and said, "Well, breakfast is almost ready, anyway. The bacon looks... oh, Ben, I'm sorry! I've been cooking bacon and I just remembered that eating pigs is forbidden in the Old Testament. Does your family follow those restrictions?"

"Yes, we do. I know that doesn't make much sense when we don't believe in God, but we treat the food laws as a cultural question rather than a religious matter."

"So, what parts of Judaism do you follow?"

"We generally follow the food restrictions, although from time to time Dad eats seafood or other things he wouldn't normally eat when he's invited to meals with non-Jews."

"What about keeping the Sabbath, or going to a synagogue?"

"We don't keep all the detailed restrictions of the Sabbath, but we do take it easy on Saturdays – most of the time. We rarely go to the synagogue."

"So you follow some things and not others. Do you mind me asking how you choose?"

"Mum and Dad like to acknowledge their Jewish heritage, but they aren't observant Jews and don't believe in God. For our family, Judaism is just cultural. We keep the traditions to feel a connection with our ancestors."

"With your ancestors," mused Dan. "Interesting. I've always thought about Judaism as a *religion* – something intended to give a connection with *God*."

"For some people it is, and they're careful to keep the laws of the Torah, but for others it's sort of picking and choosing the bits you like – sometimes the bits that don't feel so religious."

"Judaism also has requirements for separate kitchens for different foods, doesn't it? I'm afraid we cook everything in one kitchen here. Including the bacon."

"We only have one kitchen at home: we don't worry about it too much. I know some Jews who have two kitchens, some who have one kitchen split in two parts, and others who simply have two different sets of utensils and use one for milk and one for meat. Somebody once explained the reason to me from the Torah, but I didn't find it very convincing. The laws they mentioned seemed to have nothing to do with mixing meat and milk."

"Well, I'm glad I'm not upsetting you in that way, at least!" said Dan. "What would you like to eat for breakfast? Since you don't want bacon, we have fried eggs, fried bread or toast, and cereal – or I'm sure Belinda would make you some juicy porridge if you like."

"Juicy porridge?" laughed Ben. "I don't want to be rude, Belinda, but that sounds disgusting."

"Would you prefer cereal with pineapple juice?"

"Maybe juicy porridge isn't so bad after all, but I think toast sounds better. Or cereal with milk."

"Killjoy," said Belinda. "What about some fresh fruit or even some succulent muesli?"

"You certainly have a way with words, Belinda," said Ben.

"She does," agreed Dan, "and it's not always a good way, either. After she's had her way with words they resemble shredded lettuce."

"I'm an appreciative visitor," said Ben, "so instead of agreeing, I'll have to change the subject and ask if there is anything I can do to help. Do you need any help with making juicy porridge? I'm willing to learn."

"I don't think I've ever had any takers for juicy porridge," laughed Belinda. "I believe this is often the fate of the innovative artist."

During breakfast, Nathan broke the news to Ben about their camping trip.

"Ben, our family and Dave are going off-grid camping somewhere in the Grampians on Monday. We haven't decided exactly where yet, but somewhere we can easily camp – probably without power or other facilities. We'll need access to water and we can treat it if we need to. We've got a camper-trailer and solar panels and we've done quite a bit of camping over the years, so we're used to it, although not so much recently. Would you like to come with us?"

Ben's eyes widened and a smile spread across his face. "You betcha!" he said. "But why would you ask me? You hardly know me."

Nathan looked serious. "Your father asked us to consider it," he said. "He's concerned you're in danger after that attack on your house. Did you ever tell him how your injury happened at the camp?"

"Not in detail."

"So you didn't tell him about Ali?"

"No."

"Well even without that, your father is concerned enough after the firebomb. If he knew about the other, he'd probably be even more concerned and glad to keep you away from school next week."

"I don't like to worry Dad, and I have to sort out my own problems anyway."

"This problem isn't just your problem," answered Nathan. "This is a problem you inherited from your ancestors. Sure, you have to sort it out, but it's not as if it's your fault."

"I really think that Ali is just a bully," protested Ben. "I don't think it's because I'm a Jew."

"Uh huh? What does he call you?"

Ben hesitated. Finally he answered, "Jew."

"Don't you think that might be a hint as to his motivation?" queried Nathan. "Once during the camp I heard someone calling that out. At the time, I couldn't tell who, or who it was aimed at. In fact, I wasn't even sure I'd heard correctly. If it had happened again, I'd have investigated until I got to the bottom of it."

"He rarely talks to me, but whenever he does, he always calls me that."

"Even in class?"

"Yes. One of my teachers doesn't stop him. In fact, I suspect that he likes it. Other teachers wouldn't allow it, so it doesn't happen in their classes."

Tanya looked perplexed and shook her head. "How does this sort of thing ever happen? When did it start?"

"About two years ago when we had a culture day and I said I was Jewish. I just happened to be locking at him as I said it, and I still remember the look on his face."

"How old were you then?"

"Fourteen."

"So he already hated Jews at fourteen."

Ben nodded.

"Why?" asked Tanya.

"I think it's his family background," sighed Ben. "He's an Arab and his parents have taught him that the Jews are evil and secretly control the world. They've told him the Jews oppress all Muslims, and particularly Arabs."

"Do you hate him?"

"No, although he does make my life miserable at times. I'd just like to be able to get on with him – or avoid him completely."

"Can I ask you a question about the camp?" asked Dan. Ben nodded. "What happened with your bracelet?"

"I lost it during the camp. The last time I saw it was on Wednesday."

"How did you lose it?"

"Well... I put it on the desk in my cabin, and that's the last time I remember seeing it. When I couldn't find it on Thursday evening, I assumed I must not have put it on properly on Thursday morning and lost it during the day, perhaps outside."

"Do you know where we found it?"

"Where?"

"Under the dishwasher in the kitchen."

Ben looked puzzled. "How could it have got there? I didn't even go into the kitchen on Thursday – or Friday, either."

"We were looking at the dishwasher on Friday morning because water was leaking out from underneath. When we investigated, the water pipe seemed to have been cut, and your bracelet was lying on the floor under the dishwasher, right next to a knife."

Ben frowned. "How could that happen?"

"I have no idea," said Nathan, "but I know that when we found the bracelet and the knife, we jumped to the conclusion that the owner of the bracelet had cut the pipe. Of course, I don't think that now I know you're the owner, but that's what it looked like."

"I wonder if we were *meant* to think that?" puzzled Dan.

"What do you mean?" asked Nathan.

"I wonder if whoever cut the pipe deliberately dropped both the knife and Ben's bracelet after cutting it. In other words, were they trying to get him into trouble?"

Tanya asked excitedly, "You only found the leak on Friday morning didn't you, Nathan?"

"It was Steve who saw it first, but yes, that was on Friday morning."

"Guess who was on the roster for stacking the dishwasher on Thursday evening?" asked Tanya.

"Ali!" said Belinda. "I was showing the helpers how to load the dishwasher Wednesday morning, and I remember he was one of them because he was complaining that he had more jobs to do than others." She looked at Ben. "In fact, he complained particularly that you weren't down for as many jobs as he was – not that I knew who you were at the time."

"He complained to me about that on Wednesday afternoon too," said Ben, sighing. "Then when he listed the jobs he had during the camp, I found that I had one more than him anyway. I pointed it out and that seemed to make him angrier than ever. Then he said he'd get back at me for it, although I have no idea what there was to get back at me for."

"So perhaps this was his plan to get back at you."

"It all seems a bit strange to me," said Dan. "If Ali cut the pipe and dropped Ben's bracelet under the dishwasher to get him in trouble, why didn't he report the leak, and how did he have the bracelet anyway?"

"I don't know how anyone had my bracelet," said Ben.

"Did Ali steal it?"

"I don't know."

"Well, we don't have any proof that Ali cut the pipe or stole your bracelet," said Nathan, "but I do want to assure you that we don't think you cut the pipe, Ben."

"Thanks," said Ben. "I wouldn't ever do anything like that."

"Just one last question before we move on," said Tanya. "Are there any other Jews in your class?"

"No. I know that there are some others in the school, but most of them keep quiet."

"Oh, this is a tragedy," said Tanya, looking up at Nathan.

"True, but let's get back to our camping trip, shall we? We plan to be away for about four or five weeks, Ben, but exactly how long we stay will depend on the weather and progress with the work here at the campsite."

"But watch out, Ben," said Dan. "Dad has one important thing he hasn't told you about. It's a serious case of oppression!"

Nathan laughed, "I think Dan means that we'll be expecting you to do some schoolwork while we're away. It's not quite the same as oppression."

"That's good, anyway. I was thinking that I'd be missing out on schooling, and although it's not always pleasant at school, I need to keep learning so I can get the best possible results."

"You have a better attitude to schooling than Dan has," said Nathan. "You should have heard him complaining when we told him that he had to read a Russian novel while we're away."

"You mean stories by authors like Tolstoy and Dostoevsky?"

"Yes, like 'The Brothers Kalamazoo'," laughed Dan.

"But don't start the puns," begged Dave, "or I'll escape through the Fyodor!"

"I think we'll all be rushin' through the fire door," said Belinda.

Ben was looking from one to the other, trying to understand what was going on and clearly finding the puns a little hard to comprehend. Eventually, he said, "Oh, I think I understand."

"Sorry," said Dan. "The family sense of humour is a little... ah, novel."

"Putting aside the trivia," said Nathan, "we'll try to allow enough time for you to do some schoolwork. Your Dad is hoping you can come with us. Do you think he'll bring some schoolwork for you tomorrow?"

"Probably. He wants me to do well, and he knows how important it is to me."

"If not, you may be able to find books in the Stawell library that would be useful."

After breakfast, they began getting ready for camping. Since the camper-trailer hadn't been used for months, Nathan wanted to check that everything was alright. After an inspection, he concluded that one of the tyres needed pumping up a little, but apart from that, everything was in good condition.

Dan and Dave showed Ben the parts of the campsite not seen by an ordinary camper, including the section of the equipment shed where the canoes and kayaks were stored. With no immediately available place to use them, these had not been used in Ben's school camp, but there were a few lakes not far away that allowed such craft, so they were always kept in operational condition.

"Do you have a canoe?" asked Dan.

"Yes, I have a favourite one, and a favourite kayak too. In fact, I have several of each, because Mum and Dad have bought me new ones as I've grown and got better at paddling. We also have some double kayaks because sometimes Dad or Mum go paddling with me. We all enjoy it."

"I've never done much canoeing," mourned Dan. "Just the occasional afternoon with the church youth group."

"I haven't done much either," agreed Dave, "but I've enjoyed the little bits I have done. It's fun."

"I love it," answered Ben, "but it's hard physical work when you're trying to go as fast as possible. I have to stay fit all the time."

Chapter 19

Fergus Follows Up

As Dan, Dave and Ben inspected the kayaks and canoes, Ben suggested which ones they should take if they decided to camp near a lake.

"Now you mention a lake, I've got an idea of a place we could camp where there's a beautiful lake," said Dan. "I'll suggest it to Dad and Mum later."

Just then, they heard a car approaching, gravel crunching under its tyres as it drove into the carpark. They quickly made their way towards the office in case there was no-one there to meet the visitor.

"It might be best for you to sneak into the living quarters behind the office, Ben," said Dan, "just in case this is Ahmed again, or one of the other four-wheel drives we saw at Troopers Creek campground."

"I'm sure Dad would share your concerns," said Ben, "so I'll wait in here." He ducked through a side door while the other two continued around to the front of the building.

A man was climbing out of the car as they rounded the corner of the office and Dan recognised him immediately.

"Hi, Fergus," he called out. "What brings you here?"

"Unfortunately, it's not a casual visit. Perhaps I should walk the Grampians Peaks Trail again. Fried eggs and a few days of walking by myself seem strangely attractive at the moment."

"You're meant to be on leave, aren't you?"

"Yes," answered Fergus with a scowl.

"So why were you at the hospital yesterday?"

"I've been asked to start working with the police here, even though they're not technically the same authority as my employer, Victoria Police. Nevertheless, we're still working together pretty well as long as we all make sure that the people who wouldn't like that don't find out about it."

"I'm sure ordinary people wouldn't mind that sort of cooperation."

"Of course not. Anyway, whether I should have agreed or not, I did. So now I'm here to try to find out more information – and possibly give you some, too."

"We'll tell you anything we can," said Dan, and Dave nodded. "Ben's staying here too, the son of Dr Ehud Cohen. I think you met Dr Cohen, but you probably haven't met Ben."

"No, I haven't, although I've heard a bit about him in my investigations."

Dan wondered how Ben could have come into Fergus' investigations, but continued, "He's just inside. Can he join us?"

"Sure. Sadly, he adds another complication – through no fault of his own."

"Hey, Ben," called Dan.

A moment later, Ben rounded the corner of the office on his crutches and approached them.

"Ben, this is Fergus Norton," said Dan. "He's working with the police here. Fergus, this is Ben."

"Hi, Mr Norton," said Ben.

"Call me Fergus," answered Fergus. "Your father did a wonderful job of saving that lad's life yesterday. You must be proud of him."

"I am," smiled Ben.

"Should we call anyone else?" asked Dan. "Dad? Mum?"

"Let's see how we go and call them if we need to. Yesterday I talked to Ahmed and found out some frightening things. As you know, Ahmed is a Muslim."

"Yes."

"His son had a gunshot wound, as you also know."

"Yes, although we didn't see him at all."

"Didn't you? Ah, so you've only met his father?"

"Yes. His father came here with three other blokes on Thursday. He got angry about everything we said and complained that everyone picked on Muslims and favoured Christians."

"He was like that with me too, but I just kept questioning him. When three other police officers joined me, that helped convince him we were taking things seriously."

"Excuse me, sir," interrupted Ben. "Can I ask how his son is now?"

"Sorry, I should have told you before I started. He's improving quickly. The doctors say he's completely out of danger and may be able to leave hospital in a few days."

"That's good. Thank you."

"He's only two or three years older than you, Ben, and it's heartbreaking to see how much hatred he's been taught throughout his life. I spoke to him early this morning and it just pours out of him. That's why I'm here."

"What sort of hatred?" asked Dan.

"Basically, his family and their friends have taught him to hate 'the infidel', as defined by their understanding of Islam. That includes all of us, and he'd consider all of us valid targets if we refused to convert to Islam."

"Would he start shooting at us if he met us?"

"Not at the moment, no. However, there's one group of people that he just *might* start shooting at." Fergus turned and looked seriously at Ben. "He particularly hates Jews, Ben. He has an absolute conviction that Jews are responsible for all of his troubles, all of the troubles of his people, the Arabs, and, in fact, all the troubles of the world."

"So, is he going to be locked up?" worried Dan. "Surely someone like that can't just be left to walk around free?"

"Police can only arrest people for certain things, Dan," answered Fergus. "Yes, we can probably keep him locked up for a short time, but most people will dismiss what he says as exaggerated and say he's not serious about his threats."

"Is he serious?"

"History shows that when people make threats against the Jews, they often – possibly even normally – have every intention of carrying them out if they can find an opportunity. They're what we call 'credible threats'."

"So did you just come here today to tell us this?"

"Partly. We'll lock up this lad and his father for the time being. The threats they've repeated in front of several witnesses will give us enough to go on with. Over time, we *might* be able to straighten him out, but I'm not holding my breath. Attempts to cure people of antisemitism don't have a very high success rate. Antisemites *enjoy* their hatred. It gives them pleasure, and they'll justify their hatred in the face of any reasoning that may be presented to them. That's why it's so difficult to know how to handle people like this."

"Can't they just be locked up until they learn?"

"They don't ever seem to learn unless they consciously choose to change themselves – and that's quite an unusual choice. What I was coming to tell you was to keep away from these people. I know it's unfair to suggest that innocent people should hide when those blokes are the bad guys, but that's the safest solution in the short term."

"We're planning to head west or southwest, camping in the wilds of the Grampians," said Dan. "Is that good enough?"

"When?"

"Monday morning, I think. We've been getting things ready this morning, and tomorrow we're planning to go to Stawell for church, then meet Ben's Dad, have lunch and join that discussion group we went to last week."

"Hmm. I think that should be alright in the current conditions. If I knew of more people like Ahmed and his son around, though, I'd say that you should keep away from Stawell entirely for a while."

"Stawell is probably safer than where we live in Horsham, though," said Ben.

"Yes. But the problem seems to be spreading quickly at the moment."

"Will we see you at the discussion class tomorrow?" asked Dan.

"I expect so, but I can't guarantee it. Ahmed and his son might keep me busy."

"I believe it's at Luke's house tomorrow, wherever that is. I'm relying on Alex to take me. I hope you can get there."

"One more thing before I leave," said Fergus, speaking earnestly to Ben. "If you see anyone around this site with darker skin and a beard, then you must hide. It might just be someone who likes sun baking and growing a beard, but if you keep away from them, you'll be safe if they're *not* just bearded sunbathers. That's really important."

Ben sighed. "I suppose I can. Although I hate the idea of running away."

"And while you're in public in Stawell, I suggest that you don't do anything that is obviously Jewish."

"I don't always know what things are considered to be 'obviously Jewish'," protested Ben.

"Of course you don't, so just avoid anything you do know of. For example, don't wear an obvious star of David or a kippah. This is just for the time being so we can make sure you stay healthy. Once we deal with the problem, you'll be able to go back to living as you choose. But I want you to survive until that can happen!"

"Well, thanks. Do you know how Ahmec's son got hurt?"

"That's my other reason for coming here. The story is a bit garbled, but both he and Ahmed said it happened near Roses Gap."

"But if it happened near Roses Gap, why would he be flown to Stawell from Horsham?" asked Dan. "After all, we're closer to Stawell than to Horsham here."

"True. He also said it had happened on Thursday, which doesn't seem possible," said Fergus.

"Why not?" asked Dave.

"How could he have survived that long? He was in such terrible condition when they flew him to Stawell."

"Maybe it happened on Thursday but they didn't do anything about it until Friday," suggested Dave.

"I suppose that's possible," pondered Fergus.

"Dave could be right," said Dan. "If it happened late on Thursday, after dark, say, they might have thought the wound wasn't so bad."

"Or perhaps they were just avoiding questions," suggested Dave. "After all, if you turn up with a gunshot wound, wanting to see a doctor, someone's going to ask how it happened."

"How *did* it happen?" asked Ben.

"He said it was an accident when he was cleaning a gun."

"Why did he have a gun?" asked Ben.

"He said it was for shooting deer."

"There are certainly plenty of deer in the park," said Dan. "I've seen quite a few on the roads and trails since we arrived."

"However, the doctors say the wound came from a handgun. You don't use a handgun to hunt deer."

"Dave and I are sure that at least one of the men who came here had a handgun in his pocket," said Dan, "although we didn't actually see it. When we arrived unexpectedly and gave him a shock, he shoved his hand into his pocket very quickly. Then he left it there, watching us carefully."

Fergus nodded. "You're right," he said, "he probably had a gun."

"And the others we saw at Troopers Creek Campground had rifles," added Dave.

"What others?" asked Fergus, quickly.

"On Tuesday, we saw twelve vehicles at the Troopers Creek Campground. They were looking for a place to stay."

"Uh-oh," said Fergus. "That possibility is just what I was concerned about. Tell me more."

"We don't really know much more. They wanted somewhere quiet to stay and train, so when one of them mentioned that the Troopers Creek Campground was on the

GPT and would have quite a few visitors, they decided to move on. As the last car went past, although the windows were tinted, we saw that the men in it were holding rifles."

At that point, Belinda opened the front door of the office and walked down the steps towards them.

"Hi, Fergus," she called.

He gave her a perfunctory wave as he mulled over the news Dan and Dave had given him.

"Do you have any reason to believe these men are connected with Ahmed?"

"Yes. Although we didn't see most of the men at Troopers Creek because they were hidden behind the noticeboard, they talked about a man who was climbing Briggs Bluff at the time to have a look around. We met a man walking down from Briggs Bluff later that afternoon, and he was one of the three men with Ahmed on Thursday."

"And there were only three people in that first vehicle," interjected Belinda.

"So, twelve cars with four people in each. Almost fifty people, and at least some of them armed." Fergus shook his head and sighed. "This is exactly what I was afraid of, but I'd hoped we'd got onto it early enough that we were only dealing with four dangerous men – and that was bad enough."

"I'm sorry I didn't tell you earlier," said Dan. "I meant to, but each time I tried, something interrupted or distracted me."

"One other thing," said Belinda. "That first car didn't have a number plate, but it had a card with writing on where it should have had a plate."

"It might be more useful for tracking them down if it had a proper licence plate," observed Fergus, "but even a card with writing on it might help us identify the car. Do you remember what it said, or was it in Arabic?"

"It was in English. It said 'AK-47'. Does that mean anything?"

"That's a type of rifle, isn't it?" asked Dan and Dave together.

"Yes," sighed Fergus. "And I don't think it's good news either. Thanks all the same, Belinda."

"I've just thought of something else," said Dan. "Having seen what Ahmed was like when his son was hurt, I'm pretty sure the accident hadn't happened yet when he visited here on Thursday."

"And that was early afternoon," said Dave.

"Hmm. I wonder when it did happen, then. And how did it happen? I'm not convinced by that 'cleaning a gun' explanation. Well, Dan, Dave and Belinda, I think this is a worse threat than NK2. I'd better get back to Stawell. Be careful, Ben. Give my regards to your parents, Dan."

Fergus climbed back into his car and drove away.

Chapter 20

More Evidence

Shortly before lunch, Steve and Sylvia returned from Stawell with the good news that the doctors were well satisfied with Sylvia's condition. They were glad to settle back into their temporary cabin.

Now lunch was over and the afternoon was warm and breezy. Despite still being confined to crutches, Ben was eager for exercise.

Originally, he'd been told to use crutches for four weeks, but when his stitches were removed, the surgeon was so pleased with his quick healing that he told Ben that he only needed to use them for one more week. He would have to be careful for a while, but his injured knee was expected to make a quick and complete recovery. In the meantime, Ben wanted to keep exercising as much as he could. There was no opportunity to paddle for now, but using crutches would provide its own strengthening exercise.

"I'd like to go for a walk," he said. "Not too far with these crutches, but maybe a kilometre or two."

"We could walk to the Beehive Falls carpark," suggested Belinda, "then you could go a little way towards the waterfall if you want to. The path is quite smooth and easy at the start."

After telling Nathan and Tanya where they were going, the four set off down the driveway to the Roses Gap Road. Ben made good speed on his crutches, but Dan was glad he wasn't having to walk too fast. His left arm ached and the cast seemed to grow heavier by the hour. He walked as smoothly as he could, avoiding any sudden movement.

At the bitumen road they turned towards the Beehive Falls carpark. The distance was short, but by the time they arrived, Dan was glad to stop for a while.

"Do you want to try the track, Ben?" asked Belinda.

"I'm not sure. I'll try walking to the other end of this carpark first," said Ben. "When I get back, I'll see if I need to go back to the camp."

"I'll wait here," said Dan. "My arm wants a rest."

"You three stay here then, and I'll go at my own speed," said Ben, swinging expertly off across the long carpark on his crutches.

The other three stood and watched, but after a while, Dan thought he heard the sound of approaching voices. Soon, there was no doubt: people were returning from Beehive Falls.

Ben reached the other end of the carpark and turned around to make his way back. Dan held up his hand, like a policeman stopping the traffic. If someone was coming, it was best for Ben to keep out of the way, just in case.

Two boys came into view along the path and Dan immediately recognised one as Ali, from Ben's school. He turned back to see if Ben had understood his signal, but saw that he was still approaching quickly and smoothly, each swing of his crutches bringing him closer to a confrontation with Ali.

Dan stepped forward a few steps to get out of sight of Ali and his companion, then waved wildly at Ben, trying to get his attention. He even held up his cast and waved it too. But Ben was obviously concentrating on his technique, reaching forward with the crutches, placing them quickly and maintaining his momentum as he swung forward between them to repeat the cycle again.

Knowing Ali must be getting quite close now, Dan put his arms down and stepped back to where he could see along the path. Belinda and Dave were alternately glancing across at Dan and staring down the path in concern. They seemed mesmerised. Dan noticed that Ali's conversation with his partner had stopped. At least Ben was still too far away for them to hear his speedy progress towards them. Dan wondered if Ali had recognised them. Now they were too close; his only way to warn Ben to hide would be to address Ali loudly enough that Ben could hear.

"Hi, Ali," he called, "you couldn't resist coming back to Roses Gap, hey?"

"Hi, Dan and Dave, and Belinda," replied Ali. His expression was more glare than smile, but at least he was being polite. "This is my friend, Omar. We've been up past Beehive Falls, collecting something."

He held up his hand a little as he spoke, and Dan instantly recognised the makeshift stove they had found in the camping cave.

"Hi Omar," said Dan, too distracted to smile but remembering to speak loudly, concerned that even now, Ben might be coming into view. "I'm Dan."

"Huh," said Omar, a sour look on his face.

Despite his anxiety, Dan couldn't help wondering where Ali had managed to find a friend even more belligerent than himself!

Of course, Omar's rude response was an invitation for Belinda to join the conversation. As she did so, Dan suddenly realised that this wasn't the first time recently that she'd taken up the challenge of extracting information from people she didn't know – and not done a bad job, either.

"Hi, Omar. Have you walked around the Grampians much?" asked Belinda, guilelessly.

He grunted and looked away.

"Ah, you can't remember the names of the places you've been," responded Belinda, nodding knowingly. "I feel like that sometimes. The Grampians have so many lovely places to walk."

Omar grunted again, but looked as if he was almost ready to say something.

"What about you, Ali?" Belinda pursued. "Have you walked many places, or can't you remember the names either?"

"I remember the names," interrupted Omar. "I've walked places around here and in other places up north and further west and south."

"Oh, have you been up to Briggs Bluff then?" asked Belinda, looking fascinated.

"Yes, I walked up there from here... when was it, Ali?"

"About a week ago. Two days after my camp here."

"Did you walk up the old track?" asked Belinda, exuding keen interest.

Dan wished she hadn't mentioned the old track. Some things were best kept to themselves. However, Omar avoided answering the question anyway.

"We followed the signposted path. It was really cold and windy at the top."

"It's a great view from up there though, isn't it?" threw in Dan.

"We didn't go there for the view," said Ali, sharply.

"Why else would you climb all the way up there?" asked Belinda, looking puzzled. Dan was impressed by her appearance of naive interest. There was no doubt she was getting a lot more information from Ali and Omar than he would have managed.

"We'd heard a claim that someone from another group had put up a flag at the top. We wanted to make sure the flag was, ah, acceptable."

"Oh, surely no-one would do anything like that, would they?" breathed Belinda, eyes widening theatrically.

"Well, there wasn't a flag there anyway," said Omar, once more avoiding a question.

"I suppose that was good news for you," persisted Belinda, pressing her opinion on them.

"Yes and no," said Omar, looking annoyed. "A flag on Briggs Bluff would be a good idea, but we wanted to make sure it was a good flag. As it turned out, there was no flag – they must have been just boasting."

"We could have put up a flag of our own if we'd thought of it earlier," said Ali.

"I'm glad you didn't," said Belinda, quietly.

"Why should we care about what you think?" sneered Ali. "After all, you helped the Jew last week."

"What do you mean?" asked Dan, wanting to force them to use Ben's name instead of hiding behind abusive titles.

"You know who the Jew is. You know who I mean."

Dan said nothing and an awkward silence fell. As it lengthened, Dan suddenly remembered that Ben had been coming. Since he hadn't arrived, he must have heard the voices and found somewhere to hide.

He kept looking fixedly at Ali, challenging him to name Ben. He was not going to be a party to using the word "Jew" when Ali clearly intended it to be derogatory.

"Can't you remember his name?" he prompted. "Surely you see him often enough at school?"

"You know who I mean, the one who fell over on the last day."

"But you don't know his name?" Dan persisted.

"Of course I do, but I'm not going to use it."

"Okay, we'd better be moving on then," said Dan. "We don't seem to have anything to talk about."

"Yes, we do," said Ali abruptly, as if just remembering. "Did you know that he cut the water pipe for the dishwasher? I went into the kitchen and saw him do it. When he saw me, he quickly dropped the knife and nudged it under the machine with his foot, hoping I wouldn't notice."

"Did you report it?" asked Dan.

"No," said Ali. "I forgot."

"Did you look at the machine to see what damage was done?"

"No, I didn't need to. I saw him do it, hold the knife, cut the pipe."

"It's a pity you didn't report it," said Belinda. "Leaking pipes waste water and can do a lot of damage."

"What would you say if we told you he'd reported that *you* cut the pipe?" asked Dave.

"How would he kno...?" began Ali, before stopping and looking at Dave doubtfully. Dan was careful not to smile. "Anyway, if you look at the dishwasher, Dan, you'll find that everything fits with what I've described. You might even find more evidence that it was the Jew," he added mysteriously.

"Come on, Ali," said Omar. "We need to hurry along to the Mount Zero Road. We're due to be picked up in five minutes."

"Okay, I'll come," said Ali. He took a few steps, then turned back to Dan, Dave and Belinda and spoke savagely. "Don't any of you take the Jew's side or you'll find yourself in deep trouble."

He turned on his heel and walked off.

Dan, Dave and Belinda exchanged glances, but stood watching in silence until the unpleasant pair had walked beyond the far end of the carpark and disappeared from sight.

"Ali gave himself away there, didn't he?" observed Dan. "Brilliant question, Dave. He couldn't work out how to answer or what you might already know."

"Where did Ben go?" asked Belinda.

"We'd better wait a while before we look for him," said Dan. "Just to make sure they've really gone."

There was movement some ten or fifteen metres away and Ben appeared, carefully negotiating the undergrowth with his crutches.

"I don't care if they've gone or not. I should have just come along at the start instead of hiding," he said.

"If you'd done that, I'm pretty sure we wouldn't have learned what we learned," said Belinda.

"So, what did we learn, then?" asked Dan. "His story about seeing Ben cutting the pipe doesn't stack up."

"No," agreed Dave. "You can't see the pipe from the doorway or anywhere near it. In fact, you can't see it without looking in behind the dishwasher. He was lying."

"He also said we'd find some extra evidence of Ben having cut the pipe. Could he be referring to anything other than the bracelet?"

"I don't think so," said Dave. "But since he said he didn't look under the dishwasher, he couldn't have known about it unless he put it there himself."

"You've got a dedicated enemy there, Ben," commented Dan.

"I know. He's been like that for a long time now."

"And he doesn't care if he tells lies to get you in trouble," said Belinda. "How can he live with himself?"

Chapter 21

Complexity

As Dan, Dave, Belinda and Ben returned to the camp site, something was niggling at the back of Dan's mind. When Ali had turned angrily back to them after beginning to walk off with Omar, the expression on his face had triggered something in Dan's memory. What was it? Something was lurking at the edge of recollection, but remaining stubbornly out of reach.

Perhaps learning more about Ali and the problems he'd caused Ben might help. He asked, but Ben refused to discuss the subject.

"Dad already talks about it too much," said Ben. "I don't think it helps."

"I understand that you don't want to concentrate on it. You'd end up thinking that everyone is picking on you," answered Dan.

"Yes, you'd start to sound like Ahmed," laughed Dave.

"Well, I want to be able to get on with life; achieve things and be useful to the people around me," said Ben. "My ancestors have always kept going in the face of difficulties, and we'll keep doing so. We must."

"When you put it like that," mused Dan, "I suppose you're right. It's a matter of life and death if people hate you and are determined to kill you."

"I don't know much about the history of the Jews beyond some of what is in the Bible and the things I used to hear on the news," said Dave. "Can you tell me anything?"

"I could, but I don't really want to. I prefer to look forward."

"Okay," said Dan. "So, what do you look forward to, then?"

"Further education. Maybe university, but it would have to be in Adelaide, since Melbourne won't accept anyone from beyond the margins. I hear that they call us all 'foreigners' now."

"Yeah. Dave lives in Adelaide, so he's okay," said Dan.

"And I'm meant to be going back there in six weeks' time," said Dave, not looking too thrilled at the prospect. "Still, I do want to go to uni there next year."

"My parents want me to go to uni too," grumbled Dan, "and Adelaide might be the only place possible. The problem is, I don't really have anything in particular that I want to do at uni, and going for the sake of it seems like a waste of time."

"I want to become a doctor," said Ben, "but I also love rowing and I'd like to do some competitive rowing if I can."

"What sort of rowing competitions are available?"

"A few years ago, if you wanted a career in rowing it was all pretty clear: the Olympics and the World Championships. Now it's not so simple."

"Are you that good at it?" queried Belinda, impressed.

"I don't know. Other people say I am, but I can't tell until I meet more competition and row in more important races. With sports, it's never enough to be just very good – to be successful, you really have to enjoy the way the competitions work in your sport. I'm not sure I would, and I've never tried anything major. I was a bit too young when everything started shutting down."

"Victoria wouldn't let you in for competitions, would they?" asked Dave.

"No," answered Ben, shortly.

"And I hear that New South Wales is the same," said Dan. "Western Australia is even stricter, if that's possible – it might as well be on the other side of the world."

"I think Adelaide and South Australia are my only options at the moment," Ben agreed.

"It's funny," said Dan. "Our family came from South Australia when I was seven, but I'd never thought about living there until Victoria started forcing me to."

"You really can't predict where the future will go, can you?" commented Dave.

"No," agreed Belinda. "Sometimes it would be nice to know more about what's coming: schooling, pandemics, dangers from extremists and so on."

"A few days ago, I read what Jesus said about that," responded Dan. "He said, 'Don't worry about tomorrow, for tomorrow will worry about itself. Each day has enough trouble of its own.' " He smiled wryly and held up his still-aching arm with its cast. "The last few days have certainly had enough trouble of their own!"

"I wonder how that young lad in the hospital is," pondered Dave.

"Do you know how old he is, Ben?" asked Dan. "Did your Dad tell you anything about him?"

"No. Someone said he looked like he was under 20, but I don't think anyone had proper details at that stage. They were too busy trying to save him!"

"It's a bit strange to have someone turning up in a helicopter with a gunshot wound and nobody knowing who he is or how he got hurt," said Dan.

"I think his father put people off a bit," said Dave. "Carrying on and shouting at everyone."

Dan was just about to ask Ben what he knew about Muslims when he remembered the attack on his family's house and thought better of it. He changed the subject instead and asked Ben, "Have you ever read the Bible?"

"No, not really. My parents aren't interested in religion. Being Jews, their families have suffered a lot over the last few generations, and they don't think much of religion."

"Do you agree with them? Have you looked into it yourself?"

"I'm not sure whether they're right or not – though I suppose that by not investigating it I'm saying I agree with them. If I were to examine any religion, I'd start with Judaism, but I'm too busy, anyway."

"I don't know much about Judaism myself," said Dan. "Dave knows a bit more than me because one of his best friends at school was Jewish and his parents were... how would you describe them, Dave?"

"I think they'd be called observant Jews, or something like that. They kept the Sabbath and many other rituals of Judaism, but my friend didn't know much about the Bible. Then again, I didn't know much myself at that time. It's only been in the last couple of years or so that I've started reading it. It was probably Dan who started me looking, but once I started, I found it really interesting."

"But you mean what is called the New Testament, don't you?" asked Ben. "Judaism only looks at what you call the Old Testament: the law and the prophets."

"I read both the New Testament and the Old," said Dave. "The New Testament quotes the Old Testament so much that I found I had to read a lot of it just to understand the context and the background. Some parts are kind of hard to read, but lots is really... really exciting, I suppose."

"I've never read it," said Ben. "Have you, Dan?"

"Yes," smiled Dan. "I've read the Old Testament a few times now, and the New Testament too. I've been interested in it for a few years, but my parents weren't and nor was anyone else I knew, so it wasn't easy to get started. Since we came here, I've spent a lot of time talking to Alex about it."

"You mean the Alex who worked for the camp?"

"Yes. He really loves the Bible. He's taught me a lot."

"Isn't it funny," laughed Ben, "that you three have read the Jewish scriptures and you're not Jews, yet I'm a Jew and I haven't."

"I hadn't thought of it that way," nodded Dan. "But you're right, it does seem strange. I do think that you Jews are very blessed to be descended from Abraham whom God chose as a friend."

"Don't think it's always been such a blessing," said Ben, drily.

"No, but that's been a choice, hasn't it?"

"A choice? You think I *want* to be hated?"

"No, I don't mean a choice to be hated. I meant the choice the Jews have made through history not to treat God the way Abraham, Isaac and Jacob did. As far as I can tell, God warned that being hated and suffering everything the Jews have suffered would be the result of not listening to God."

"I thought God was meant to be a God of love," said Ben.

"Of course," said Dave, "but that doesn't mean he has no standards! It's not just love, love, love and you can do what you want! Just like sensible parents have requirements!"

"How do you know that?"

Dave looked questioningly at Dan. "Where could we show Ben that?"

"Does it have to come from the Old Testament?" asked Dan.

"I'd prefer it," said Ben, slowly.

"Oh, that's a bit tougher..." Dan stopped and thought for a moment, then his face lit up and he said, "No it's not. It's easy. In the Ten Commandments, I think it's in Exodus chapter 20, God told your people to have no other gods but him and describes himself as a jealous God who will punish those who hate him but show lasting love to those who love him and keep his commandments."

"So loving God is doing what he tells you?"

"Yes. It makes sense, because a life that follows his commands is the best sort of life for a human being to live. God is the creator, so of course he knows what's best for the people he created."

"It's like following the user's manual for a piece of equipment," added Dave. "The designer and manufacturer know what works and what doesn't, so it makes sense to follow the instructions. When people don't follow the instructions, that's when they get into trouble."

"I guess that does make sense," said Ben. "I've never heard it expressed that way before."

"I think that once people stopped thinking of God as the creator, it was inevitable that they'd stop listening to his commands," said Dan. "It's a tragedy."

"Well, there, you've got a starting point. I want to be a doctor, like my Dad. Doctors learn lots about the human body, and scientists explain everything by saying that our bodies came about by chance. They talk about evolution and say that God has nothing to do with it. Why should we believe the Bible rather than what science has proved?"

"Whew, this discussion keeps getting bigger and bigger," said Dan. "Has your Dad ever talked about just how complex the human body is?"

"Yes, he talks about it often. In fact, I've never thought about it before, but he says it's a miracle. It's funny that he should call it a miracle when he doesn't believe in God or anything else that could cause a miracle. Surely a miracle requires a... a... a person or a power to drive it?"

"That's how it seems to me," said Dan, "but that's not all. The body is unbelievably complex. I'm no doctor, but from what I read, science can only explain a very small part of the operation of the human body. There are all sorts of chemicals in the body, all sorts of messages sent from one part to another, all sorts of unbelievably complex chains of events that scientists just don't understand. They can observe that things happen, but they have no idea of *how* they actually happen. It's easy to say that we're gradually understanding more and more, and it's true. But to make the leap that says we'll eventually be able to understand everything – well, I don't think there's any reason to believe that."

"Why not?" asked Ben.

"It requires a certain level of intelligence to understand something, doesn't it? You wouldn't try explaining rowing to a slug. So anything we understand has to be simple enough for our brains to comprehend, or we won't be able to understand it. Some people can't understand addition, whereas others understand complex mathematics and physics. But nobody understands our brain in detail, and I don't believe anyone ever will be able to. There's just no reason to think we will."

"As I understand it," said Dave, "we can't even understand *in detail* how any animal or insect brain works."

"No," agreed Dan. "We like to talk about simple organisms, but there's no such thing. We don't understand how single-celled organisms work, let alone our brain. I remember a quote I read in Year 11: 'If our brains were simple enough for us to understand, we'd be too simple to understand them,' which was saying that a brain that was simple enough for us to understand would be way too simple to be capable of understanding how our brain works – in detail at least."

"I think I know what you mean," nodded Ben. "What it's really saying is that a brain can only understand things that are simpler than it is."

"That's a good way of putting it. And so far, I think all the evidence points to that being true. There is no such thing as simple when it comes to life, and humans have never been able to create life – other than using the methods God designed," said Dan.

"I thought you said you didn't know much about this?" teased Dave.

"I don't," retorted Dan, "but I've read quite a lot and watched videos too – before the internet started breaking. One of the things that stands out in explanations of biology is the frequency of statements like 'we don't know exactly how this works...' or 'by a method that is not fully understood, this happens'. Certainly, scientists understand a lot, and that's a testament to the complexity of the brains God has given us, but if people expect to understand everything eventually, I think it's wishful thinking."

"You said that people have never created life," said Ben. "I understood that they'd created life in petri dishes and stuff like that."

"Only ever by starting with *living things*. Not starting with dead things like dust. And it isn't due to a lack of trying," answered Dan.

"That's always been one of the things that convinced me about God creating," said Dave. "If humans, the most intelligent beings in creation, can't make life from dead things, how can anyone believe that it can happen by pure, stupid chance?"

"I'm sure you know the answer people give: it just takes time. Deep time. Billions of years," said Belinda.

"Yes, I know, but it still defies logic. If something can't be done, it can't be done. If creating life is so simple that blind chance can do it, how come humans can't make it happen with the best efforts of intelligence? Is blind stupid chance really so much smarter than humans? How can anyone believe life could start by chance, and not only start but continue, and not only continue, but improve? The evidence just isn't there." Dan paused for a moment and grinned. "And my unbiased logic says it couldn't happen."

"So why do people believe it then?" asked Ben.

"They prefer it to the other option."

"What other option?" asked Belinda.

"That there is a God who made everyone. Because if there *is* a God, humans aren't the best living things, and also if there is a God, he just might want something from the things he's created."

"Hmm. That makes sense, too," nodded Ben.

"It explains why people act how they do and why they fight so hard against anyone who says there must be a creator."

"Can mainstream science really be so wrong?" asked Belinda.

"It's not hard to look through history and find lots of cases of people who've made new discoveries and been ridiculed by mainstream science," answered Dan. "Science is said to be unbiased, but it isn't. Science is often very attached to existing science, and scientists have egos, just like the rest of us."

"I think science allows some advances to be made easily," said Dave; "advances that don't have an impact on people's worldview. But others are fought every step of the way. The useful thing about physical science is that processes are reproducible. Enough proof can eventually force science to adjust its beliefs. That's why we now know as much as we do about hygiene, despite the scientific and medical establishment dismissing and ridiculing the evidence for a long time. Lots of people lost their jobs for those advances. Some even lost their lives."

"So you think proof can eventually force science to accept things it doesn't like?"

"Yes – but funnily enough, none of the ideas of progressive evolution that science is so attached to can currently be demonstrated by reproducing them. And none of their interpretations of fossil discoveries or other ancient things can *ever* be proved."

"Hey, but what about Christianity?" teased Belinda. "Can't it be proved?"

"No, I don't think so," answered Dan, seriously. "The past is the past, and what happened can't be proved. That's why courts talk about things being demonstrated 'beyond reasonable doubt'. It's an acknowledgement that you can't prove things you can't reproduce."

"And sometimes courts have to reverse their decisions because later evidence suggests that what was believed to be 'beyond reasonable doubt' was actually wrong," added Dave.

"True," said Belinda.

"And Belinda, if we could prove Christianity, we wouldn't need faith," said Dan, "yet God says that without faith it is impossible to please him."

"I really will have to think more about all this," said Ben.

"That's what I decided," said Dan. "I could've followed what my parents did, but I thought it was worth investigating myself. One of the frustrating parts of having no access to the internet is that I can't easily do much more investigating. If we go to the library tomorrow to get school books, I might be able to find some other books to look at."

Chapter 22

Who Was That?

During the evening meal, they told Nathan and Tanya about Fergus' visit and their meeting with Ali and his friend.

Tanya wasn't happy with any of the news.

"The sooner we go camping, the better," she said.

"Then we need to decide where to go," said Nathan.

"If we're trying to keep away from people, we can't go to places like Halls Gap," said Tanya.

"And places near the boundary of the national park are too easy for people to get to," said Dan. "Somewhere more remote would be better."

"But not so remote that there isn't any reasonable access," said Nathan. "Don't forget we'll be towing the camper-trailer."

"Would Moora Moora Reservoir fit the bill?" asked Dan.

"Oh, that was a lovely place," smiled Tanya.

"I don't remember it much," said Belinda, "but I think it was nice."

"Quiet and beautiful," said Nathan, "and with a deep feeling of calm."

"I've never been there," said Ben, "but it sounds nice compared with most of what's been happening recently."

"I remember seeing someone in a canoe last time we were there. Do you think we could borrow a canoe and a kayak from the camp equipment here?"

"Would they be safe, tied on top of the camper-trailer?" asked Dave.

"I think so," said Nathan, "but first, we'll have to ask Steve and Sylvia if we can borrow them. Would you like that, Ben?"

Ben's face was all smiles. "I sure would, Mr Turner. Being able to get some exercise and maybe some training would be a great help. I still hope to get to the Olympics somehow, and this knee has had me worried."

"Are the Olympics more important to you than university?" asked Dan, curiously.

"No," said Ben, definitely. "Competitive rowing is important alright, but education is more important to me. I want a job that's useful and challenging, and I think being a doctor is more useful than paddling fast!"

"That sounds sensible," said Dave.

"What canoes or kayaks would you like us to take with us – if we can?" asked Nathan.

"One canoe and one kayak would be good, perhaps ones we could all use, not just me. Would others be interested?"

"I'd like to," said Dave, and Belinda chimed in too.

"I'd love to," said Dan, ruefully, holding up his arm with the cast, "but with this...."

"Then what about a double kayak and an open canoe? I saw a couple of each in the equipment shed."

"That sounds good," said Nathan, "as long as they're not too big for us to tie on top of the camper-trailer. I'll just go and check with Steve that it's okay."

It took only a few moments to get Steve's permission, and then Nathan and Dave carried the canoe and kayak across to the camper-trailer. Dan was forced to watch, frustrated at another limitation caused by his broken arm, while Ben selected paddles and Belinda carried them to the camper-trailer where Nathan and Dave were tying the kayak and canoe on top.

When Ben pulled out life jackets, Dan laughed. "Lifejackets? Isn't Moora Moora reservoir only about two metres deep?"

Nathan said they would take them anyway, and places were dutifully found for them.

By the time it was getting dark, the camper-trailer was ready to be attached to the car, but it would be left standing under the tree until Monday morning when they were ready to go.

"Did we ever actually decide that we were going to Moora Moora?" asked Dan.

"I think it was carried without any need for discussion," said Nathan.

"I'm already picturing the beauty and starting to feel the tranquillity," said Tanya. "Monday morning can't come too quickly."

☙

Sunday, however, came first and saw them attending the same church again.

Belinda had suggested that they could go later, since this time they were all going to the discussion class in the afternoon, but Nathan reminded her that they had to meet Ehud before lunch time and Tanya was eager to see Linda again in the morning. The idea of church as a place to meet trusted friends was more attractive to her than ever before. In the past, they might have travelled in separate cars, but having only one car had forced them to do more things together as a family. Overall, Nathan and Tanya thought it was an advantage, although it was not always so convenient.

Dan enjoyed the church music again, but found the sermon less engaging than the Bible readings and discussions the family had shared with Alex. At one stage, the clergyman spoke of loved ones watching their families from heaven and Dan wished he could ask Alex about it.

Ben had never been in a Christian church before and felt very uncomfortable, not knowing what to expect. In truth, though, he wouldn't have felt much more comfortable in a synagogue, having grown up in a home that avoided religion. He did, however, enjoy some of the music, and listened with interest to the reading of a small section from the Bible.

At the end of the service, the family and Ben went outside and stood chatting with Terry and Linda. Ehud met them at much the same time as he had the previous week, and Nathan duly reported that they would be pleased to have Ben camping with them. Ehud beamed and thanked them all sincerely. He passed over a bag of clothes and school books for Ben, and hurried off to the hospital where he was to see Ahmed's son. The others continued to chat until the growing heat of the sun made them decide to find somewhere a little cooler to talk. They agreed to move to Cato Park again, where they had picnicked the previous week. It was only a short distance away, but as they were passing the steep hospital entrance road, Dan noticed two men making their way down the hill. They looked to be in a hurry, but what attracted Dan's attention was the fact that the younger of the two was not clothed above his waist and had his arm in a sling, with a substantial bandage around his upper arm and shoulder. The older man appeared to be hurrying him along.

"Hey," called Dan as they passed the road, "was that Ahmed?"

"Where?" asked Nathan.

"Walking down the hill from the hospital," said Dan, craning his neck back to see behind them as Nathan slowed down to turn into the carpark of Cato Park.

As he watched, he saw Ahmed reach the lower roadway and wave at a four-wheel drive standing a few metres back along the road. The Turners had driven right past it, noticing nothing unusual except, perhaps, that it occupied a place where parking was not allowed. Now it was pulling out from the curb and hurrying to where Ahmed and his son were waiting.

"Can we go back, Dad?" implored Dan.

"I'm just turning around," said Nathan, doing a U-turn instead of turning into the carpark. He drove back towards the hospital, while on the other side of the road, the four-wheel drive stopped and the back door opened from inside.

"The man in the passenger seat has a rifle," said Dan, urgently.

"And Fergus said we should keep away from Ahmed because of Ben," added Dave, his voice equally urgent.

"Then I'll just drive past," said Nathan. "Don't even look at the other car, everyone. And once we go past, don't try turning around to look – they may be watching us."

They drove past, followed a slight kink in the road and slowed as they approached a roundabout. Nathan, watching the rear-view mirror, reported: "The young man has been helped up into the car and now Ahmed is climbing in. The door's shut. They're driving away. Uh-oh. They're doing a U-turn. They're following us."

"Oh no!" said Belinda.

"If they're heading for Horsham," said Nathan, tensely, "they may not follow us past the roundabout, but if they do, I'll turn right at Patrick Street. At least that's heading away from Horsham."

The four-wheel drive did follow them through the roundabout and was quickly catching up with the Turners when Nathan turned right onto Patrick Street. "Don't look back!" he ordered.

They obeyed, but the knowledge that there was a car behind them containing at least one man with a rifle made Dan's back crawl with fear.

"Don't worry," said Nathan a few seconds later. "They turned left."

"Phew," said Belinda, and everyone else heaved a sigh of relief.

"What do we do now?" asked Dan. "We just drove past the Police Station. Should we stop?"

"Maybe turning right was smarter than I thought. They might not have wanted to go near the Police Station. Will it be open now?"

"Oh, I hope so," said Tanya.

"Let's go and look," said Dan.

Once again, Nathan did a U-turn, then stopped opposite the Police Station.

"Can I come in?" asked Dan.

"What made you think anyone else was going in?" asked Nathan.

"Well, I knew you'd go," teased Dan. "Leader of the family and all that."

"Yes, but I also want to be out here to look after the family if anything unexpected happens."

"I hadn't thought of that," admitted Dan. "You think they may come back?"

"I don't know what to think, Dan," said his father, gently. "This is not within my range of familiar experiences."

"Fair point, Dad."

"And I'd like it to stay that way, dear," said Tanya. "There has been much too much excitement in the last four months."

"So who *is* going in then?" asked Dan, like a terrier who won't let go of a bone.

"I'll come," said Dave.

At Nathan's nod, Dan and Dave climbed out of the car and crossed the road to the police station. The front door was open and they went in. Inside the foyer they found a vacant reception desk in front of an open door that led into an office.

Leaning casually against the doorpost was Fergus Norton.

"Fergus!" said Dan, feeling that he'd said that quite often recently.

"What are you doing here, young man? Shouldn't you be in church?"

"We went to church. It's what happened afterwards that made us come here."

"Come in," said Fergus, waving them into the office, where they found Les Talbot seated at a desk. "We've just been speaking about you and your Muslim friends."

Fergus followed them in and shut the door.

"Hey, mister boss man," he said to Les. "I hope you're happy with me running your office like this!"

"Of course. I was watching how skilfully you were doing it. Perhaps you'd like to take my chair as well?"

"No thanks," said Fergus. "Sitting closer to the door allows me to escape quicker should the job become intolerably difficult. I can write a letter of resignation quicker than you can blink!"

"No doubt," said Les, comfortably, "but you don't ever seem to get around to it. You just keep coming back for more and more work. Even when you're meant to be on holiday. Would you like to look after the security arrangements for that special visitor on Friday evening?"

"Sit down, lads," said Fergus, ignoring the question and waving casually to a pair of chairs in front of the desk.

As they sat down, he found a stool to squat on and smilingly prompted them, "Tell us your news."

"We just saw Ahmed and his son escaping from the hospital," blurted out Dan.

Fergus stopped smiling and Les leaned forward, his face suddenly serious.

"You what?"

"We just saw a four-wheel drive pick up Ahmed and his son from the bottom of the hospital entrance driveway. The son was half-dressed and they helped him into the back of the car. The front passenger had a rifle."

"Where did they go?"

"They did a U-turn and followed us up the road until we turned right onto Patrick Street, just out there. Then they turned left."

"How long ago?"

"Maybe four or five minutes at the most?"

"Hey, Les," asked Fergus, "do we have a couple of cars to see if we can catch them?"

"Where would they be going?"

"Probably out of town on the back road, then onto the Western Highway heading towards Horsham."

"Do we want a shootout on the highway?"

"Probably not, but it may be better than having one in the middle of either town!"

"Well, in this case, I'll defer to your expertise, Fergus. You're the marksman."

"I have a conflict here," said Fergus. "A shootout on the highway would put ordinary citizens at risk. We may be able to stop the car and arrest its occupants without trouble, but we won't have control over the situation, so the risk is high. Of course, if we had lots of time on our side, we could wait to find a better opportunity to confront these people. But I don't think we have much time." He paused for a moment in thought. "It's a difficult choice, but on balance, I think we're best avoiding a confrontation on the highway."

"I agree with you," replied Les, "but letting them leave means we don't know where they are. We could try following them without looking for a confrontation – using an unmarked car."

"We could, but we don't need to."

"Why not?"

"Very early on in this business I decided that location tracking might be important. Ahmed was so belligerent and confrontational that I felt having some aces in hand could be worthwhile."

"Which means?"

"While the young man was still unconscious, I put a GPS tracker on his arm and covered it with bandages. A nurse helped me, so he shouldn't notice it at all."

"How big is it?"

"Only small. I took it from an ankle bracelet. It's tracked by wireless or mobile data and the monitoring centre is in Horsham."

"The way mobile systems are nowadays, once they leave the Stawell area, surely we won't get any communication for most of the way along the highway until they get near Horsham?"

"That's right. I believe it used to take about 45 or 50 minutes to get to Horsham, so now it's probably 75 to 90 minutes. I'll contact the monitoring centre to make sure they've been getting the tracking data and check what movement they've seen today."

Fergus left the office and went to another where he could more easily speak to the officers in the monitoring centre. He returned a few minutes later to report that the monitoring centre was only receiving occasional updates at the moment from along the highway, but that the tracking device had reported in detail the travel from the hospital and across town towards the highway.

"I asked them to let us know when or if they receive location data from near Horsham, or anything unexpected," finished Fergus. "They also mentioned that there seem to be two different groups in Horsham causing trouble at the moment. They don't like each other, either. Some conflict near town last night, apparently. I'll get more information later."

"But you should be able to find where these people live in Horsham?" asked Dan.

"Yes, if they live in the built-up area of Horsham. Of course, it's possible they live beyond the limited mobile coverage we have at the moment."

"And then you'll go and arrest them?"

"I should, and in the past I'd have been leaving now, but I've decided I'm not available this afternoon. Sorry, Les. I can go this evening if that seems worthwhile, but not this afternoon."

"Why?" asked Les.

"It's simple. All my life I've allowed work to control what I do, but when I was reading the Bible last night, I came across a few verses that convinced me it's time to stop letting work control my life."

"What do they say?" asked Les.

Dan and Dave looked at each other. They could guess what the verses were, having discussed them between themselves just two weeks before.

"The most important part of the most important verse says, 'seek first the kingdom of God and his righteousness'. I've decided to listen to it, so I resolved last night that whatever happened, I was going to a Bible discussion class that I've been to before and need to keep going to."

"Well, that sounds quite alright to me," answered Les. "After all, you're actually on leave anyway."

"I'm still determined to track down these people, but this afternoon I've got something more urgent, so policing will have to wait until later."

"Will you come back here after the meeting?" asked Les.

'I intend to. Theoretically, this tracking should make it all easy, but I have a feeling something's not going to work."

The phone at reception began to ring, and Les leaned over and picked up the phone on his desk. "Stawell Police Station," he said. "How can I help you?"

The others in the room couldn't hear the response, but they watched as Les nodded and smiled to himself.

"Yes, yes," he said. "Thanks very much for letting us know. We'll be over there soon."

He hung up the phone.

"Guess who that was?"

Dan and Dave looked at each other. This time they had no idea.

"Someone at the hospital?" suggested Fergus.

"Exactly," nodded Les. "They were ringing to report that the gunshot victim has disappeared, along with his father."

"They didn't take long to notice. Quite impressive," said Fergus.

"I think I'll go across to the hospital now," said Les. "Coming?"

"Did you have anything else to tell us, boys?" Fergus said to Dan and Dave.

"No, not that I can think of," said Dan. "We were just about to go to Cato Park for a picnic, so if you're up at the hospital, we can drop in if anything more occurs to us. Or we should see you at the Bible class, anyway."

"That sounds good," said Fergus. "Let's go."

Chapter 23

Another Discussion

When the Turners and Ben reached Cato Park, they found Linda and Terry waiting for them with Alex.

"Where did you go?" called Terry. "You left before us, but we've been waiting for twenty minutes. We were just about to give up and start eating."

"We had to go to the Police Station," said Nathan. "We'll explain while we eat."

Terry and Linda had chosen one of a pair of adjoining empty tables, so Nathan and Tanya sat with them, while the young people sat at the other table.

"Can I start the meal with thanks to God?" asked Alex as he sat down.

Ben looked surprised and Belinda pursed her lips a little, but everyone else nodded.

"Our father in heaven," said Alex, "thank you for giving us our food. We pray to you through Jesus, your son. Amen."

"Thanks, Alex," said Tanya. "Short but grateful."

Belinda probably wasn't trying to cause trouble, but if she had taken the time to think, she wouldn't have asked what she did. "Ben, what did you think of the prayer?"

Nathan frowned, but said nothing.

Of course, Ben had two reasons to feel uncomfortable with the prayer: firstly because his family did not acknowledge God, and secondly because any prayers he had heard in his Jewish community didn't mention Jesus.

"Ah... I..."

"You don't have to answer, Ben," said Alex, "although I don't mind if you do."

"I'm not used to prayer," said Ben, slowly. "My parents don't pray and I've never tried it myself."

"Sorry, Ben," said Belinda, contritely. "I didn't mean to make it awkward for you."

"That's fine. I'm also more used to the way Jews speak of the Lord – modifying names and titles a little to avoid taking his name in vain. It's a bit like using code. I'm not used to this sort of open discussion about him."

"We didn't talk about God much in our family before we left Melbourne," said Belinda, her tone suggesting she preferred that.

"Well, I'm glad it's changed a bit," said Dan, "though I don't think it's changed as much as you're suggesting."

The awkward moment passed and everyone started eating, except for Nathan, who began explaining to Terry and Linda why they were late. He had no problem describing the happenings near the hospital, but when he tried to recount

Dan and Dave's discussions in the police station, Dan and Dave had to correct him continually.

After the fourth correction, Dan laughed. "Shall I tell it, Dad?"

"I thought I was doing a good job," said Nathan, joining in the general laughter. "Maybe the information I was given was deficient."

"The important part was that Fergus put a tracker in Ahmed's son's bandages, so the police are tracking their car back to Horsham – or wherever they go, as long as there's coverage. When we left, Les and Fergus were heading to the hospital to see what the hospital could tell them."

Glancing at Belinda, Dan added, "You may not be interested in this, Sis, so don't listen if you don't want to. Fergus said he wasn't going to chase Ahmed and his son immediately because he had something more important to do this afternoon. He's going to the Bible discussion instead. I thought that was good."

"A brave decision for a policeman to make," pondered Terry. "What happens if everything suddenly blows up?"

"Presumably someone else will have to look after it," answered Dan. "For what it's worth, he's currently on leave anyway."

"Fair enough."

"Perhaps I should have kept away from the police in the first place," said a voice from behind Dan.

"Fergus!" Dan exclaimed, swinging around.

Fergus threw back his head and laughed. "You really do like saying my name in that shocked manner."

"You keep turning up when I least expect it," complained Dan.

"Good afternoon, everyone," said Fergus, waving to them all. "Dan mentioned that you were going to be here, so once I finished at the hospital, I came over to see you."

"Welcome, Fergus," said Nathan. "Did you get any news from the hospital?"

"Nothing significant. Ahmed was in his son's room when Ehud visited and examined him briefly before the nurse delivered an early lunch. When she next visited the room, it was empty. It seems they sneaked out through a back door. Anyway, they've headed off and we hope to track them down soon – perhaps this afternoon."

"After the Bible class," added Dan.

"Yes," Fergus agreed.

"I think our whole family is going to the Bible class."

"And Ben?" asked Fergus.

"I *think* he's coming too. Ben?"

"If you'd prefer to come to our house, you'd be welcome," said Linda, quickly.

"Thanks very much," said Ben, "but I think I'd like to go along – as long as nobody expects me to become a Christian on the spot!"

"No!" said Dan. "I've only been there once, but nobody tried to push anyone into anything. It was clear that most people agreed with some of the things said and not others. Above all, most people seemed to concentrate on the Bible."

"I'll see what it's like, then," answered Ben.

"At least no-one there should have any guns," said Tanya. "I don't like seeing so many people with guns! Getting shot seems the natural result of having guns."

"It is if you're careless," observed Fergus.

Two o'clock found the Turners, Ben, Alex and Fergus at Luke's house. Luke was an avid reader of the Bible, but his wife Angela did not believe in God. Luke had not been sure about God when they were married, but had subsequently found faith and belief. Angela not only accepted the change in her husband's direction in life but appreciated the changes she continued to see in him. She was happy to have him invite people to their home to discuss the Bible, but was not convinced herself – although she sat and listened whenever the class was held in their house.

On this particular Sunday afternoon, Luke had selected 1 Thessalonians chapter 4 verses 13-17 to start off a discussion on resurrection. After a prayer, he read the passage and talked for a few minutes about the return of Jesus and the resurrection that would happen at that time.

After that, he welcomed comments from others and a lively discussion began. Some wanted to discuss meeting Jesus in the air, while others spoke of Jesus judging when he returned. People referred to various parts of Scripture, and Dan found everyone's willingness to listen patiently to others very encouraging. Once again, it was clear that there were differing opinions. Thinking back to the previous week as he listened, Dan began to realise that some of those present were more familiar with the Bible than others – more often able to suggest connected passages that helped to explain or confirm their points.

One word had struck Dan as the passage was read: "sleep", which occurred a few times. It reminded him of what he'd heard in the sermon. The word "sleep" here was clearly referring to *death*, so how did that fit in with the preacher's idea that righteous people were watching from heaven after death? This passage seemed to hint that the dead were being raised first so that they wouldn't miss out on something special, which seemed peculiar if they had already been enjoying the pleasures of heaven ever since their death!

He tried to concentrate on the discussion, turning to 1 Corinthians chapter 15, where Paul spoke about resurrection throughout the entire chapter. And as Dan skimmed the chapter, he saw the word "sleep" used again in a way that could only refer to death. After stating that more than 500 people had seen Jesus alive after he rose from the dead, Paul observed that most were still alive, although some had "fallen asleep". There could be no question about his meaning.

The discussion continued, but Dan's mind was elsewhere. His glance through the chapter found the word "sleep" used another three times. The second of these seemed to be very important, explaining that if resurrection was impossible then Jesus couldn't have been raised and therefore all believers who had fallen asleep in Christ had *perished*. Of course, Paul went on to show that resurrection did happen and will happen again, but the point of his argument was clear: the hope of Jesus' followers was *resurrection*. If there was no resurrection, they would *perish*. Was he reading this correctly?

Suddenly, Dan decided he needed to investigate further – now. Resurrection was a fascinating subject, but he felt he needed more background to make sense of it.

He pulled from his pocket the phone he still carried out of habit, though it was more useful for its standalone apps than for accessing the internet. Opening his Bible app, he looked for a way to find the information he wanted. He had done some searches before, but normally to locate just one verse from which he remembered specific words. Now he wanted to find out how the word "sleep" was used in the Bible and whether it mattered. He found it was easy to search for all the places where the word "sleep" occurred in the Bible, and apparently it wasn't a very common word. Most of the time it just referred to nightly sleep, but there were various places where it clearly referred to death. An aging David was to "sleep with his fathers" and had earlier written in a Psalm about "sleeping the sleep of death". Later, Daniel was told that many who slept in the dust of the earth would awake. In the New Testament, using "sleep" to refer to death was more common and Jesus himself used it that way a few times, including once needing to explain to his confused disciples that he was referring to death.

It took a while, and Dan heard nothing of the discussion going on around him during his search. In the end he felt that he had learned something important. If death was described as sleep, how did that fit in with loved ones watching from heaven?

Dan was deeply absorbed in exploration when he was jolted to an awareness of his surroundings by Luke saying, "I think we've just about finished our discussion for this afternoon. I think we've all found or confirmed some answers, but I think many of us also have some new questions to think about, so I hope we'll all be able to pursue them during the week. Resurrection is an important theme throughout the Bible, but was brought to centre stage in the resurrection of Jesus. I wanted to find just one verse to sum it up, and I couldn't. The best I could come up with was John chapter 11 verse 25, where Jesus said, 'I am the resurrection and the life. Whoever believes in me, though he die, yet shall he live.' "

The discussion was closed with a prayer asking for God's guidance in understanding his word. A few had to hurry off, but others stayed for afternoon tea and conversation, which continued for some time. Dan enjoyed the atmosphere of cooperation and was a little sorry that he hadn't listened to the discussion on what he found a fascinating subject.

"What were you doing when you pulled out your phone?" Belinda asked quietly as she was enjoying a cool drink. "Were you playing games?"

Dan smiled and shook his head. "Nope, I was searching for a few things in the Bible."

"I suppose I'm pleased," she commented. "I was a bit surprised. Shocked, almost."

"Did you enjoy the discussion?" he asked.

"It was better than I expected. I've never looked at the Bible as a... a whole. As something that makes one big picture. To be honest, I've always thought it was just full of quotable quotes so people could pick out something that said what they wanted it to say."

"Well, I don't think we should ever use it that way," Dan answered firmly. "We should be learning about God from it, not trying to make it say what we want it to say."

Soon afterwards, the Turners and Ben left, thanking Luke and Angela for their hospitality. Fergus accompanied them, taking the opportunity to speak quietly to Dan as they walked along the footpath.

"Obviously, I don't have any new information, but for your family's safety – and Ben's – I strongly recommend that you get back to Roses Gap as soon as possible and go on that camping trip you've been planning. Have you decided where you're going?"

"To Moora Moora Reservoir – we plan to leave tomorrow morning. But if you don't think it's safe there, Mum and Dad might prefer to go somewhere outside the Grampians."

"No, I don't think so. Moora Moora is far enough from the hotspots we know about: Stawell, Roses Gap and Horsham. It should be safe."

"Oh, and before we leave Stawell, we're meant to be going to the library to pick up some books that Dad's insisting we need for education." Dan paused, then added slyly, "Though you did say we should leave Stawell as soon as possible, right?"

"I don't think you need to worry about visiting the library, Dan," smiled Fergus. "Sorry, but I can't give you an excuse to avoid that."

"Ah, well, it was worth a try! Anyway, I want to get some books on biology, too."

Map of Moora Moora

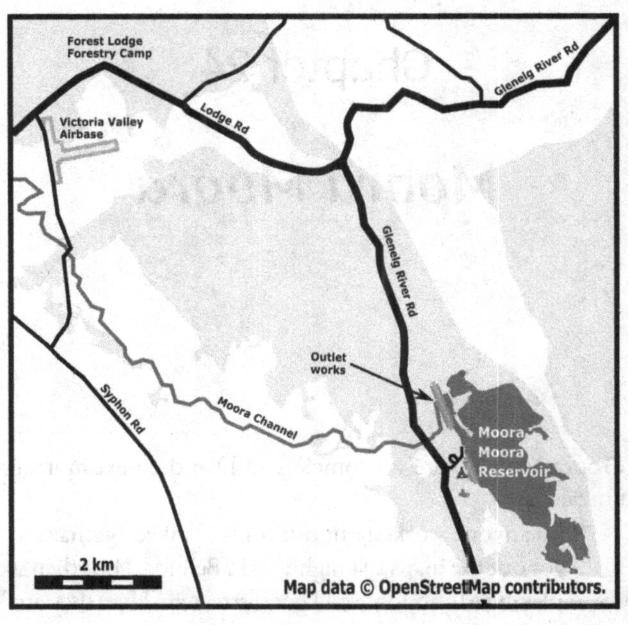

Chapter 24

Moora Moora

"Moora Moora, here we come!" said Dan the next morning at breakfast.

"Has anyone worked out our route?" asked Nathan.

"I got out the maps last night," said Belinda, "but then we started playing Monopoly and I got distracted. Here they are."

She picked up a map and studied it.

"We're here in Roses Gap, and there is Moora Moora Reservoir, quite a way south. There's no direct way there, but it looks like the shortest path would be through Halls Gap."

"It might be the shortest," said Nathan, "but is there another way that doesn't take us through any towns?"

"Ah... yes, I think so. But why do we want that? The roads through towns are likely to be the best maintained nowadays."

"That's true, but Fergus suggested that we should keep away from places with people while we're in the Grampians with Ben."

"There are a few ways we could go that use unmade tracks. Would those be okay?"

"It's hard to tell," answered Nathan. "Some unmade roads should be good enough, but I'd stick to ones with 'highway' or 'road' in their name rather than 'track'."

"Okay..." Belinda studied the map for a while and then continued, "I think we should go along Roses Gap Road to the far end, then head south on Mount Victory Road through Zumsteins to the Glenelg River Road, and follow that until we get to Moora Moora. Will there be any people in Zumsteins? I don't think we can dodge it very easily."

"No need to worry. Zumsteins isn't a town like Halls Gap. There might be a few houses around, but nothing much. How far is it altogether?"

"It's hard to tell with such winding roads, but perhaps 50 to 70 kilometres."

"That could take quite a while, depending on the condition of the roads. At least we'll have a chainsaw with us – Steve is happy for us to take one of his."

They left immediately after breakfast, hastily cramming in the last few items while Nathan made sure the trailer was properly attached and all its lights were working.

With six passengers, the car would be crowded. Fortunately, there was a bench seat in the front where Belinda could sit between Nathan and Tanya.

With the trailer, roof box and back of the car already crammed full, those in the back seat would be carrying extras on their laps, including Ben's crutches.

"The car looks ridiculous," said Nathan, shaking his head. "Extras on top of the trailer, extras on the roof and extras across the back seat."

"We could leave one of the extras behind," suggested Dan, winking at Dave.

"No," said Belinda, guessing immediately what he meant. "It's a good luck charm for the family."

"Perhaps we should tie it to the bull bar then," suggested Dan.

"No," replied Belinda firmly.

Ben sat in silence, not sure what to make of this obscure discussion.

"What are you squabbling about, children?" asked Tanya.

"My teddy," said Belinda, holding up the bedraggled item for inspection. "It travelled beyond the Western Margin with us to Roses Gap, then climbed up into the wilds near Briggs Bluff, and now it's accompanying us to Moora Moora Reservoir."

"All to keep a poor insecure little girl happy!" said Dan.

"At least I acknowledge my weaknesses," said Belinda loftily. "Not like others, who try to paper over the cracks – and end up even more insecure."

They all climbed in, closed the doors and distributed the extras.

"See you in four or five weeks," called Steve and Sylvia, who had come to wave them goodbye.

Nathan let out the clutch and they all waved as the heavily loaded four-wheel drive rolled along the driveway.

When they reached the made road, Dan and Dave cheered, singing, "We're off to Moora Moora. The wonderful Moora of Oz."

Belinda groaned. "I think I prefer my insecurity to your delusions of lyrical genius!"

Nathan picked his way carefully along Roses Gap Road, dodging fallen branches and the occasional tree without too much difficulty. When they turned towards Zumsteins, however, progress was more difficult. The road was very narrow in places, and three times Nathan decided that he couldn't fit past a trunk or branch lying partially across the road. Each time, he, Dan and Dave piled out of the car and used the chainsaw to clear the road sufficiently to allow them passage. Ben remained in the car rather than slow things down struggling with his crutches. Dan could almost have done the same, but was determined to contribute despite his broken arm and did genuinely help. When they reached the Glenelg River Road, however, the unmade road actually proved easier. Although the surface was not as smooth, the road was wider and they safely negotiated the difficult places, including a couple of areas where the road was quite badly washed away. Without a four-wheel drive, they couldn't have continued.

"I'm glad that we've got a map," said Belinda as they neared their destination. "The signs don't seem to help much. I haven't seen a sign to the reservoir yet. Oh, Dad! Look out! Three, no... four kangaroos!"

Nathan slowed quickly as the kangaroos jumped onto the road, saw the car and seemed to panic. One turned suddenly, and Belinda gasped as it hopped straight towards them. Nathan slammed on the brakes and the car ground to a halt, metres from the kangaroo, which swung around once again, leaping past the car's bull bar before crossing the drain beside the road and disappearing into the bush.

"Whew!" said Nathan, rubbing his forehead. "That was close."

The other three kangaroos had turned as one and were bouncing along the road in front of them, weaving from side to side until one by one they too headed off the road into the bush.

The Turners and Ben sat motionless in the middle of the road, with no visible evidence of the sudden danger they had narrowly avoided. Starting off again, Nathan drove cautiously along the road for a kilometre until they came to an intersection where a road joined from the right.

"There's a sign," sang out Dave as Nathan slowed down. "It seems Moora Moora Reservoir is back the way we've just come."

"And if we keep going this way, we'll get to the Victoria Valley Airbase," said Dan.

"I wouldn't expect an airport here," observed Tanya.

"Well, we're not going to visit it now," said Nathan. "I guess we need to do a U-turn and go back."

"Did we miss a turn somehow?" asked Dan.

"There was a road going off to the left where we saw those kangaroos," said Ben.

"Ah, I was busy dodging the kangaroos and didn't notice," said Nathan. They retraced their route and found that, although Nathan had chosen what seemed to be the main road, they should have veered left to follow the Glenelg River Road, which led past the reservoir. Belinda warned them all to watch carefully for the track to the reservoir, and they finally spotted it after a few false alarms.

It was in poor condition. Not only did branches obscure the track, but large potholes also slowed their progress. Nathan and Dave lifted the branches out of the way and Nathan avoided the deepest potholes. Eventually, they reached a parking area where gates and fences prevented further progress towards the dam wall, visible just one or two hundred metres ahead.

"Let's stop here for a while and work out where to camp," said Nathan, climbing out with Tanya and Belinda.

"Coming to the dam wall, Ben?" asked Dan.

"Yeah, but it'll take me a while. You go on ahead, if you want."

Dan and Dave ran off towards the wall and shortly afterwards could be seen climbing a rough set of stairs.

Ben walked with Belinda, Nathan and Tanya, making slower progress because of his crutches.

Nathan was scouting for a camp site as he walked. When they passed an area that showed signs of having been used for campfires, he made his way across and had a look. The others kept walking and soon Nathan caught up with them, saying, "That looks like a good place to camp. It's nice and flat. Clear of trees, too. All we have to do is find a way to drive in there, but that shouldn't be hard. A track seems to lead over to where we're parked."

"Sounds good, but let's go and look at the reservoir first," said Tanya.

"Yes, there's no hurry," said Nathan.

The wall wasn't very high, but it did look higher as you got close to it. Ben looked up with some trepidation as he approached the first step. Step by careful step, he climbed the stairs and was the last to reach the orange-coloured gravel road on top of the wall. It was wide enough for a vehicle to drive along and the water side of the wall was faced with large rocks.

Overhead, soft grey clouds filled the sky and tempered the light. The clear, tranquil water of the reservoir spread out in front of them, ruffled from time to time by gentle breezes. Some distance away, clumps of yellow-green rushes formed living islands, and beyond them, dead trees stood like silent sentinels, their branches and twigs pointing up to the heavens.

Beyond the water's end rose tree-covered hills, grey-green with eucalypts, rising to rocky mountain ranges that stretched away to the horizon. On the skyline, a distinctive hill stood alone above its neighbours, topped with a squarish rock pillar.

For a few moments, they stood without speaking, taking in the scene, overcome by the peaceful, pensive silence.

"I think that's Tower Hill," Nathan said quietly, pointing to the unusually shaped hill, then lapsed into silence again.

Even Dan and Dave appeared to be affected by the silence. They were walking along the dam wall away from Nathan, Tanya and Belinda, but no voices disturbed the silence.

"I'm going with them," said Belinda, her voice fading to a whisper as if the sound of it surprised her. She seemed about to run off when she turned and asked Ben, "Do you want to come?"

He nodded and together they made their way along the wall after the others. Before long, Dan and Dave saw them following and stopped to wait. Soon the four had met and Dan and Dave were pointing out something on the beaching stones between them and the water.

Tanya and Nathan stood and watched as Dan, Dave, Belinda and Ben walked to the end of the dam wall.

"What a beautiful place," breathed Tanya.

"True, and the utter emptiness of it all makes it seem a little unreal. It's as if the reservoir was built for a town, but once they finished it, the town went somewhere else to live, and the reservoir was left all alone with this deep silence."

They stood in silence for a few more moments, then Tanya smiled wryly. "I've no doubt the young ones will get used to the place soon enough, and the silence will become less... profound."

CR

"Ah, this is the place to be," said Nathan, leaning back in his camp chair and sipping a steaming mug of tea.

After spending some time on the dam wall, they had all returned to the carpark and found a way in to their chosen camping site. There was no available power, piped water or other amenities, but they had what they needed and could do without the rest.

They set up the camper-trailer with its annex and Dan struggled once more to accept the limitations imposed by his broken arm.

Belinda would sleep in the annex while Dan, Dave and Ben slept in a four-man tent set up nearby.

Occasional flies droned around, making themselves heard from a surprising distance. Mosquitoes contributed their own annoying noises, not so loud, but more threatening.

Lunch was over and the boys and Belinda were getting ready to take up Nathan's education challenge, which included one Russian novel for each of them.

"These novels are the size of textbooks," grumbled Dan, holding up the one he had borrowed from the Stawell library. "You wanted exercise, Ben! We're getting weightlifting exercise."

"Maybe we shouldn't have agreed to this quite so quickly," said Dave.

"Once you start reading them, you might actually enjoy them," said Ben. "I did."

"That's not the point," grinned Belinda. "We're getting our complaining in beforehand."

"Well, I don't know very much about the Bible," said Ben, "but I do know that complaining isn't too popular with Hashem." He stopped, looking awkward. Dan knew that Hashem was one of the titles Jews used for God, and guessed that Ben would have liked to explain but wasn't comfortable with using more direct names.

Belinda looked confused, so Dan explained, "'Hashem' means 'the name', referring to God. Feel free to use it, Ben. We'll know what you mean."

"Thanks. I also didn't want to seem 'holier than thou' by complaining about complaining."

"No, you're right in what you said," observed Dan. "I'm trying to learn it. What do you think, Dad, should I be suggesting that Russian novels are the best thing since sliced bread?"

"I don't think so. If you've never read one, then it doesn't make much sense to either complain about them or praise them."

"Fair enough," said Dan. "I won't say any more."

"At least, not until later," laughed Belinda.

"I suppose I'll be thinking a lot of Russian thoughts for a while," said Dan.

"Oh, I'm sure you'll find other thoughts to think too," replied Nathan. "For example, you could think just how good it is to be camping out here in peace."

"Away from Ahmed and his son, and all those men we saw at Troopers Creek," added Tanya.

"And Ali and his friend," said Belinda, glancing at Ben.

"And those blokes we met in Cato Park. Remember how friendly the one I hit with a ball was?" asked Dan.

"Exactly," said Nathan. "Instead, you're in the back of beyond enjoying the peace with enough free time to read 'War and Peace'."

"This is the holiday we expected when we set out from Melbourne to go beyond the western margin," said Dan, stretching. "It just took a few months to happen."

"And it won't be all sitting around reading books," said Nathan. "Ben wanted some training, so we need to get the kayak and the canoe up to the water soon."

"Can it be this afternoon?" asked Ben. "I'm afraid I can't do it myself, though, or even help much."

"Good idea," said Dan. "Shall we do it now? I'd do it by myself if it weren't for this arm."

"How about starting your novel first," suggested Tanya.

"Oh, I suppose so," sighed Dan. "And there's another thing I'd like to do while we're here: I want to visit that airbase. I wonder how big it is?"

"I was wondering how much it gets used," mused Dave.

"Is it an air force base?" wondered Dan. "Is that why it's called an airbase rather than an airport?"

Chapter 25

Camping

The Turners and Ben settled down quickly into the rhythm of camping. Tanya's smiling prediction was right: the teenagers soon lost their awe of the profound silence and the local noise level gradually rose. However, the deep peace that pervaded the place remained and they all revelled in it.

Ben was thoroughly self-disciplined and began some informal training that very first afternoon. Crutches would make getting into kayak or canoe quite difficult, particularly when wearing a lifejacket. However, Ben decided the canoe would be easier, and asked for it to be taken up to the water first.

"It might be best to have someone with you at the start," suggested Nathan. "The reservoir is quite shallow overall, and many places are probably very shallow. Two pairs of eyes might save you from getting stuck."

"Can I go with you, Ben?" asked Belinda. "I'd love to go out in the canoe, and I think I can trust *you* not to tip it over."

Dan and Dave understood her meaning, but Ben merely looked embarrassed and said, "That's alright with me, as long as your parents think you'll be safe."

"Just take care that Belinda doesn't tip *you* over," warned Nathan. "You may be safer with Dan or Dave!"

"We should take the double kayak, Dave," said Dan. "We can be ready to rescue them."

"It's not long since you broke your wrist, Dan, so you need to keep that plaster cast dry," said Tanya, sounding like the nurse she was. "You'll have to wait at least a week or two before using the canoe or kayak."

Dan sighed. "Oh, I suppose that makes sense, but this wrist is stopping me doing all sorts of things I didn't expect." After struggling with his frustration for a few moments, he offered nobly, "Can I help get the boats ready? I can at least carry the lifejackets."

Dan carried the lifejackets to the top of the wall while Nathan and Dave carried each craft to a suitable place for embarking. He watched as the others paddled across the reservoir and wished he could join them. Ben showed his skill at paddling, while Belinda kept watch. Dave showed his enthusiasm, but evidently found managing the double kayak alone hard work at times.

After watching for a while, Dan returned to the camper-trailer and read his novel. He had been using his broken arm a little too much and it ached.

⚭

Tuesday and Wednesday passed with a mix of relaxation and physical activity – at least for those who could do the latter. Since Ben couldn't walk far and Dan couldn't use his arm much, there wasn't much physical exertion they could all share.

Ben and Belinda continued to paddle together in the canoe, although Ben did most of the paddling. With a limited amount of open water on the reservoir, having a double load to move allowed him to work hard without running out of space too soon. Belinda sometimes joined in paddling, but her lack of expertise too often rendered the canoe unstable, demanding all of Ben's skill to prevent it capsizing.

The double kayak was mostly used solo by Dave, but Nathan and Tanya took it out a couple of times, laughing at their own difficulty in keeping a straight line.

Towards the end of Thursday afternoon, while Ben and Belinda were paddling across the reservoir again and Dave had just freed the kayak from the clutches of a dense mat of rushes, Dan decided to go for a walk by himself.

"I'm going to the end of the wall there to see what's beyond," he told Nathan and Tanya, who were just heading back to the camper-trailer, pointing out the direction as he spoke. "I saw a track going further along. Maybe it'll take me around the lake."

"That'd be a long way," warned Tanya. "Don't take too long or you'll miss out on tea."

Dan walked along the dam wall with its mix of orange and grey gravel until he came to the northern end, where he found an open area and on the opposite side, a sandy track leading onward. Following this track, he walked through varied heathland until he eventually emerged onto a levee bank edging what seemed to be a branch of the reservoir, its waters lapping against the bank. He could see that the levee continued for at least a few hundred metres, so he kept walking. There was no-one around and the only sounds were the calls of a flock of birds wheeling overhead. Yet as he passed a slight bend, he suddenly heard the sound of a car. It came from his left, away from the reservoir, but not far away from him. He peered into the trees, but could see nothing through the dense foliage.

He stopped to think.

Was it wise to continue? Fergus had told them to avoid people, so perhaps he should retrace his steps.

Yet surely one car was nothing to worry about? After all, the troublemakers were far away – even Fergus had said there was no need to worry about them out here.

He kept walking as the sound of the car gradually passed him and moved away. It appeared to be travelling more or less parallel to him, so perhaps their paths wouldn't cross. But wait, was that another car? It was, and presumably following the same track as the first car.

This was more serious. He stopped. In fact, he almost turned back immediately, but as he stood there listening, the sound of the cars diminished, almost fading away completely. In the stillness, he began to notice a new sound: flowing water, perhaps water leaking under pressure. And now that he heard it, it had swallowed up the sound of the cars.

Was water flowing out of the reservoir? He knew that there had been a lot of rain in other parts of the Grampians, so perhaps the reservoir was spilling over. But maybe there was a dangerous problem that he should investigate. What if there was a leak somewhere?

He hadn't forgotten the cars, but the possibility of a leak had piqued his interest. He had to find out where the sound was coming from.

Dan began to walk again, covering another one hundred, two hundred metres, concentrating on the growing murmur of flowing water. Just ahead of him he could now see concrete walls and what looked like a small bridge. This must be a place where water could flow out of the reservoir when it was full. Perhaps it *was* full and the sound he was hearing was just the water overflowing.

Suddenly, through the trees to his left, he saw movement beyond the bridge. Men! Men, making their way towards the bridge that must span the outlet. Once they reached it, he would be as much in their view as the bridge was in his.

Quickly, he dodged off the path, hurrying down into the trees. Near him, the shrubbery was thick and he easily found a tree to hide behind.

Looking back toward the bridge, he could now see that concrete walls must permit water to be either kept in the reservoir or allowed to flow into a channel leading away. The bridge spanned the channel and the men were now approaching it. Each was carrying two large black containers, and Dan couldn't help being thankful. He was sure that if they hadn't been paying attention to those containers, they must have seen him. He counted eight men, then froze in shock as he recognised the leader: Ahmed!

How could Ahmed possibly be here in the peace and quiet of Moora Moora Reservoir? Surely he wasn't a man who would look for peace and quiet!

Dan made sure that he was as invisible as possible while he stood watching the men. He felt confident that his clothes would merge into the hues of the bush, but his new white plaster cast was a different matter. He positioned himself carefully to ensure the tree trunk was between the men and that white cast with its blue sling. He must keep them hidden – they would stand out like a sore thumb. A glimpse would be all it would take.

As Dan craned his neck to see what he could, Ahmed put down his container and stepped onto the bridge. He gave orders in a foreign language – Dan guessed it was Arabic – and the other men found places where the water was easily accessible and began to fill their containers with clean reservoir water.

Ahmed, meanwhile, was standing in the middle of the bridge, examining its footway and handrails as well as the equipment attached to it. He seemed to be peering underneath it too.

Once more he spoke in Arabic, and Dan had no idea what he said. It was frustrating – and worrying. For all he knew, Ahmed could have been saying, "I've just spotted a bloke hiding in the trees, get ready to jump him!"

Fortunately, there was no sudden rush toward his hiding place, and the men soon finished filling their containers. One of them took Ahmed's containers and filled them too.

After stowing them all in the cars, the men returned, chatting among themselves. Dan noticed that the younger ones seemed to use English, while the older ones used Arabic.

The men gathered around the bridge and Ahmed began pointing to parts of the structure and apparently making suggestions or asking questions.

At first, answers were given in Arabic, but some of the younger ones seemed to find something funny and perhaps found it easier to enjoy their joke in English.

"It's all very well to hide it down in the water," said one, "but if we do, it won't work!"

"No. Won't even fizzle," laughed another.

"Hiding it is a good idea, but..."

At that point Ahmed spoke sharply in Arabic, and suddenly there was no more English. The young men hurriedly wiped the grins off their faces and answered in Arabic.

After more discussion, two of the men went to the car and returned carrying a bag, from which they removed a steel box.

Placing it on the decking of the bridge, they pulled a chain out of the bag and used it to fasten the box against the mesh decking and one of the handrail stanchions. Once they were satisfied with its position, they padlocked the chain tightly in place.

At this point, one of the young men went under the bridge. Dan couldn't see what he was doing, but he saw the other man remove something black from the bag and pass it down to him. Some rope and a roll of duct tape soon followed.

The work continued for another few minutes, but well before it was complete Dan was grimly sure of its purpose.

Ahmed intended to blow up the dam's outlet works!

Chapter 26

Eavesdropping

"Eventually, they left," said Dan, breathless between excitement and having run much of the way back from the outlet works. "I waited until I couldn't hear their four-wheel drives any more, then I went to the bridge and had a look at what they'd put there."

The Turners and Ben were gathered around their cooking fire, listening to Dan's retelling of his eavesdropping.

"That was brave of you," said Belinda. "What if they'd set the bomb to blow up just after they left?"

"They wouldn't have done that when they were driving down beside the channel themselves," scoffed Dan. Actually, it hadn't even occurred to him as a possibility.

"Oh."

"How many men did you say there were?" asked Nathan.

"Eight," answered Dan.

"With two water containers each?"

Dan nodded, still breathing heavily.

"16 biggish containers – so probably about 300 litres of water." Nathan looked thoughtful. "Enough drinking water for quite a crowd."

Dan nodded, but was clearly eager to continue. "Do you want to hear the rest? There's a lot more to tell!"

"Tell on, then," nodded Nathan.

"I found a black box chained to the bridge, with a black-plastic-wrapped package below it. I was about to have a closer look, when suddenly I heard a car coming."

"Ahmed again?"

"No, it was coming from a different direction – the north. I hadn't even realised there was another track coming from there, running along beside the reservoir. As soon as I heard the noise, I ran back into the trees."

Belinda gasped, eyes like a lemur's.

"I'd only just got behind my tree again when a four-wheel drive came into view and stopped near the outlet works. It seems silly to hide just because I heard a car coming, but I'm glad I did. Guess who got out, Ben?"

"No idea," said Ben – then suddenly held up a finger. "Was it Ali?"

"Well done!" beamed Dan. "Yes, it was Ali, but not only Ali."

"Omar?" asked Dave.

"Brilliant," nodded Dan. "Our friends Ali and Omar."

"But they can't be old enough to drive by themselves," objected Belinda.

"They weren't by themselves, Sis. They were with two men we met in Cato Park a couple of weeks ago. Remember the bloke who got so angry at me when the ball hit him? He's Ali's Dad. The other man was the one who calmed him down – I think he must be Omar's Dad."

"What are they doing here?" asked Tanya, lifting a pot of vegetables off the fire.

"Apparently they belong to a rival group that hates Ahmed and his men. Hasim, Ali's Dad, seems to be the leader, or maybe second in command. Interestingly, almost everything they said was in English, not Arabic, which was handy."

"Why were they there?"

"They drove in slowly and looked around carefully when they climbed out of the car. Once they were sure there was no-one around, they hurried to the bridge – obviously looking for something. When they spotted the things I'd just been looking at, Ali's father said, 'You're right, Ali'."

Pausing, Dan pictured the scene, but his memory was fixed on the pitbull. It was enormous and terrifying. From the moment Ali had let it out of the car, the dog had strained at its leash, almost dragging Ali along behind it. It had sniffed the ground, then the grating on the bridge, eager to pick up a scent and chase it down. His scent? Dan remembered the instant he'd locked eyes with the beast as it suddenly looked up from the grating. How could it possibly have known he was there? Was it scent or sight? Dan's blood had run cold as the dog jerked suddenly at the leash, nearly escaping Ali's grip entirely. What would've happened if Ali hadn't made that sudden grab at the leash with his other hand?

"Hey, boy. Calm down," said Ali, hanging on and pulling hard.

"He's excited," said Omar. "Maybe it's the smell of Ahmed and his men. He'd like to make a meal of them."

"Don't let him escape, Ali," said his father. That had been the instant when Dan had recognised him and known the relationship between father and son.

"I won't," Ali had answered, "but why is he so annoyed?"

"Perhaps there's a kangaroo over in the bush," suggested the other man.

"Maybe I should let him go then," said Ali. "See what happens."

"I've heard kangaroos can kill dogs," warned Hasim.

Dan had willed Ali to believe his father. The dog looked vicious, and the thought of trying to fight it off barehanded and with only one useful arm wasn't pleasant.

"What's up?" interrupted Belinda, staring at him.

Dan shook his head to escape the picture of the dog with its slavering wide-open jaws and terrifying stare.

"They had a pitbull with them. Somehow or other, it spotted me. It would've loved to attack me."

"I'm glad it didn't," said Tanya. "I don't know why people have those dogs. I've seen the results a few times as a nurse."

"Keep going," prompted Nathan.

"Omar went to have a look at the wrapped-up package under the bridge. From the sound of it, some of the younger boys in each group go to the same school. Is that your school, Ben?"

"Yes," answered Ben, "or, it's one of them. They actually attend a couple of schools in Horsham. They mostly stay in their own groups and there's a lot of competition between them, a bit like two gangs. They're always boasting to each other about how great they are, and from time to time they fight, but occasionally they work together."

"What for?" asked Dan, suspecting he could guess.

"Mostly to attack me or anyone who supports me."

"Charming," said Dan. "Enemies unless brought together by a shared hatred. Anyway, it sounds like the boys in Ahmed's gang have been boasting about their plans to take over Victoria and turn it into an Islamic state."

"Surely no-one would believe that sort of incredible idea?" said Nathan.

"Of course not," agreed Tanya.

"I'm sure no-one would," said Dan, "but what if it's true? Sometimes people's boasting and sneering has some truth to it. Apparently Omar heard talk of blowing up something important in two weeks' time and then publicly threatening to do more. Ali heard independently about plans to take over a large area around Moora Moora to use as a training ground. Those two things wouldn't mean much except that Hasim heard another snippet when the two groups worked together to attack your house, Ben."

"Did they really work together just to attack my house?" asked Ben, shocked.

"Yes, and one of Ahmed's men said that *next time* they came to attack your house, they should do what they were doing to Moora Moora. Hasim decided the three things were probably linked."

"Sounds like he was right," said Nathan.

"Yep. But that mixture of bragging, competition and cooperation just might help us stop them."

"We're not going to be stopping anyone," said Tanya. "That's not our job."

"Your Mum's right," agreed Nathan. "As soon as you finish telling us the details, we'll be heading to Stawell to pass on everything we know."

Dan screwed up his nose. "Wait until you hear the rest of it," he protested.

"It's not likely to change my mind," said Nathan, emphatically.

"What else did they say?" asked Dave.

"Firstly, they said an important visitor is coming to Halls Gap tomorrow evening. From the sound of it, someone important to both these Islamic groups."

"A private visitor?" asked Nathan.

"It didn't sound like it. They sounded rather excited about it – talked as though it were a public victory against the Christians and Jews they reckon run Australia."

"What sort of victory?" asked Belinda.

"I'm not certain, but it sounded like an important international visitor of some sort."

"How can that happen when the pandemic has messed up international relations? We don't get many visitors from America, England or Europe now."

"I don't know," said Dan, "but it's clearly someone important, and he's going to be at Centenary Hall, wherever that is."

"I think it's in the Halls Gap shopping strip," mused Nathan.

"I'll see if I can find it on the map," said Belinda.

As she went to find the map, Dan's mind slipped back to the conversation he'd overheard near the outlet works while praying that the terrifying dog would not slip his leash.

It was Hasim who'd mentioned the delivery.

"These explosives aren't much, but I guess they'll do the job," he said. "The delivery will give them a lot more to work with if we don't intervene. Lots of weapons, too."

"When's it coming, Dad?" asked Ali.

"We don't know exactly, but probably towards the end of next week. When it does come, we'll be ready to deal with them before the plane lands."

"We're ready now, aren't we?"

"Yes. We've had men placed around here since this morning. They all have access to wireless communication and they know the signal to attack. We'll send it as soon as we hear the plane overhead."

"What are we going to do with the equipment when we get it?" asked Ali.

"Spend a few months training the men to use it. We'll also arrange for further supplies, more deliveries. This one shipment won't be enough to achieve what we want – we need..."

It was at that instant that the dog snarled and started barking furiously. Dan suddenly realised that he must have leaned too far to one side of the tree trunk, giving the dog another glimpse of him. He moved out of sight immediately, but the dog continued baying, and from what he could hear, Ali was having difficulty holding him. Dan's fear of the dog suddenly appearing around the tree was too great to allow him to remain completely hidden. He had to keep an eye on that dog. But each time he peeped around the tree, the ferocity of the dog's snarling barks redoubled.

Once again, Belinda prodded him out of his reverie as she returned with the map. "Anything else?"

"Yes," answered Dan, and quickly explained about the expected delivery of weapons and explosives.

"This gets worse and worse!" complained Tanya. "We should leave straight after tea and hurry to Stawell to report all of this."

"But didn't you notice what Hasim said?" asked Dan. "He said that they've got enough men in the area to be able to attack Ahmed's group. I don't think it's safe to leave now."

"Can you think of any time that will be safer?" asked Nathan.

"I suppose we should wait for them to blow up the dam and drown us all?" asked Belinda, sarcastically.

"If they'll be occupied with a special visitor tomorrow evening, that's probably the best time to go," answered Dan.

"What time, though?" asked Dave.

"They only said 'evening'. What time would you mean by 'evening'?"

"At this time of year, probably about six to eight pm," suggested Dave.

"I agree," said Nathan, "but that's a wide range if we're trying to avoid dangerous watchers."

"Do you still want to go tonight, Mum?" asked Dan.

"Ah... no," answered Tanya, slowly.

"And what about the trailer?" asked Dave. "Should we take it with us?"

"I think so," said Nathan, "but let's talk about that tomorrow. What a ridiculous 'holiday'! Sorry for all this, Ben. You chose the wrong people to travel with!"

"No, I don't think so, Mr... Nathan," said Ben. "Some things are beyond our control."

'That's why they're called 'acts of God'," said Dan.

"A good description," answered Dave.

Night was falling when they finished their meal that night and there was an atmosphere of uncertainty as they prepared for bed.

Were they safe for the night? What would the next day bring?

As Dan drifted towards sleep that night, he remembered a few extra details from the two confronting conversations he'd overheard. He must remember to mention them to the others. They might be important.

In the meantime, he was glad to have escaped both situations without getting caught – or attacked by that pitbull. He hoped fervently never to see that ghastly dog again!

Chapter 27

Just You Wait!

Dan woke early on Friday morning. His arm, which had been getting much better, was aching. Running back to camp from the outlet works had shaken it up badly.

Light was already filtering into the tent, but it would be quite a while before the sun crested the hills and gilded their secluded camping paradise. Looking around the tent, he saw Dave and Ben were still asleep, and he didn't want to disturb them.

Nevertheless, he was eager to get up and check their surroundings. Not only did thoughts of that dog prey on his mind, but he couldn't forget Hasim's comment about having men around. Between Ahmed's and Hasim's groups, there must be lots of people in the area. And all of them seemed to be armed and eager to use their guns.

Dan had told the others most of what he had seen and heard, but he hadn't mentioned Hasim's behaviour when the dog refused to stop barking. First, he had angrily told Ali to keep the dog quiet, then he had shouted and struck at it. Watching furtively from a distance, Dan couldn't see every detail, but Hasim's rising anger reminded Dan of his behaviour in Cato Park when disturbed in prayer. As the dog continued to bark, Hasim suddenly flew off the handle. His hand flashed towards his pocket and in an instant came out with a deadly-looking pistol. His face wore the expression Dan had seen on Ali's face in the Beehive Falls Carpark.

"Shut that dog up or I'll shoot it!" shouted Hasim, pointing his pistol at the barking dog.

Ali did what he could to calm the dog, while Omar's father tried to calm Hasim. Ali was only partly successful, but Omar's father seemed to clinch the matter when he warned, "Don't shoot, we don't want to attract attention!"

Gradually, Hasim calmed down until once again he was outwardly a reasonable, rational leader of men. Fearing the unpredictable result of another outbreak of fury, Dan quashed his desire to see what was going on and hid completely behind the tree to avoid provoking the dog again.

At some time during the night, while reliving the incident yet again, Dan had suddenly understood that Hasim's anger in Cato Park was no religious disappointment at having his prayers disturbed or his connection with God broken. No, Hasim's anger was like an unstable explosive, apt to go off at any moment. Dan marvelled that a man could be so undisciplined as to intend to kill his son's dog because of a few barks.

In a moment of insight, Dan pictured a future in which the uncontrolled anger of father or son would cause one to murder the other. Wasn't there a line in the Bible: "they sow the wind, and they shall reap the whirlwind"? Hasim and Ali were welcome to each other – but could they be kept from hurting others in the meantime?

Yet Hasim was not alone. Ahmed was also an unstable leader – but excitable Ahmed seemed slightly less terrifying than explosive Hasim. In another flash of insight, Dan wondered if Ahmed might be more frightening if he used English instead of Arabic. It was a terrifying thought.

Dan looked around again in the growing light, but Dave and Ben were still fast asleep. He decided to spend time in prayer, something which seemed more important than ever with all of these dangerous men around. After some time, Dave stirred, stretched and yawned, then saw that Dan was awake. "Seems like the bad guys haven't come during the night," he said quietly.

Dan nodded.

Dave yawned again. "During the night I was thinking over what you said and realised that you never said what happened to the explosives."

"No. I didn't want to worry Dad and Mum."

"What do you mean?"

"The blokes discussed taking the explosives, so I checked after they left. It all looked the same, superficially, but then I found that the package under the bridge had nothing in it. Some wires went in, but they weren't attached to anything."

"Why would that worry your parents?"

"What if Ahmed comes back and finds his explosives gone? What if he looks around and finds us?"

"Oh!" mouthed Dave, silently.

"I'm not worried myself because it seems to me that if they're not going to use the explosives for a couple of weeks, they're very unlikely to come back and look the next day."

Dave pondered Dan's explanation and was about to answer when another voice said, "So now Ali and his Dad have some explosives." Ben had woken and heard their discussions.

"Morning, Ben," said Dan. "It's not good news, is it?"

"No. In fact, I'm not sure which of the two groups I'd like to have the explosives less."

"I'm not happy with Ahmed and his men having access to a detonator, either," answered Dan. "If they have more explosives, how long would it take them to set it all up again?"

"Did Hasim do anything about the detonator?"

"It was chained to the bridge and padlocked. What could he do?"

"Putting glue in the padlock might slow them down," suggested Ben.

"That's a good idea," said Dave, impressed.

"Maybe we should do that ourselves this morning," said Dan. "Dad always keeps superglue in the car just in case."

"I don't think your parents are going to want us going back to the outlet channel," said Dave. "In fact, I wouldn't be surprised if they decide to head south to Dunkeld this morning, away from the airfield, the outlet works and these crazy terrorists."

"I hadn't thought of that," said Dan. "You're right. If we want to mess up their lock, we might have to do it before breakfast. Having run back from the outlet works, I can tell you they're not nearby!"

"Shall we go now?" asked Dave.

As it happened, Dan was already having second thoughts. His arm ached and the idea of hurrying to the outlet works and back was far from appealing. However, he'd suggested it, so he couldn't pull out now. "Yeah, let's get the glue from the car. I know where Dad keeps it."

"Can you get it out without waking your parents?" asked Ben.

"I think so," said Dan. "I'll close the door as gently as I can."

Dan and Dave got dressed as quickly as they could, though Dan was still hampered by his broken arm. Creeping out of the tent, they walked as silently as they could towards the car.

Belinda was standing next to it.

"What are you doing up?" hissed Dan.

"You didn't say what had happened to the detonator and the explosives," she answered quietly. "Are they still there?"

"They took away the explosives."

"What about the detonator?"

"It's still there in the steel box."

"I thought it might be, since you said it was chained in place. It occurred to me during the night that it wouldn't take long for Ahmed to wire up more explosives, but we could slow him down by putting some superglue into the padlock. I was about to get it."

"Have you been talking to Ben?"

"No," said Belinda, looking puzzled.

"We're about to go and put some glue in the padlock because Ben suggested it," said Dan, torn between irritation and amusement.

Dan opened the car's front door and looked for the superglue in the glovebox. He couldn't locate it immediately, so he started quietly removing the other items that must be obscuring it. Soon, he was sure the glue wasn't there.

"Uh oh," he heard Belinda murmur, and turned around. Nathan was emerging from the annex, dressed for walking. Seeing Dan, Dave and Belinda standing near the car, he looked puzzled for an instant.

"Why are you kids up?" he asked.

"Ah…" prevaricated Dan, trying to work out what to say. "We were just…"

Nathan suddenly grinned and held up a hand. "Looking for this?" he asked. A tube of superglue was in his hand.

Dan groaned. "Does everyone here think of nothing but superglue?"

ↀↀ

Despite Nathan's suggestion that he should stay and rest his arm, Dan went with Nathan and Dave to visit the outlet works and apply some judicious superglue to the barrel of Ahmed's padlock. No-one disturbed them, and the damage they left behind was invisible to all but the most careful investigator.

When they returned an hour later, everyone enjoyed breakfast together and Dan answered many more questions about his undercover surveillance. He also told them about "the leader". Hasim had frequently mentioned "the leader", but it wasn't clear who he was or what he led. What made him important in Dan's mind was that he seemed to be connected with the event planned for Halls Gap that evening.

"So, is he the real leader of Hasim's group, with Hasim as his second?" asked Nathan.

"I'm not sure," answered Dan. "It sounded like he's been away for a few months. This'll be the first time they've seen him this year."

"Any idea where he went?" pursued Nathan.

"No, except that it was a long way away."

"Or what he went for?" asked Dave.

"None whatsoever."

"Maybe we'll see him this evening."

"Hasim expected to have a big crowd there, most of them nothing to do with either his group or Ahmed's. Important people too, from the sound of it."

"So when should we set off for Halls Gap?" asked Nathan.

"Should we leave now?" asked Tanya. "And I don't mean going to Halls Gap. The more I hear about this, the less I like it. I think we should pack up right now and head south for Dunkeld, then contact the police from there."

Dan winked at Dave: his prediction had been right.

"Some of Hasim's men might be south of us, dear," answered Nathan. "I think it's safest for us to wait until they leave to attend this important event, whatever it is."

"That's all very well, but we don't know when they'll leave," protested Tanya.

"True. So we wait until we're confident they've left. Dave's guess of evening being about six to eight o'clock seems reasonable, and travelling to Halls Gap will take about an hour to an hour and a half."

"Hasim and his men will probably want to arrive a bit early," Dan pointed out.

"I'd say leaving at half past six should be safe," said Nathan. "What do you think, dear?" he asked Tanya.

"I suppose if we're going through Halls Gap, we don't want to completely miss the important gathering," said Tanya. "It should be safe enough there, though I'm not sure what we'll find."

"Will it be safe for Ben?" asked Belinda.

"I'll stay in the car if I need to," said Ben. "And I'll keep my star of David bracelet in my pocket. In fact, I'll take it off now so I don't forget." He took it off and put it in his pocket.

"As for knowing when we can leave, we may see or hear signs that the bad guys are leaving," suggested Dave.

"Like we did when they arrived?" laughed Belinda.

"Mmm. Maybe not," Dave admitted.

"Is it safe to leave our camping things here while we go to Stawell?" asked Dan.

"We don't know what we'll be doing afterwards," answered Nathan, "so I think we'd better take everything with us."

"It's a lot of work if we just end up back here again," said Belinda.

"True, but what if we don't?" asked Tanya. "The kayak and canoe aren't ours. We don't want to leave them here when they might be stolen."

"I think we should pack up and take it all with us," said Nathan.

"And then we can be ready to leave whenever we want," said Dave.

"Shall we pack up straight after lunch then?" suggested Tanya.

Everyone agreed.

Although no unwelcome visitors disturbed them that morning, they all felt a little on edge. Nobody wanted to leave the campsite to go for a walk or to paddle on the reservoir. Even reading was hard to concentrate on.

Dan found himself listening all the time, straining to hear any unusual noises. In the end, he, Dave and Ben packed up their tent early, just to keep themselves occupied!

After an early lunch, packing began in earnest. Soon the annex and camper-trailer were finished, and Dan was helping Nathan and Dave with the boating equipment – as much as his broken arm allowed.

Ben had also helped where he could, but when there was nothing else to do, he decided to follow the track out towards the Glenelg River Road. Belinda offered to walk with him to make sure nothing went wrong.

Nathan reminded them not to go too close to the road.

As they walked off together, Ben now expert on crutches but Belinda looking at him sympathetically, Dan saw his father wink at his mother. For a moment he wondered why, then suddenly guessed: Ben was a friendly and agreeable young man and shared a few interests with Belinda. It was an interesting possibility, but Dan knew that many Jews – even secular Jews – would not marry non-Jews, so it probably wouldn't work out.

Dan was holding the kayak in place on the top of the camper-trailer with one hand while Nathan tightened a rope around it when they heard the sound of a car approaching out on the road.

They all froze, gazing towards the road. Nothing could be seen through the bush.

The car seemed to slow and stop. They all looked at each other.

Surely Ben and Belinda would have kept out of sight?

Once more the car engine revved and soon it was clear that the car was coming towards them.

"Quickly, Dan and Dave," snapped Nathan. "Let's finish tying these on before they arrive. That way, we can leave immediately if we need to."

A car stopped in the main parking area and Nathan was just tightening the last knot when they heard a voice shouting in Arabic. Someone had seen their car.

Dan soon saw a four-wheel drive approaching along the track. By this time, Dave had finished stowing the last few items in the car's roof box and Nathan and Dan were checking that the lights on the camper-trailer worked properly.

The car came closer and Dan drew in his breath sharply as he recognised it as Ahmed's. The car stopped and Ahmed opened the front door. Saad climbed awkwardly out of the other side, although Dan, focusing on Ahmed, paid him little attention.

Ahmed wasted no time with polite greetings as he climbed out and slammed the door. "You!" he snarled in recognition. "Why you here?"

"Oh, we've been camping here for a few days," answered Nathan, calmly climbing out of the car. "What brings you here? Are you camping nearby?"

Advancing aggressively, Ahmed ignored Nathan's questions and snapped, "We see peoples hiding near road. Are yours? Why spying on us?"

At the edges of his hearing, Dan began to hear a distant pulsing sound. What was it?

"I'm not sure who you saw," said Nathan, trying to be careful with the truth. "But what've you been doing that would make anyone want to spy on you?"

The question seemed to enrage Ahmed, and his voice became a shout. "We do Allah's work. Infidels try to stop us. Muslims persecuted in this country. Must fight. Fight against Jewish plots."

The humming drone grew more distinct. Could it be a plane?

Saad had come to stand quietly near his father and obviously heard the same sound. As he turned a little and looked at the sky, Dan suddenly noticed that he was wearing a light jacket with only one arm in a sleeve. The other arm was supported by a sling inside the jacket!

Immediately Dan saw the truth. Saad was Ahmed's son, the young man on whom Ehud had worked so tirelessly. Obviously Saad would have no idea that his life had been saved by a Jew, but would it make any difference if he did?

"I hear a plane, Dad," said Saad. "We should go. It must be the one we're waiting for."

Ahmed listened for a few seconds, then spoke a little more calmly. "Need get back as soon we can." He began to turn away, ignoring the Turners.

"Well, don't let us keep you," said Nathan. "But I do hope you'll learn that Muslims are not persecuted in this country. They live here freely like everyone else, including Christians and Jews."

Ahmed's anger flared again and he spewed agitated Arabic until Saad put a hand on his arm and spoke a few quiet words.

After taking a deep breath, Ahmed snarled, "Idiot! Jews pull strings in world. Muslims must destroy them. Rule all countries."

Despite the absurdity of Ahmed's claims, Dan would have left it at that. The man was like a pistol with a hair trigger, likely to explode without warning. Nathan, however, had other ideas.

"Nonsense," he said, firmly. "You're always blaming the Jews for everything. Jews don't control the world. In fact, Muslims control many countries, probably including the one you came from. So why did you leave it?"

Dan agreed with everything his father said, but he wouldn't have been brave enough to say it!

Ahmed's face turned purple and he began to scream incoherently in Arabic. Suddenly, he turned and ran towards his four-wheel drive, but Saad stood in his way. Ahmed tried to dodge around him, brushing past his injured arm, but the younger man reached out the arm to stop him. Ahmed pushed him away roughly, and Saad winced as he stumbled back against the car.

Despite the obvious pain, Saad didn't give up, speaking quietly to his father. The Turners had no idea what he said, since he used Arabic, but Ahmed's voluble anger slowly died away. As it did so, Dan listened to the growing hum, confident now that it was an approaching aeroplane.

At length, Ahmed issued an angry instruction and Saad hurried to the passenger door and climbed in awkwardly. Ahmed wrenched open the driver's door and got in too. As he started the car, he shouted at Nathan, "Urgent work. When finished, we deal with you. Just you wait!" He slammed the door and drove forward.

The Turners stepped quickly to one side, concerned from Ahmed's expression that he might use the car as a weapon. With his targets out of reach, however, the furious terrorist drove a quick circuit around the camper-trailer and sped off towards the road.

Chapter 28

Where's Ben?

"That was too close," said Tanya, bursting into tears.

"It was," agreed Nathan, slowly, "but don't worry, I think God kept us safe this time."

Dan stood listening. Although Ahmed's car had started driving north on the main road, he was convinced it had stopped almost immediately before starting again a minute later. The buzz of the approaching plane continued to grow louder.

"Did any of you see the men in the back seat?" asked Dan in a subdued voice, once the car was out of earshot.

"Yes," said Dave. "Two men with rifles."

"Dressed in black and wearing balaclavas." added Dan.

"I guess Ahmed was trying to get a rifle from them when Saad stopped him," said Dave, soberly.

"I didn't see any of that," admitted Tanya, "or I might've screamed. "Oh, Nathan, what should we do? When will they come back?"

"Impossible to know. They're probably driving to the airbase now, but how long they'll stay there, I've no idea."

All of a sudden, they heard the sound of running feet, and soon they saw Belinda running towards them.

"Was that Ahmed?" she called urgently as she came closer.

"Yes," answered Dan.

She ran into the clearing and dropped to a walk, her face red, her eyes wild. "Ben and I were near the road when we heard the car coming. We tried to hide in the bush, but the crutches made it hard for him. Ben thought they must've seen us, but when they turned in here and didn't try to chase us, I decided they couldn't have."

"They *did* see you," said Dan.

"Really? We did our best to hide, but the bush isn't very dense there. We decided to stay where we were until they came out again. Then, when they didn't come back, we got worried about you lot. I decided Ben should stay put while I came back here. On my way here, I heard the car coming, so I hid behind a tree while they went past. The tree wasn't very big, but I hope they didn't see me that time. After that, I hurried back here. Since you're all okay, I'll go back to Ben."

"Hang on!" interjected Nathan. "Ahmed threatened to come back and 'deal' with us, so I want to take the car and trailer out there anyway. Climb in, everyone."

Everyone got in, with Belinda in the back seat. Nathan was just about to start the car when suddenly there was a volley of distant explosions. Nathan paused and they all looked at each other.

"Sounds like Hasim's men are attacking as planned," said Dan.

"Could be," said Nathan. "If so, that might keep Ahmed busy for a while. Let's go and find Ben."

He started the car and hurried out to the main road. Belinda kept scanning the bush for Ben, but there was no sign of him.

When they reached the road, Belinda pointed to two not-very-large trees not far from the road. "That's where we hid," she said. "I'd better check there first."

"Okay," said Nathan, stopping to let her climb out. "While you look around here, we'll search along the road to see if he's gone along there for some reason. The road is wide enough, so I'll be able to turn around easily."

Dan suddenly remembered the pause he thought he'd heard as Ahmed's car departed. Had Ahmed or Saad seen Ben as they went out?

Nathan drove slowly along the road while everyone scanned the bush for signs of Ben. After a few hundred metres, they were sure there was nothing to see, but Nathan kept going, just in case. They were almost a kilometre down the road when he said, "What's that up ahead?"

'That' turned out to be two objects near each other: Ben's crutches. Both broken.

Nathan stopped while Dave climbed out and fetched the pieces.

After looking around a little, he climbed in again. "There are no footprints nearby. I think they must have been thrown out of a car."

"Ahmed," said Dan immediately. "That pause must have been them stopping to kidnap Ben."

"Oh, no!" gasped Tanya, covering her mouth with her hand. "And we brought him here to keep him safe!"

"What do we do now?" asked Dave.

"We must get Belinda," said Tanya. "There's always a chance she's found Ben back there and that Ahmed just stole his crutches."

Nathan did a U-turn and they went back to the track leading to Moora Moora Reservoir. Belinda was waiting for them alone, looking worried.

"Ben's not here, and the only clues I can see are crutch end impressions with a footprint in the middle every metre or so. They lead from the bush at the side of the road to here," she said, pointing to the ground. "They end here, next to these tyre marks."

"I'm afraid Ben's probably been kidnapped by Ahmed," said Tanya.

"We found his crutches further up the road," said Dave.

"Broken," added Dan, thoughtlessly.

Belinda's face was the very embodiment of shock – her eyes open wide, her mouth forming the shape of an 'O'. Her gasp and the hands she held to her mouth added the finishing touches. "How? What? Where could..." she said, floundering.

"We don't know, dear," said Tanya, sympathetically, "but we'll find Ben somehow."

Belinda was just about to climb into the back again when Nathan said, "Here in the front, Belinda, just in case we find Ben and need to get him in quickly."

As soon as she was in, Nathan turned around again and they drove north.

"Where are we going, Dad?" asked Dan.

"We've got to head towards the airbase," said Nathan. "I think we're probably safe from Hasim's men until we get close, but I'm not sure how we're going to find Ben."

Dan opened his window to listen, but the tyres and the wind made so much noise that nothing else could be heard.

"Let's go to that intersection where we saw the kangaroos," suggested Belinda. "Then we can look around and listen."

As they drove, Belinda got out the maps. It was sobering to think that the information they held could be the difference between life and death in the next few minutes.

It was the most terrifying six kilometres any of them had ever travelled. All eyes were staring ahead, while Nathan kept an eye on the rear-view mirror as well.

Finally, they approached the triangular island at the intersection. Nathan stopped just short of the left turn that led towards the airbase and turned off the ignition.

Frequent explosions and the crack of gunfire could be heard in the distance, due west. Dan listened carefully in quieter moments, but he could no longer hear the aeroplane.

"Sounds like a war zone!" said Nathan. "How far is it to the airbase, Belinda?"

"Another six kilometres, Dad."

"Why don't we go along to the signpost that turned us around when we arrived? We can stop there and see what's going on."

"I don't think we have any choice about going on," said Tanya. "We must find Ben."

"And the road that went off at that signpost goes up to Mount Victory Road, so we could escape that way if we need to," said Belinda.

Nathan was about to start the car again when Dan said, "Hang on a moment, Dad – can anyone hear a car coming?"

"With all this gunfire, how could we?" asked Nathan.

"Shhh," said Tanya, listening carefully.

"I think I can," said Dave.

Dan put his head out of the window, listening carefully. "Yes, it's definitely a car, and I think it's coming from the airbase," he said. "It could be Ahmed! He said he'd come back."

Nathan quickly started the car and inched forward until he could see along the road leading to the airbase. "I can't see a car coming yet," he said. "You know, I don't think we need to worry about Hasim's men anymore, so we can safely head towards Halls Gap and if we do, we should be out of sight around a corner on that road before the car gets here."

"Then, assuming it's Ahmed, we can come back and find Ben after they've driven south towards the reservoir," said Tanya tenaciously.

"Yes," agreed Nathan. "I'll just reverse a bit so that I can go around the other side of this island. They won't be able to see us there."

As he reversed, Tanya suddenly squealed, "Oh no! I see the car!"

Along the road leading from the airbase, a car had just appeared around the corner, surrounded by a cloud of dust.

"From their point of view, our car would be almost completely hidden by trees," said Nathan, "so I don't think they'll have seen us. I think we still have time to escape, as long as I hurry and don't get tangled up with the trailer."

Expertly, he finished backing, then veered to the right along the road to Halls Gap.

As the road straightened out in front of them, Nathan gasped and Tanya squealed again. Coming towards them was another car!

Nathan made a snap decision and continued driving. There was no way to tell who was coming towards them, but surely it couldn't be worse than Ahmed!

As the vehicle passed them, Dan said, "Hey, that's Fergus' car."

"Are you sure?" asked Nathan.

"It's got the same number plate."

By this time, Nathan had reached a bend in the road. As he steered around it, he cocked his head and began to move the steering wheel backwards and forwards as if it felt strange. Dan also noticed that the sound of the car had changed. The tyre noise was different.

"Looks like we might have a flat tyre," said Nathan, tensely.

"Oh, no!" said Tanya, voicing the thoughts of everyone in the car.

"At least we're round the corner," said Belinda as Nathan brought the car to a stop at the edge of the road.

"What now?" asked Dave.

"We change the tyre," said Nathan.

He was getting out the jack and other tools they needed when a car rounded the bend behind them, and quickly slowed as the driver saw them.

"That's Ahmed's car!" shouted Dan.

"Get ready for some fast talking," said Nathan.

The car pulled up beside them, and the first thing Dan saw was Ben, sitting in the back and waving at them! He wound down the window and called out, "Saad is taking me to the police in Stawell. What's up?"

Meanwhile, the driver's door opened and Saad jumped down, his arm in a sling. "Don't worry about me," he said to Nathan. "I'm trying to help."

"What's going...," began Nathan, then suddenly fell silent as another car slid around the corner, engine revving as if the driver was pushing it hard. Fortunately, the driver reacted quickly and the car skidded to a halt close behind Ahmed's car.

The driver's door was opening even before it stopped, and on the instant of stopping, a man leapt out and trained a large rifle on Saad.

"Don't move!" he called out.

"Don't shoot," said Dan. "Saad is helping us."

Fergus lowered his sniper's rifle a little and said, "That's good news, Dan, but how do I know it's true? Are any of his comrades with him?"

"No, just Ben. We don't know any details yet."

"*Ben?* Okay, Saad," said Fergus, lowering the rifle further. "Please explain what's going on."

"My father, Ahmed, took Ben prisoner. He wanted him as a hostage. When we got back to our camp, it was chaos. We could hear gunfire and explosions, and the men said there was fighting near the airbase. My father jumped out and left Ben in the car, sure that he couldn't escape without crutches. He gave me the keys and told me to look after Ben." He smiled. "So I did."

"Saad got into the car and drove us here," said Ben, "steering one-handed and dodging all sorts of things on the way."

"Why did you help Ben?" asked Fergus, stowing the rifle in his car.

"Since I got shot and Dr Ehud saved me, I've been thinking a lot about my loyalties," said Saad. "I've decided that I can't work with my father or his men any more. Their mission is all about hatred and power, and I think there should be more to life than that. It was Dr Ehud who really made me think. I woke up for a few moments after he'd been operating on me and noticed his star of David necklace. I went back to sleep again immediately, but I still remembered it when I woke up properly. And the nurses were always singing his praises – at least when my father wasn't around."

"Ehud saved you, and now you've saved his son," said Fergus.

Saad looked at Ben in amazement. "Are you Dr Ehud's son?"

"Yes," smiled Ben, reaching into his pocket and pulling out his bracelet. "Here's a star of David bracelet he gave me for my birthday. It matches his necklace."

"I'm glad you weren't wearing that when my father caught you," said Saad seriously. "If you had, I doubt I could've saved you. My father's hatred for Jews is beyond any reasoning."

"Even if he knew Ben was the son of the doctor who saved your life?" asked Dan.

"That would make no difference," said Saad. "I know that's ridiculous, but it's true."

"Tell us why you changed, then," said Fergus.

"I'll keep listening," interjected Nathan, "but I need to swap our flat tyre. Can you help me, Dave? You haven't got a sling or crutches!"

Saad began to explain how knowing that a Jew had saved him had triggered all sorts of questions in his mind. He'd tried discussing them with his father, but got nowhere. He'd also talked to his mother, which went better, but seemed to worry her greatly.

"Your mother?" enquired Fergus. Naming an address in Horsham, he asked, "Is that where you live?"

Saad looked surprised. "Yes. How do you know?"

"When you were in hospital, we put a tracking device in your bandages. It's probably still there, though the battery will be flat by now. When your Dad took you away from the hospital, we tracked you to that address. The police were just getting ready to visit when the device showed you were leaving Horsham again."

"Yes. My father took me to the so-called 'Forest Lodge Forestry Camp'. There's no lodge there – no camp at all. But it's remote, and that's what my father wanted. We all camped in tents and started training."

"Training?" queried Fergus.

"Training for fighting, using weapons and explosives. I'd call it terrorist training."

"If you don't mind me saying so, you've changed your outlook very quickly," said Fergus.

"Yes and no," said Saad. "I'd already been having doubts, and when Dr Ehud used his brilliance to save a man who probably hated him, that was the final straw."

"Your mother was also very thankful to Ehud."

"Yes, she saw that Dr Ehud's attitude of helping was better than my father's overwhelming hatred."

"She was very worried about you, too."

"She was terrified that my father would kill me," said Saad simply.

"With good reason," said Fergus. "What I've learned from my enquiries about him hasn't been encouraging."

"And that's what I was like too, I'm afraid. I hope he can change in the same way I'm changing."

"So do I, Saad. So do I. But I won't be holding my breath, even though I've been learning more about God's amazing willingness to forgive."

Saad said nothing.

"I have a few more questions, prompted by my interview with your mother," said Fergus. "Did a plane land here?"

"No," said Saad. "We thought it was meant to, but it just kept flying on."

"Good," said Fergus, rubbing his hands together and smiling. "A beneficial case of mistaken identity."

"What do you mean?" asked Dan.

"I'll explain later. Do any of you know why the shooting started?"

"There are two terrorist groups here," answered Dan. "They hate each other, and I overheard a leader from the other group discussing plans to attack Ahmed's group as soon as they heard the plane approaching. They wanted to defeat Ahmed's men before the plane landed with extra weapons and ammunition."

"Is that The Leader's group?" asked Saad.

"Yes, whoever 'the leader' is."

"He's an important imam, and a bit of a diplomat too. He has powerful connections overseas. We were very proud of ourselves when we arranged deliveries of weapons and ammunition from overseas before he could."

"Well, now the two groups seem to be fighting each other over the equipment," observed Fergus. "That should make the army's job easier."

"The army?" asked Saad, concerned.

Fergus looked at his watch. "We should hear a few heavy vehicles rumbling through that intersection soon. It's a long story, but our enquiries showed that this delivery was likely to go astray, which was very convenient. The police in Stawell involved the army, and they're approaching the airbase in a pincer movement from the south and the northeast. They should be able to deal with whatever's left of these two groups."

"I do hope there aren't too many people killed," said Saad, "even though killing was my father's intention. And I hope he hasn't been killed himself. Perhaps he can still learn not to view everything through a lens of hate."

A feeling that something was incongruous had been gnawing at Dan's mind for some time, and he had finally identified it. "Can I ask you a question, Saad?" he asked.

"Sure."

"When we first met your father and his men, they mostly spoke English. Now they always speak Arabic. Why?"

"Ah, that's easy," said Saad. "My father suddenly made a rule that everyone had to speak Arabic. It suited him because he doesn't speak English well, but he also said that the infidels were so stupid that if we discussed our plans in a language they didn't understand, they'd never believe we were capable of doing such things until after we'd done them and destroyed their society. I believe the idea was suggested to him by a leader of a group in New South Wales," he finished, apologetically.

Dan shook his head and took a deep breath. His fears had tended in the right direction.

By this time, Nathan and Dave had swapped the wheel and the car was ready to go again.

"I think I hear those army vehicles coming," said Fergus. "I don't believe there's anything we can do to help, so it might be safer to move out of the area."

Chapter 29

Generosity

"So far, so good," said Nathan as he turned onto Mount Victory Road towards Halls Gap.

It was mid-afternoon and the Turners, with Ben, were following close behind Fergus' car. During the uneventful journey Ben had recounted his terrifying experience of being kidnapped by Ahmed and his men.

"They made all sorts of threats about what they'd do to me," he said, "but they clearly had no real plans."

"At least they didn't know you were Jewish," said Tanya.

"If they had, I think Saad's probably right – they would have killed me. I wasn't with them for long, but almost everything they said in English was against the Jews."

"I'm glad you weren't with them for long or they might've found out!" shuddered Tanya.

"I've never realised before just how fixated these people are on hating the Jews. Hating us seems to be their only reason for living, and killing us is their only goal in life."

"What a waste!" said Dave.

"And how different from what Jesus taught about loving your enemies," said Dan.

"Christians have been killing their enemies for centuries," scoffed Belinda.

"They've never had the words of Jesus to support them in their killing," argued Dan. "These extremists often quote their prophet's words to support what they do. That's a big difference."

"I've never quite thought of it that way, Dan," said Nathan. "So, what do you think of Christians attacking Muslims?"

"Jesus and his disciples never told believers to commit any sort of violence. In fact, Jesus encouraged his followers to accept any cruelty or violence against themselves without retaliation."

"But that can't be practical," said Ben. "If people attack you, surely you have to fight back?"

"That's not what Jesus did, or any of his disciples – except Simon Peter once, and Jesus told him off for that."

"So why do Christians do it now?" asked Belinda.

"I think they use the same argument as Ben, but that's not what Jesus or his followers did. It seems to me it's the difference between..." Dan paused, searching for the right word, "ah... *pragmatism*, I suppose, and real faith. God says it takes faith to please him and he'll take care of the practicalities for people who have faith."

There was silence for a while as everyone reflected on Dan's comments. Tanya couldn't help thinking that her family's problems with Christianity might have been reduced if the churches her parents had attended had followed Dan's explanation.

"I'll have to think about it," said Nathan finally, "but I have to say it sounds impractical. Can you imagine Australia or America working like that?"

"The way of life Jesus and his followers taught was for individuals and congregations to follow."

"Not countries?" enquired Ben.

"No. In your scripture, what I call the Old Testament, God gave commands about how Israel should operate as a nation. But things change in the New Testament, when people from other nations are explicitly offered salvation," answered Dan.

"I'm glad the army is dealing with those extremists," observed Belinda.

"It doesn't sound like there was much to deal with," said Dan. "The extremists were dealing with each other!"

They all sat in silence for a few moments, wondering what sort of disaster had unfolded in and around the airbase.

Nathan changed the subject. "Have you noticed how tidy the road is here?" he said. "No trees, no branches, not even piles of leaves."

"It makes driving much safer," said Tanya.

"And quicker," agreed Nathan.

Plenty of work had been done to clear the road, but Nathan still drove cautiously on the windy road. As they neared Halls Gap, they found a straighter section where on their left a steep hill climbed to the top of a range, while on their right, a cliff fell away into a deep valley where they knew a delightful creek flowed gently between boulders. Beyond the creek rose Elephant's Hide, an inclined slab of weathered and fractured sandstone leading up to a peak that overlooked

Halls Gap. A group of climbers could be seen halfway up, carefully choosing their path up the steep rock.

"Looks like holiday-makers," said Dave.

"Perhaps we're finally getting organised out here beyond the margins," said Belinda.

"Could everything go back to how it was before?" asked Ben, wistfully.

"With even the Olympics, perhaps," suggested Belinda, sympathetically.

"I don't want to disappoint you, Ben, but I think there's a long way to go before that," said Tanya.

"In the meantime, let's enjoy the improvement and hope they start cleaning up other roads soon too," said Nathan.

Reaching the floor of the valley in which Halls Gap lay, they followed Fergus into the small town. They had not visited it since leaving Melbourne, and it was more crowded than they expected.

Before they reached the shopping strip, Fergus pulled over and parked beside the road, leaving room for the Turners' camper-trailer.

"What will you do without your crutches, Ben?" asked Belinda.

"Actually, it's a bit embarrassing," replied Ben; "I only had to use them for another week after my last appointment, and today is one week. I could've stopped using them this morning. I never would've believed I could've forgotten that."

Laughing, they all climbed out and looked towards the town centre. The main street was crowded with cars, and several small trucks were parked at the far end of the small shopping area, clustered near the information centre.

"Busy," said Dan, surprised.

"And do you see the police cars?" asked Dave, pointing at the other end of the shopping area where a small carpark seemed full of police cars.

"I think that's just about opposite Centenary Hall," said Belinda.

"How does it feel without crutches, Ben?" asked Dan.

"A little strange, but it doesn't really hurt at all."

By this time, Fergus had locked his car and approached them. "Do you see any of the cars from Ahmed's group here?"

They looked carefully around the crowded street and parking areas. There were several black four-wheel drives like those Ahmed's men seemed to prefer, but none were driven by men they recognised.

"I suppose it's too early for them to come," said Fergus as they all shook their heads. "If they come at all. The town looks much busier than it was when Craig and Brad were in control here.[2] Hopefully it's friendlier too!"

"Is everything safe here, Fergus?" asked Tanya.

"It looks safe enough at the moment, doesn't it?" said Fergus, scanning the town. "But I can't be sure the danger is over yet. Let's go and see where the special do is to be held tonight. Les is meant to be providing security. He might be interested in your information from Moora Moora."

They walked along the main street to where people were carrying boxes from parked trucks into the hall. Peeking in through the front door, they saw a group of technicians setting up audiovisual equipment while others set up tables with various displays and chairs for an audience.

"Les doesn't seem to be here," said Fergus, heading across the road to the smaller carpark. There they found Les, snoozing in the back seat of a police car with the door open.

---

[2] See *"Beyond the Western Margin"*.

"Hey, mister boss man," said Fergus, tapping him on the shoulder. "How come you're sleeping while I work? I'm the one who's meant to be on holiday."

Les opened a bleary eye. "I'm preparing myself for a busy evening. You should try it."

Fergus looked around, but there was no-one near. "It could be a dangerous evening," he said quietly. "We may have a few determined terrorists on hand, if any of them are still alive."

"I think you'd better explain," said Les, yawning as he climbed out of the car. Noticing the Turners and Ben, he nodded a greeting.

"A quick summary to bring everyone up to date. We learned that a plane was to deliver an illegal arms shipment to the Victoria Valley Airfield today. That's a private airfield near Dunkeld, so on Wednesday, we sent police to question the owners. There was no-one there and neighbours said the owners were on holiday. They also said there was no way the owners would ever be involved in such a thing. Due to the size of the delivery, we advised the Victorian army, but something didn't seem quite right. It was all too quiet. This morning, I was looking at a map and noticed the Victoria Valley Airbase, and all of a sudden, I guessed there'd been a mix-up with the names: airbase and airfield."

"Ah," nodded Les. "So where is the Victoria Valley *Airbase*, then?"

"About 40 kilometres further north, not far from Moora Moora Reservoir – which rang alarm bells for me since I knew the Turners were camping there with Ben. The army brass decided to send trucks with men up from the south on two roads, so I hot-footed it up the road to Halls Gap and approached Moora Moora Reservoir and the airbase from the north."

"Was your guess right?"

"It seems so. However, what we didn't realise was that there wasn't just one group of extremists waiting for that shipment, but two – and neither wanted to share it. Ahmed's group kidnapped Ben this afternoon, but he was freed by Ahmed's son Saad, the lad Ehud saved last week. He brought Ben to us, then went back to try to find his father. I sure hope he hasn't been hurt in the melee."

"Are they really so dangerous?" asked Les, sceptically.

"Yes," interrupted Dan, "they are. This afternoon, Ahmed came to our campsite and was very aggressive. He would have grabbed a rifle and killed Dad if Saad hadn't stopped him. He left because he heard the plane coming, but said he'd come back and deal with us."

"Dan's right," said Nathan. "And I don't think all the gunshots we heard were just harmless target practice. Each group was quite happy to kill the other to get their hands on more weapons and ammunition to help kill more people."

"But we don't know yet how successful they've been?" asked Les.

"No," answered Fergus. "Except that we do know they didn't get the extra weapons and ammunition. As I expected, the plane didn't land, it flew on south, presumably to the Victoria Valley Airfield."

"That's good news – and I suppose their fighting was using up their ammunition," observed Les.

"True. However, there is one matter of particular concern. It seems that both groups planned to attend the event here tonight."

"Here? With our special overseas guest and various government ministers attending? That could be a problem, Fergus."

"It certainly could. Can you communicate with the army to find out what's happened at the airbase?"

As the afternoon drew to a close, Tanya was having second thoughts. They'd left Moora Moora Reservoir with the intention of escaping dangerous terrorists and informing the police about them. Those goals were satisfied at the moment, but camping at Lake Fyans or Stawell would keep them further away from the terrorists who intended to come to Halls Gap.

"Can we go somewhere else to camp soon?" she asked Nathan as he returned after making sure the camper-trailer was parked well and truly out of the way.

"I thought we were staying for the presentation or whatever it is," he answered.

"Is there any advantage in doing so? It could be risky."

"I'm sorry, Tanya, but I thought we were staying, so I took the flat tyre to the petrol station to be fixed. They've organised for someone to come into town and fix it soon."

"Oh! How long will that take?" asked Tanya, worried.

"They said he'd take it to his farm, where he has the right equipment. He's going to bring it back just before seven o'clock, which is when the presentation begins."

"Could we do without a spare tyre?"

"I suppose we could," said Nathan, doubtfully, "but I never like being without a spare. That's why I was so glad when they said they could fix it straight away. You never know when you might need one."

"Okay," sighed Tanya. "I suppose that means we stay."

"Frankly, I don't think there's anything to worry about. I doubt either Ahmed or Hasim will turn up, let alone their men. It'll just be a presentation where officials announce some special local development and pat themselves on the back. I hear there are even some politicians visiting from Melbourne."

"Are they allowed to cross the margin?" asked Tanya.

"Perhaps Victoria is having second thoughts about the margins. After all, the areas outside the margins are going very well economically."

"I suppose it should be alright then," said Tanya, reluctantly. "Where are the children?"

CR

Dan, Dave, Belinda and Ben had made their way across the main street to the grassy park beyond. Ben's knee wasn't bad, but he was glad to sit down all the same.

As they sat chatting on the grass, trucks and cars continued to come and go from the hall in final preparation for the important presentation. Some consequential people with their attendants had even begun to arrive in Victorian government cars.

Dan couldn't help wondering if this entire performance was safe. Politicians, cabinet ministers and foreign dignitaries were gathering in a small country town to spruik their achievements, and two groups of militant terrorists planned to attend. Dan doubted they were attending just to enjoy a simple supper! Still, Fergus and Les didn't seem too concerned, so why should he worry?

He lay back on the grass and closed his eyes. Once these extremists were all sorted out, they could return to Moora Moora and enjoy the delightful calm and solitude once more. His arm was definitely feeling better, but it would still be a couple of weeks before the plaster could be removed.

CR

"I'd like you to welcome the Iranian Ambassador," announced the Minister for Foreign Affairs, clapping politely to set the tone.

The smiling ambassador, in suit and open-necked shirt, approached the microphone.

"Thank you for your generous welcome," he began. "As ambassador of the Islamic Republic of Iran, I am honoured to join you in this celebration of international cooperation. The Iranian government wishes to contribute generously to the development and ongoing operation of several educational camps in Victoria. With the support of the Victorian government, the first will be constructed here in the Grampians. School children will enjoy week-long camps with structured educational activities. Using land provided by the Victorian government, Iran will provide funding for construction as well as ongoing staff and equipment costs. Iran will also fund scholarships allowing underprivileged children to enjoy the benefits of these camps at no cost. Outstanding educational materials designed to build and support a united society will provide ongoing advantage to all."

Applause rippled around the room after each sentence. Dan, standing near the back door with Dave and Ben, exchanged troubled glances with them as the ambassador continued.

"While final details are still being worked out, the Islamic Republic of Iran will gladly contribute most generously to the entire plan, even funding the development of a leadership team with exceptional international talent."

Cheers sounded as the ambassador stepped away from the microphone and went to stand next to a man dressed in a long robe whom he obviously knew well. The two shared smiles and a few hurried comments as the applause died down.

"The other man is a popular imam in Horsham," said Ben quietly.

The foreign minister began speaking again, singing the praises of the entire program and predicting extensive advantages to Victoria.

"The most exciting feature of this joint venture is the generosity of our friends in Iran and their contribution to culture in Victoria," he concluded.

Next, the imam Ben had recognised was introduced as a community faith leader. He began, "Our friends from Iran have made an honest and generous offer of support in this vital project. I have been asked to describe how this first campsite will be built and how quickly it will generate benefits for the community..."

From outside, Dan suddenly heard angry barking and his flesh crawled. He'd recognise that bark anywhere: Ali's pitbull.

The barking drew closer, and suddenly Ali stood in the doorway, holding his dog on a short leash as it tried to rush into the hall, barking frantically. His father stood at his side, and Dan noticed his left arm was roughly bandaged. Attendants moved towards the pair, but cautiously. No one was eager to tackle the dog! Two policemen also began to move from their positions at the front of the hall, one easing his gun from its holster as he walked.

The imam's voice quavered and fell silent as the pitbull strained still harder on its leash. At last, Ali lost his grip and the dog leapt forward. For a moment, Dan feared that the dog was coming for him, but it ignored him, charging instead for the side of the hall where the imam was now pulling a pistol from under his long robe.

With frightening speed, the dog lunged for the man before he could free his weapon. Fastening his jaws on the man's arm, the dog began to jerk and shake his victim. The imam fell to one knee, screaming in pain.

Suddenly a shot rang out, deafening in the enclosed space, and the dog collapsed, its teeth still locked on the imam's arm.

"Dad!" cried Ali's anguished voice.

"Shut up," said Hasim. "Help The Leader."

"Don't move!" shouted a policeman, his pistol now in both hands.

Everyone stopped except for the other policeman, who also held his pistol ready as he moved to a better vantage point. "Drop your gun," he shouted to Hasim.

Hasim ignored him, spinning around instead and sprinting from the hall, pistol still in hand.

Unable to fire safely in the crowded hall, both policemen followed him, disappearing quickly through the doorway. The sound of their running feet echoed strangely in the silence of the hall.

Ali stood where he was for a moment, then ran forward to examine his dog. When the imam finally freed his arm from its grip, the dog slid to the floor and lay unmoving. There was no doubt that it was dead.

Ali sat on the floor beside the dog, then picked it up and cradled it in his arms. Glaring at the dog's victim, he ground out, "I told you he hated you. I wish he'd killed you."

The imam ignored him and wrapped his savaged arm in his robe, forgetting for a moment that he still held a pistol.

At that instant, the paralysis that had seized everybody in the hall broke and, almost as one, they began to rush towards the doors, their noise almost muffling the single gunshot that sounded outside. Dan found himself carried along by a flood of humanity as the hall emptied in seconds. Ali, his lifeless dog and the injured imam were left alone.

What Ali and the imam may have said to each other, Dan never knew, but when several policemen entered a few minutes later, Ali was gently rocking his dog, ignoring the imam who stood motionless, cradling his arm with no sign of his pistol. Perhaps he hoped everyone would forget it.

CR

Fergus, meanwhile, had not been idle.

He and Les had been standing outside the hall, watching for any terrorists who might have survived the confrontation at the airbase and made for Halls Gap. Fergus held a rifle as inconspicuously as possible, hoping he'd have no call to use it.

He was at last growing confident that no terrorists would arrive when suddenly he saw a car he recognised driving slowly towards them. "That's Ahmed's car," he said, pointing.

"AK-47," snorted Les. "What an imaginative number plate."

Fergus peered through the car's tinted windows as best he could in the failing light. "I *think* there's only the driver in it," he said.

"I think you're right," said Les.

The car drove past the hall then turned onto the road that led behind it. Fergus and Les followed.

After parking, the driver climbed out. It was Saad. He walked slowly towards them.

"What did you find at the airbase?" asked Fergus.

"Not much good news for my mother," sighed Saad. "My father is dead and so are most of his men. I think the same is true of Hasim's group. Thanks for letting the army guys know that I wasn't with the rest."

Nearby, a dog barked furiously, but none of them paid any attention.

"Was there much fighting still going on when the army trucks arrived?"

"No. By then most of the men were either dead or injured, and the survivors all surrendered with very little resistance. I don't think any of the army blokes were hurt."

"That's good news."

"Yes."

"Are any other cars coming here?"

"I don't think so. Of course, people can hide in the bush pretty easily, but I doubt there are any left to come. Not from my father's group, anyway."

"What about Hasim's group?"

"I don't know them so well."

A sudden gunshot rang out.

"That was inside the hall," said Fergus urgently, turning and running towards the main street. It was less than 50 metres away, and as he rounded a corner, he saw a man with a pistol and a bandaged arm run to a car parked just outside the hall.

He stopped near a wall and stood still, breathing shallowly and steadying his rifle against the wall.

The running figure yanked open the door and climbed in, starting the engine as he did so. The engine revved and the car rolled forward as Fergus squeezed the trigger. From that distance, he couldn't miss.

Chapter 30

Surprises

"My father's body was found at the outlet works of Moora Moora Reservoir," said Saad, regretfully. "Someone must have taken him there during the fighting, shortly after I took his car. He was lying on the bridge, right next to the detonator. It looked like he couldn't open the padlock, so he tried to shoot it off and was killed by a ricochet."

"What was he doing there?" asked Les.

"I suppose he was trying to set off the explosives," said Saad, quietly.

"Trying to destroy the dam?"

"That was his plan. One of his many plans to sabotage local infrastructure, and the first one to be acted on."

"Did you help him with that plan?" asked Les, seriously.

"No."

"What about other similar plans?"

"No. My father liked to run things his own way. I enjoyed the excitement of war games at first, but I was having increasing doubts about it all. I didn't like the hatred that underpinned everything my father and his men did."

"Yet you placed a terrorist flag on Briggs Bluff?"

"I did. I should've refused when my father ordered me to do it, but I was afraid to. If it hadn't been for Dr Ehud's example, I'd probably still be reluctantly going along with things."

"How did you get shot?" asked Les. "Your father would only say that it was an accident."

"That same afternoon, we found a place for target practice near Horsham. I was fastening a target on a tree when someone shot me. They were probably aiming at another target, but missed badly and hit me instead. The bullet went right through my arm and my father said it should be alright. He didn't want to take me to a doctor because they would ask too many questions."

"He very nearly killed you," said Les, seriously.

It was Saturday afternoon and Les was doing his best to get to the bottom of the terrorist uprising that had begun so quickly and ended with such tragic loss of life.

Saad was an important element in the investigation, but his position before the law was tricky. What had his position been in Ahmed's group? His action in saving Ben would be worth a lot in court, but his previous actions could well be serious crimes.

"You made a good moral choice yesterday," said Les. "And the best part about it is that you made it before you knew your father's plans were going to fail. And they always *were* going to fail, you know. They had too many flaws: too much boasting; too little planning; too much hatred; too much anger; too much unjustified confidence;

too many claims of persecution. Your father shot himself in the foot at every step. Fortunately, Hasim did the same."

"My mother will be sad, but my father's death will also take a weight off her mind."

"Is there anything else you want to tell me about this affair?" asked Les.

"Have you heard of 'The Leader'?"

"Yes, but I know nothing about him."

"He was the true leader of Hasim's group. He's been overseas for several months organising Iranian funding and several arms shipments that haven't happened yet. My father planned a quick revolution. The Leader planned a slow takeover, working from within using the power of money."

"He sounds like an important target. How can I catch him?"

"I think you already have him. The imam bitten by Ali's dog."

"Ah, that's good news. We locked him up last night on firearm offences, but it sounds like he has a good deal more to answer for."

❦

When Saad left Les' office, he found that the Turners and Ben had arrived while he was inside. The small Police Station waiting room was crowded.

"Hello, Saad," smiled Ben. "I was wondering how I'd get to see you again. I really want to thank you for your courage and kindness."

"I'm just sorry it took me so long to find them," said Saad. "Now I'll have to work out what's left of my old life and where I need to start from scratch."

"I'm a few years younger than you," said Ben, "but if you need any help, I'd be happy to give it, and so would my parents."

"That could be difficult," said Saad, wryly, "since all of my family and friends think they hate you."

"Don't forget where that hatred has got them," said Nathan.

"I suppose so," sighed Saad.

"I know you're not a Christian, Saad," said Dan, "but the Bible and history both make it clear that nations who hate the Jews never do well in the long run. Look it up and check."

"Is Islam so badly wrong about the Jews?"

"You'll have to decide that for yourself."

"I think I need to look into religion more carefully than I have before," said Saad. "I'll start with the Jewish religion, because that's what prompted Dr Ehud to behave how he did."

Ben looked embarrassed for a moment, then thoughtful. "I suppose you're right to some extent. Judaism probably *is* Dad's starting point, but not the ceremonial parts. You see, Saad, in my family we don't even believe in Hashem – the name!"

Saad looked taken aback. "So, is Dan wrong about Israel?" he asked.

"I don't know. I know that Jews don't have everything easy and that Jew-haters don't have everything hard. At the same time, history does have a feel to it, as Dan says. Many nations come and go, but Israel always continues, despite being the most hated nation in the world."

"You're right," nodded Dan, and Dave agreed.

"You're very quiet today, Belinda," said Ben. "What do you think?"

"Oh, I don't know. Religion used to be easy: I just ignored it. Now it seems to demand my attention more."

"And what about you, Tanya my dear?" asked Nathan.

"Belinda's right. And I'm starting to think that Dan might be too."

"Perhaps pandemics and danger make us all think more about religion," suggested Saad.

"I was just thinking that Fergus must have thought a lot about religion then," laughed Dan, "and now I see him walking up the path."

Fergus entered the waiting room and looked around in surprise.

"So I'm not the only one wanting to talk to the boss man. I guess I'll have to wait my turn."

"Saad's already spoken to him, and I think he wants to talk to the rest of us together," said Nathan. "If you're in a hurry, you can go first."

At that moment, the door to Les' office opened and he stepped out, smiling at them all.

"Welcome to the Stawell Police Station where all problems big and small are solved within days – as long as we have our valuable assistants at work. Thank you all for your help in solving this particular problem."

"You were the one who arrested the last two dangerous men," said Fergus.

"Ali and the imam?" asked Les. "Not dangerous really. And you fired the last shot."

"You're right," nodded Fergus. "The last shot," he repeated thoughtfully. "The very last shot."

"What do you mean?"

"I've fired my very last shot as a policeman. I came to tell you the news. I've contacted my official bosses in Victoria and told them that I quit."

"Why, Fergus? Are you upset about the outcome of that last shot?"

"Not particularly, but I've been reviewing my life and considering my direction. As you know, I've been turning more to religion recently, and it's making me question what I do for a job. You might have heard the question 'What would Jesus do?' Well, I've been asking myself if Jesus would be a police marksman and decided he wouldn't, so I've quit."

Dan couldn't help it – he clapped.

"Obviously it's up to you," said Les, "but I've really enjoyed your company over the last few months and I'll miss you. I must also say that your last shot had an amazing result."

"Quite spectacular," agreed Fergus.

At that distance, he couldn't have missed, and he hadn't. His aim was impeccable. The bullet passed through the side window and shattered the windscreen in front of the driver, so that Hasim was driving blind. The four-wheel drive sped away south towards Lake Bellfield, weaving all over the road as he tried to get rid of the shattered windscreen. As his speed increased, so did his zigzagging gyrations, until finally he lost control completely. The car left the road and crumpled against a tree. A second later, a shattering explosion shook the air and lit up the dusk. Hasim's attempted escape was over.

"You may not have heard the extra detail Ali whispered to me later as he wept over his dog. 'Dad made a bomb with Ahmed's explosives. He said that if things went wrong, he'd throw it into Lake Bellfield.' "

"No, I hadn't heard that. I wonder how much damage *that* would have done to the dam wall."

"In the end, it didn't matter," said Les. "Ali lost his dog and his father within minutes. What path in life will he choose now?"

There was silence for a few minutes as each pondered the sudden violent deaths that Ahmed and Hasim had planned to unleash on others and then suffered themselves.

"I'm sure there are many other details that we'll be wondering over for months," said Les, "but did you hear what happened to the aeroplane that flew on to the Victoria Valley Airfield? The runway was too short for it, so it overshot the end and damaged its landing gear. The army blokes captured the pilot and the rest of the crew and impounded all the weapons, ammunition and explosives. It couldn't have been easier."

"A most satisfying case of mistaken identity," said Fergus.

"Indeed," agreed Les. "Now, I invited the Turners and Ben here to give them some good news, but since it'll certainly extend to you, Fergus, and possibly even to you, Saad, listen up.

"The Victorian government is quite embarrassed about last night and not eager to have the news spread far and wide. Having dispensed with the land beyond the margins, it was hardly reasonable to still treat it as their sovereign property when they saw a naive opportunity for easy money. Give away some land and rake in the dough, they thought! As if the Iranians would ever give funds without a reasonable expectation of results – normally terrorism and violence. The local councils beyond the margins have expressed their displeasure in no uncertain terms.

"As a result, the Victorian politicians were quite eager to leave last night and quickly decided to offer rewards to the people directly involved in catching the terrorists. The reward is surprisingly generous: each of you will be given freedom of passage between Victoria and the lands beyond the margins, as well as full citizenship in Victoria with none of those pesky distance limits."

"Wow!" breathed Dan and Belinda together.

"I could go to uni in Melbourne," cried Ben.

"And enter elite rowing competitions," added Belinda.

"We could fetch our goods from Melbourne," said Nathan.

"And I could bring my little car up here," grinned Tanya.

No-one suggested going back to live in Melbourne.

Notes

This story is fictional, but based in many real locations in the state of Victoria in south-eastern Australia. All of the characters are fictional and any similarity with any existing people or names is purely coincidental.

There is an existing resort near the Beehive Falls parking area, but I have never visited it – beyond a brief look at their website.[3] The camp site described in this story may or may not bear much similarity to that resort – I don't know.

The roads, mountains, tracks, lakes and distances mentioned reflect the true locations of places in and around the Grampians in western Victoria. See the Parks Victoria website for information about the National Park,[4] and the Grampians Wimmera Mallee website for more information about Moora Moora Reservoir.[5]

Placed a few years in the future, this story makes many guesses and assumptions regarding the effects of the COVID-19 pandemic and possible subsequent pandemics. These may or may not prove to be well-founded: only time will tell! The story is not intended as any sort of praise, criticism, or deep analysis of past or existing government policies or actions; any references to suggested future policies are simply part of the storyline imagined by the author.

Maps were made using Open Street Map data[6] with additional features added to fit the story. The margins are completely imaginary.

---

[3] www.rosesgap.com.au/

[4] www.parks.vic.gov.au/places-to-see/parks/grampians-national-park/

[5] www.gwmwater.org.au/using-lakes-and-reservoirs/our-reservoirs/moora-moora-reservoir/reservoir/

[6] www.openstreetmap.org/

About the Author

Mark Morgan was born in Australia during 1963; the youngest son of Peter and Meryl Morgan. Deeply involved in religion all of his life, he has worked as a lay preacher, Sunday School teacher and missionary – trying to balance the many demands of spiritual life with those of family and paid employment.

After graduating, he worked in engineering for several years before concentrating on software development. Happily married and blessed with eight children, he has spent many years reading the Bible and learning to teach its lessons.

Writing Bible-based novels now fills much of his time.

Free Download

Paul in Snippets

A 109-page PDF novelette by Mark Morgan.

The life of Paul painted from the Acts of the Apostles.

Get your free copy of *Paul in Snippets* when you sign up for the Bible Tales mailing list. As well as the eBook, you will receive a weekly email newsletter with micro tales, informative articles and special offers.

Visit https://www.BibleTales.online/free-pins

Bible Tales Online

Other books by Mark Morgan are available from Bible Tales Online.

Terror on Every Side!
THE LIFE OF JEREMIAH

From a family of priests in the peaceful reign of good King Josiah, came a young man Jeremiah, bringing words from God to his people. It was no message for the fainthearted, either. It was a message of *Terror on Every Side!*

> **Volume 1 – Early Days**
> **Volume 2 – As Good As It Gets**
> **Volume 3 – Darkness Falling**
> **Volume 4 – The Darkness Deepens**
> **Volume 5 – No Remedy**
> **Volume 6 – That Broken Reed**

Hardcover, paperback, eBook and audiobook.

Other Bible-based novels

Joseph, Rachel's son (p'back, eBook, audiobook)

The King's Armour-bearer (h'cover, p'back, eBook)

Young Adult novels and other genres

Beyond the Western Margin (YA adventure: p'back, eBook)

Upside Down with Paul (h'cover, p'back, eBook)

Micro-tales

Collections of short stories about Bible characters or events, available in paperback, eBook and audiobook. Written by Mark Morgan and others.

Fiction Favours the Facts
Fiction Favours the Facts – Book 2
Fiction Favours the Facts – Book 3

Coming soon (God willing)

Daniel, Man of Light
Fiction Favours the Facts – Book 4
Chief and Commander

Bible Tales Online continues to publish books. To find the list of currently available books, visit

https://www.BibleTales.online/books

Bible
Tales

www.BibleTales.online